Praise for the Elizabeth Blair . . .

'An interesting and credible cast of characters and
a good twisty-turny plot'
Ms London on *Turkey Tracks*

'A sprightly mystery debut . . . Murder and
Elizabeth's sharp-eyed forays into the village
society add interest to the credible plot'
Publishers Weekly on *Broken Star*

'Reveals Brown as a stylist with a line in sharp
dialogue. Part-time PI Elizabeth Blair and partner
Max are hired to prove a man innocent of murder
. . . The crackling relationship between the
principles makes for a higher entertaining read'
Crimes Writers' Supplement,
The Times on *Double Wedding Ring*

'Lizbie Brown's novel bursts open with all the
fanfare of the wedding march . . . She unpicks the
flaws in the characters of this intricate mystery'
The Oxford Times on *Double Wedding Ring*

Also by Lizbie Brown

Turkey Tracks
Broken Star
Shoo-Fly
Double Wedding Ring

Jacob's Ladder

Lizbie Brown

NEW ENGLISH LIBRARY

Hodder & Stoughton

First published in Great Britain in 2000
by Hodder and Stoughton
First published in paperback in 2000
by Hodder and Stoughton
A division of Hodder Headline

A New English Library Paperback

10 9 8 7 6 5 4 3 2 1

A CIP catalogue record for this title
is available from the British Library.

ISBN 0 340 76819 3

Printed and bound in Great Britain by
Mackays of Chatham plc, Chatham, Kent

Hodder and Stoughton
A division of Hodder Headline
338 Euston Road
London NW1 3BH

For Susy, Ian, Parker and Hazel

Prologue

Daisy Pluess closes the back door behind her, calls out, 'Anyone at home?' Apparently not. The place is as still as the grave. There's a smell of lemons. It's a miserable kind of day. The rain has held off, but at three forty-five in the afternoon, it's almost as dark as night.

Strictly speaking, Daisy isn't supposed to be on the premises. She's an intruder. But it's Christmas week . . . Does that make a difference? Daisy would say so. It explains why she is to be found creeping — tiptoeing with almost clandestine intent — into the warmth of the vicarage kitchen. The woman who cleans; bad hair, thin and straggly, a tendency (no more than that) towards buck teeth. A woman with too much to do, too many people wanting their houses put straight, too many blasted things swillocking around inside her head. All the ker-fuffle that goes with the festive season. Turkeys, wrapping-paper, marzipan, second-class stamps. Easy to see, then, why she had absent-mindedly left her bag behind that morning. The bag with her pills.

Diabetes, in case you're wondering.

Also blood pressure, so she can't be without them.

Daisy side-steps (with surprising grace) the three bags of groceries dumped on the floor just inside the door. Balances her considerable bulk between the table

1

and the cooker. Calls out, as she usually does, 'Yoo-hoo!'

No reply. Daisy gives a shrug, waits a moment longer, then drags her weight over to the door that leads into the hall. Yes, there it is on the hall table, right where she left it. Forgetful head makes weary feet, she tells herself, waddling over to pick it up.

That's all right then.

She has the bag in both her hands and is turning to leave, when she hears the voice in the study. He's rabbiting away on the phone. The vicar. Daisy clutches the bag (scuffed black leather) to her more than ample bosom, stands perfectly still on the polished parquet to listen. Her mind is like a vacuum cleaner, sucking up all sorts of scraps that she finds lying around the village. Dirty bits, on occasion. Titillating. Oh, yes. You'd be surprised what a cleaning lady hears as she progresses from house to house. Nothing wrong with listening. Good fun. We all do it given half a chance.

'Mrs Bartram,' Philip Fletcher is saying. 'How are you? And where is your husband at the moment? Samarkand or Timbuctoo?'

Daisy rolls her eyes heavenwards. Him and his so-called jokes. Pathetic. But then, so is Marian Bartram. Lady Bloody Muck. Daisy's mouth tightens. There's a movement behind her; Jasper, the vicarage cat coming to rub himself against her leg. She kicks him away. Can't abide cats. Claws. Pee all over the cabbages. Drown the lot of them, if I had my way.

'Tomorrow?' the vicar is saying. 'I think I can squeeze you in. Later rather than sooner, I think. Let's see now—'

Through the crack in the door, Daisy watches as he leans over to consult his diary. Big ear glued to the phone; jowls soft and baggy; glasses halfway down his nose. A man of God? Daisy thinks not. God doesn't wear boots that big.

'Yes. Four thirty. Will that do? Good. Now comes the million dollar question. Your place or mine?' He turns, his smile big and smarmy. Oh, he can charm, the Reverend Philip

Fletcher, when he chooses. He can also tell lies. Daisy knows that for a fact. She is dumbish, but crafty with it. Thick, but not stupid.

'Yours. Fine, fine. If it's about the tower fund—'

It isn't, but Mrs Bartram won't let on what her business is. There is more banter (on his side, at least), then the phone drops back on the receiver. Jasper circles Daisy with some suspicion and disappears into the kitchen. She moves away from the door. Time to scarper . . .

But she is still on the premises, hovering in the kitchen, a moment later, when the doorbell shrills. Now who might that be? Will she wait to find out? Is the Pope a Catholic? Daisy, being Daisy, is always on the look-out. Always nosing around other people's houses, oozing with inquisitiveness, taking little sniffs at the air in front of her.

He's out of the study. Calling up the stairs, 'Catharine. She's here.'

No reply.

'I said she's here.'

'I heard you.' Mrs F's voice from the landing.

'I'll let her in then, shall I?'

'That's up to you.'

'Darling—'

'You asked her. I didn't.'

Daisy, listening through the crack in the door, is all ears.

'Look – we talked about this—'

'You talked. I listened.'

'All right. Have it your own way.'

'My way? That's a laugh.'

'Catharine – darling – it'll be fine. I'll let her in. You promised to do your best.'

'Do my best?' Almost a laugh. 'Don't I always?'

'That's what I love most about you.'

'I bet you do!'

'So it's OK?'

3

No reply. There's a pause and a click and the sound of the front door opening. His voice booms out, 'Vivienne! Right on time. Come in out of the rain.'

Mrs McNeil. Daisy knows all about *her*. Widow in her late thirties; Lavender Cottage; Secretary of the Church Restoration Committee; posh voice and even posher ash-blonde hair.

'Dreadful day,' he says boomingly. 'We'll shut the door on it, shall we?' She comes in, they stand there looking at each other, the two of them in the hall. Mrs F. is coming down the stairs. She says nothing, merely turns to go into the dining-room. The other two follow her. A distant clock chimes.

Now at this point, Daisy has two choices. She can creep furtively out by the back door, whence she came. Or she can hang around and listen. To be fair, she does hesitate, but why break the habit of a lifetime? Daisy is good at eavesdropping. Practice makes perfect. Isn't that what they say? She inches her way into the hall.

It's very quiet in there. Seems a bit awkward. The vicar is clearing his throat, gently, but purposefully. 'Well, now, I think we all know what's to be discussed.'

A heavy silence.

'Catharine?'

'You discuss. I'll listen.'

His voice is a tad reproachful. 'We shan't get very far with that attitude.'

'I may not want to go very far.'

'Darling, you promised me we could at least talk about it. The three of us.'

'A promise made under duress.'

'Never duress—' He sounds reproachful, disappointed in her. 'But a promise is a promise.'

'All right.' She seems to have come to the end of her patience. Something has snapped. 'We'll talk about it. She can start.'

'I'll start.' He sounds happier. 'What I want . . . what I'd

4

like . . . is for us to come to some sort of equable arrangement.'

'Oh, yes. I bet you do!'

Mrs McNeil says, 'Look – if this is going to be awkward—
Only Philip persuaded me—'

'Oh, he's good at persuasion.' Mrs F. sounds weary. 'It was his
best subject at school.'

'Darling, sarcasm isn't going to help.'

'It helps me.'

'Nevertheless . . . you promised—'

'All right, so I promised. I haven't got to be possessive or
narrow. I haven't got to mind your *friend* here moving in with us
for three weeks. I have to tell myself that a *ménage à trois* will be
fun.'

Daisy, who never got beyond a supermarket day trip to
Calais, has trouble with this last sentence. Manage a what? But
she knows all about fancy ladies. She can scarcely contain herself.

'That it will be a bit of a lark. A really exciting adventure –
once I've got used to the idea.' An ironic tone is slipping in.

'Catharine—' His tone is reproachful. 'Don't be – negative.'

'Negative?'

'It's simply a question of helping Vivienne out. Her builders
want to start next week. Monday morning, in fact.'

'And this is Saturday. What happens if I don't play ball?'

Mrs McNeil says, 'Look – I'm not sure—'

'Oh, I think you are,' Mrs F. snaps back. 'Pretty damned sure
of yourself, it seems to me.'

'Catharine . . . Vivienne has nowhere to go while the
builders are in, so we're offering her . . . sanctuary. Temporary
shelter.'

'Are you sure it'll be temporary? Are you sure it's not just the
thin end of the wedge?' The question hangs in the air. Daisy, a
quivering blob by this time, holds her breath and waits for the
reply. But she is to remain disappointed, because at that moment
– exactly seven minutes past four – the doorbell interrupts the
proceedings.

'Who on earth?' His voice for once sounds uneasy.

Daisy tiptoes backwards, three awkwardly long steps and then a short one. Time for a tactical retreat. She is just in time. The vicar is already at the front door and turning the catch. Safely hidden again, Daisy opens the door very slightly and puts an avid eye to the crack. She watches him open the door, but the porch is empty.

Odd.

He steps out into the porch, opens the outer door – but he needn't have bothered. Nothing but wind and rain in the gathering dusk. The short, straight path is deserted. That thrashing, black thing is the hydrangea bush being taken this way and that. A wild draught sweeps into the hall and lifts the rug. He looks to the right and the left, reaches an arm back in to switch on the porch light. He has spotted something on the quarry-tiled floor. A dark shape. The porch light snaps on. The vicar bends to examine the contents of a box just inside the porch.

Odds and ends for the January jumble sale, Daisy decides, in response to the appeal that went out in church last week. She is not a churchgoer (except for weddings and funerals), does not profess to be a Christian, but she misses nothing.

The vicar is about to lift the flap and examine the contents when he stops. Changes his mind, for some reason, stands gazing at it intently. Daisy clutches her bag, clocks the startled expression on his childish-looking mouth. He steps back, then forward again. Pauses for a moment, as if to say something, then, gingerly, lifts the cardboard lid.

Daisy sees, from the corner of her eye, a faint movement. Hears a mewling sound that she can hardly believe. A tiny hand waves and falls again. As thick drops of rain go on falling outside, the Reverend Fletcher bends over the box. Slowly and cautiously, he reaches in and lifts something out. He can hardly believe his eyes.

Someone has left him a baby for Christmas. A newborn with

a very red, almost raw, face. As he holds it up, it stares at him like an old man. There is a moment's suspense and then it opens its mouth and yells.

Chapter One

Mid-January. Cheerless rain outside. Elizabeth Blair, in the middle of a monumental fit of the blues, sat writing a letter to her daughter.

> *I spent Christmas on my own in bed with the flu. I'm over it, thank God, but it's left me with a hacking cough. The doctor says I have a respiratory infection. I've been on antibiotics for a week now, but I'm still feeling lower than a snake's belly. Caroline won't have me in the shop — she says I'll frighten the customers away. What customers? I ask. Anyway, here I am, incarcerated at home, bored out of my skull, patching and piecing to save my sanity.*

She put down the pen, grabbed three tissues (man-sized) from the packet in front of her and gave her nose a resounding blow. Bad idea. Now her sinuses were jumping on top of everything else. Infections, she thought. Who needs them? My eyes are gritty, I've got a damn fine headache and if I have to sit here many more days with cocoa coursing through my veins, I'll shoot myself.

Her hand once more moved, crab-like across the page.

> *Life seems to have been more miss than hit lately. In the past month, the roof has sprung a leak, the stupid car blew up on me, also the gas*

9

heater. And if all that isn't enough, it has been raining for weeks. All through Christmas (wasn't that fun?) and the New Year and the holidays. Right this minute, you could take a boat across the fields behind the cottage, Or swim across. Maybe I should. Maybe a spot of exercise would do me good.

Or kill you off. Her hand was tired. She sat back and pushed her gold-rimmed glasses up high on her forehead. Green eyes, sharp and troubled, stared down at the crazy plaid block on her lap.

They say history is written in letters. Day to day stuff. What happens (or not, as the case may be) in this house. Well, God help us if this catalogue of moans is history. But at least I haven't hit the booze, she thought. Yet. There was a stash of it, untouched, in the rack in the kitchen. She had felt too ill even to raise a Christmas toast. Couldn't bear the thought of the stuff. Ill at Yuletide; what a fate. No eating, no drinking, nobody to tell good stories, nobody to minister to you; lying around ransacking heaven and earth for something to think about.

What's happening to me? I feel old and ugly and morbid and depressed. Where had it come from, this feeling that life was no longer real? Until now, she had always been so sure of where she was heading. Sure-footed. Reasonably optimistic, even on the darkest of days.

It was unlike her to feel so down. Even when the very worst had happened, when Jim, her husband, had died in a car accident back home in the States — what was it? . . . ten years ago now — she had managed to haul herself out of the abyss and book a vacation in England. It had taken every ounce of her strength and courage to set off alone and she had done so with some trepidation, but the venture had paid dividends. She had tracked down one or two of her ancestors and had fallen in love with the West Country and in particular with the city of Bath. Buying a small shop in a Georgian mews and an even smaller cottage in

South Harptree just outside the city had seemed entirely logical. 'I'm going to soak up this beautiful place for a while,' she told her stunned family. 'I've decided to sell quilts. The shop will be called Martha Washington and I've already hired me the cutest little assistant. She's called Caroline and she looks and sounds just like an English duchess. Much too posh to take orders from yours truly, but we'll give it a go and see what happens . . .'

Five years on, she still adored the place. She had friends, a thriving business, a whole new world. There was no real reason for this descent into the slough of despond. In the middle of all this heart-searching, the phone rang. She picked it up.

'Is that the convalescent home for old broads?'

'Oh, very funny, Max.' She imagined him leaning back in his office chair, feet propped on the desk, toes fidgeting away inside his scuffed shoes as he chatted.

'So how are you? Feeling better?'

She croaked some kind of answer. It was good to speak to the boy. Max and the detective agency that he ran from a ramshackle office above her shop in Pierrepont Mews could usually be relied upon to provide the odd rush of adrenaline. A wet log spat a spark on to the carpet. She trod on it hard with the toe of her slipper. Outside, the sky was lowering, though the rain was easing off. The wind had dropped, though the trees were still a good deal disturbed.

Max said, 'You sound lousy.'

'Thank you.'

'You sound like you're taking part in your own funeral.'

'Did anyone ever remark on your wonderful bedside manner?'

Max laughed. 'Now and then. Fancy a little job? Get you out of the house? Spread a few germs abroad?'

'What kind of a job?' When, a couple of years back, the Shepard Agency had experienced cash flow problems, Max had invited Elizabeth to become a partner in his business. Financial involvement had led to other things. She now found herself (bemusedly at times) shunting her Martha Washington duties sideways to make space for helping Max with the odd investigation.

'New case. Interesting. That explorer bloke who was stabbed just before Christmas. Remember?'

'I remember.' She searched her thick head for a name. 'Connor Bartram.'

'That's the one. Well, I had a call from a woman called Ellen Helmsley. Bartram's sister. She's anxious to see us. Today, if possible.'

'Today?'

'Yeah, I know. But she was rather insistent. Pushy type. Wouldn't take no for an answer. Rides to hounds, I shouldn't wonder. Used to cracking the whip.'

Elizabeth wasn't sure. 'You do it, Max. I don't think I'm up to it.'

'Nonsense! Do you good. Get you out of that—' He stopped.

'That what?'

'I was going to say that foul mood you're in.'

'Listen, if you felt like I feel—'

'I know. I know. I'd be on my last legs. But you're made of sterner stuff.'

Elizabeth started to cough.

'Finished?' he said when it was over. 'So are you coming?'

'I can't.'

'Of course you can. Listen, she's your type.'

'Which is?'

'Bossy as hell. You'll know how to deal with her. Dose yourself up with something and get your coat on. I'll give you the address and meet you there at three.'

'But it's two thirty now.'

He ignored the comment. 'We're looking for The Malthouse in a village called Little Gifford. The house is next to the churchyard. So you won't have far to go if you peg out.'

* * *

It was the middle of the afternoon. Elizabeth pulled up at a halt sign and peered this way and that. No signpost. You couldn't see a hand in front of you. Rain drizzling through the fog. No sign of any kind of civilisation, just sodden hedges, a disused barn, swelling mud and luminous grey water in the ditch.

She sat there in the driving seat, wondering why the hell she had been persuaded to come out on such a god-awful day. I'm not well enough to be doing this, she told herself. I should turn right round and go home again. It's just the weather for trouble. She felt it in her bones.

For the first time in ages, she almost wished herself back home in Virginia. She'd spent Thanksgiving there – a big family reunion – at Jim Junior's house – her elder son – in Turkey Creek. Couldn't remember the last time they'd all been together. Jim Junior, Ed and Holly (the twins) and finally Kate and her new guy, Saul. Plus husbands and wives and partners. Needed a sheepdog to round them up. They'd had a great time and ever since her return, she'd felt unreal. Unsettled. As if her centre had somehow shifted. Ridiculous, when she'd lived alone in her very English cottage for the last few years and had planned to go on doing so indefinitely. Had planned? Planned. Before you know it, you'll turn into a sad, clinging old woman. Pull yourself together. Get your backbone back in working order.

She reached into the bag on the passenger seat and found her mobile. Dialled a number.

'Shepard Agency,' Ginger's voice said. From the minute she had walked into the office two years ago – a lively, red-haired little temp wearing granny glasses and a breezy air of confidence – Elizabeth had liked the girl. She kept Max in order, wangled cheques out of clients and generally drove things along with an efficiency that should have been daunting, but wasn't.

'Hi. It's me.'

'Elizabeth! How are you? Feeling better?'

If only they'd stop asking. 'Better than I was. Listen, have you got a map anywhere at hand? I seem to have lost my way.'

In more than one sense.

It transpired that she'd taken a wrong turning after Brassknocker Hill. 'So if I take a right and head on down-hill—'

'You'll be right there. I think. I'm not brilliant at maps. Your voice sounds dreadful. How come you got up from your—'

'—deathbed? Ask Max. Listen, I'll see you later. Thanks for the help.'

Max was waiting for her in his car outside the house. Sitting with hunched shoulders, impatiently waiting as she parked across the way. A pale sun was now filtering through the clouds, covering the village with a dusky mauve light. 'Hmm,' he said. 'Only twenty-five minutes late.'

'Think yourself lucky I'm here at all.'

'I thought it would perk you up. Clear the old tubes.' He looked as if he'd slept in his jacket and might yet drop back into bed in it when he returned to his flat in Edward Street. But for the moment, his blue eyes were alert, his mind already on the woman they were about to interview.

'She sounded a bit – well – fierce.'

That's all I need, Elizabeth thought. Some tough nut to wrench my headache several notches higher. The rain had now stopped, but the trees were still dripping in single, separated hard plops. A gang of rooks shattered the quiet. The Malthouse was a long, low, eighteenth-century farmhouse standing in the middle of a fantastically complicated garden. There was a pergola (bare wood, now, in the middle of winter), a knot garden and a whole series of dropping terraces.

A middle-aged woman with blue eyes and frazzled chestnut hair jerked open the door. 'You're late,' she said.

'Yes, I'm sorry. I couldn't find—'

'Well, now that you are here, come in. Don't stand dripping on the doorstep.' Max was right. Her voice was fierce and well bred Scots.

Max made a comic face behind her back as Mrs Helmsley led them through the hall into an old-fashioned sitting-room that had faded apricot walls, a tall wooden fireplace (green-tiled), some uncommonly arty-crafty chairs and an easel set up by the window.

'You paint?' Elizabeth asked. Unnecessarily.

'Gardens mostly. It's how I make my living.' She was tall, demanding, restless.

Elizabeth took a closer look at the canvas. 'I like it. It's not wishy-washy.'

'I try to avoid that. I was trying to get down a few impressions of this brooding light. The sun trying to get out . . . the way it's filtering through.'

'It's a very unusual garden.'

'I made it that way. I like complicated compositions.' Those curious, green-blue eyes – almost turquoise – met Elizabeth's gaze.

'Do you exhibit?'

'I've had one or two shows in London.'

Elizabeth brought herself back to the matter in hand. 'We were sorry to hear about Mr Bartram. It must be hard to lose a brother. And under such dreadful circumstances.'

'It is. Con and I are – were – pretty close. Only two years between us.'

'Are the police keeping you up to date?'

'The police?' A hard, humourless laugh. 'All they do is harass my nephew, Kit. He's the elder of Con's two sons. That's why I called you in. I'm worried about the boy, if you want to know the truth. Terrified they're going to arrest him. They've had him in three times for questioning. He seems to be the prime suspect.'

'Any particular reason?'

15

'Yes, a perfectly sound one, I suppose, coming at it from their angle. My brother was stabbed with one of the boy's chisels.'

'Chisels?'

'Yes. Kit's a stonemason.'

'A stonemason?' It was the last thing you would have expected from such a family.

'What — graves and tombs?' Max asked.

She gave him a glare. 'Ecclesiastical work and private commissions. He's also done a lot of work for the National Trust. Crumbling old mansions that need restoration. My brother totally disapproved, of course. He thought it a waste of a very expensive education. But Kit is as stubborn as his father. He's found a vocation and he's sticking to it . . .'

Elizabeth felt a cough coming on and was forced to let it rip.

'I hope you're not going to give me that cold,' Ellen Helmsley said.

'I'll try not to. What did his mother make of your nephew's . . . vocation?'

'She agreed with Con. But then, she never understood the artistic temperament. I always encouraged Kit's artistic abilities. My brother didn't like it. It was one of the rare things we didn't see eye to eye on. "The boy has to earn a proper living," that's what he said.' A tear was swiftly wiped away. 'I thought he'd come around to it in time. Con could be alarming, but he was a pussy-cat inside. Cried buckets when they lost their infant daughter. Mind you, he never let Marian see. Came over to me and let it all out.'

'How old was the little girl when she died?'

'Three and a bit.'

'And what was wrong with her?'

'Hole in the heart. They tried to operate, but she didn't survive. Blessing in disguise, if you ask me. The child was pretty frail.'

A slight pause. 'So what precisely is it that you want us to do for you, Mrs Helmsley?'

'I want you to do some nosing round. Find out who killed my brother, so that my nephew can get his old life back.'

'Then perhaps you'll tell us all you know about the night your brother was murdered.'

Chapter Two

'I'll tell you what I can. I called at the house myself that evening at a quarter to nine. My sister-in-law had gone out to one of her damned committees. Con and I – I suppose we had about ten minutes together. I wish to God I'd stayed longer, but I had other Christmas presents to drop off after his, so I was in a dash.'

'And how did your brother seem that evening?'

'Fine. Perfectly normal.' Her voice quavered for a moment and she had to turn her head away. 'Well, I have to admit he'd been a bit glum lately. I'd pop in now and again to try and cheer him up.'

'Any idea what caused the glumness?'

'Nothing in particular that I could find out. You know what men are like. It's a devil of a job to get them to talk about their feelings. A mid-life crisis of some kind, I'd say, probably fuelled by overwork. Those expeditions of his took so much organising, you know? Sometimes it drained him. He wasn't a young man any more.' She gazed, watery-eyed, out at the garden. 'Perhaps like the rest of us, he was losing his fizz.' She got herself back together. 'I gave him his Christmas present. We had a brief chat.'

'About?'

'Oh, the usual kind of stuff. Our plans for Christmas Day. Stuff like that.'

'Which were?'

'My two daughters were both coming home. Con planned to spend the day quietly with Marian. I asked him to join us, but he wouldn't. Piers would be dropping by to see his mother in the afternoon, he said, so she wanted to be at home.'

'Piers?'

'His younger son.' There was something about the way she said it.

'Not your favourite?'

'Not exactly.'

'Could you tell us why?'

'Do I have to? Yes, I suppose I do. He had a twin who died at birth, so they spoiled him to death by way of compensation. He has – how shall I put this? – wide-boy tendencies. Expensive tastes that he can't always support and a tendency to manipulate situations for his own ends. The boy's unstable. Never stuck at anything. Started off working for an estate agent in Bath, but after a couple of years he got bigger ideas and left.'

'To do what?'

'He's supposed to be buying up dilapidated old properties and selling them on for a profit. But I'll believe it when I see it. He's notoriously unsafe with money.'

'You said something back there – something about Piers coming to see his mother on Christmas Day. His mother. Not his parents—'

'Con had had some sort of argument with Piers. Nothing major, but they weren't speaking—'

'An argument about what?'

'I don't know, but my guess would be money. Piers was always on the cadge. Unlike Kit, who doesn't seem to care about it at all.'

'Kit's your favourite?'

'Yes, I always liked Kit. He has more about him, only my blasted brother could never see that. Kit had the strength of mind to go off and do his own thing. Just as Con did, of course, when he was young. They were perhaps too alike in some ways. I don't mean to look at. Kit's looks come from her side.'

Elizabeth popped a throat sweet into her mouth and signalled for Max to take over. 'Did Kit visit his father?' Max asked.

'Sporadically.'

'Can we go back to the night of the murder?' he asked. 'You say your brother was fine when you left him. Did anyone else call at the house that evening?'

'Piers's partner dropped in just after I left, so they tell me.' Another purse of the lips. A glint of derision. 'In my day, a partner was someone you took to the dance floor with.'

'Piers's partner? Her name?'

'Rosie Angel. She's a midwife. She's been shacked up with Piers for a couple of years now.'

'Do you know why she visited the house that night?'

'Well, it wasn't to deliver a baby, that's for sure. Though they could have done with her across at the vicarage earlier that day. Did you hear about the abandoned baby? Extraordinary!'

Elizabeth had read about it in the local paper and had been intrigued and concerned about the poor little thing. 'Did they find the mother yet?'

'Not as far as I know.'

Max returned to his earlier question. 'So if she wasn't delivering a baby, what was she doing at the house?'

An infinitesimal pause. Then, 'You'll have to ask her that.'

'Were they friends, Miss Angel and your brother?'

'I suppose so.'

That was a bit grudging. 'You didn't approve?'

'They were too friendly, if you ask me. Not that the poor old sod didn't need friends. Marian was never much of a wife to him.'

'Do you know what time Miss Angel arrived and left?'

'Not exactly. All I know is that she didn't stay long. She had an emergency call from one of her mothers who had gone into labour early. Only when she got to the patient, they hadn't called her at all. It must have been a hoax call.' She delved into her cardigan pocket and brought out a packet of cigarettes. 'Filthy habit. I almost ditched it last year, but now and then it saves your life.'

Max waited until she had lit up and then said, 'Tell me about your relationship with your sister-in-law. Did I detect friction?'

A grim smile. 'You're quite right. I never got on with Marian. Better leave it at that.'

'But you still called to see your brother, even though you didn't see eye to eye with Mrs Bartram?'

'Good God, yes. I just went when I knew she would be out. Marian's a creature of habit. As long as you knew her committee nights—'

'Was your brother's marriage a happy one?'

'You'd better ask Marian that. They'd survived thirty-five years. Mostly, I should imagine because he was away for months at a time. I didn't like the way she put Con down in public, but there was damn all I could do about it.'

Max said, 'I'm sorry to have to ask this, but what time exactly did your brother die?'

'He was attacked just before nine thirty, as best they can judge, and died about an hour later.' She said, 'It might have been different if my dear sister-in-law had found him earlier. If she hadn't gone to bed without looking in on him.'

'She didn't find him until the morning?'

'Unfortunately not. He was up in his den and she said he never liked to be disturbed when he was working. As I said, he'd been stabbed in the heart with one of Kit's chisels. The wound was a very small one. There was little exterior bleeding and no indication of the damage done underneath. My one comfort is that the internal bleeding would have rapidly made him lose consciousness. The police immediately arrested Kit for questioning, but they had to let him go in the end. He had a solid alibi – he was travelling back from London when his father was killed. Also the blow was delivered by a left-handed person and Kit's right-handed. So they couldn't pin any-thing on him, though they clearly would like to do. But they keep coming to see him, which is why I have to do something to help the boy.'

Max said, 'How many people had keys to the house?'

'No idea. You'd better ask Marian.'

'Do you know of anyone else who visited your brother's house that night?'

'According to the police – no.'

'But?'

'But—' Her voice betrayed the tension she was under. 'I think there may have been someone else in the house when I left.'

'Someone apart from your brother?'

'Yes.'

'You saw someone?'

'No.'

'Then you heard someone?'

'No. Not exactly.'

'Then how—?'

'I can't tell you exactly. It was just a feeling.'

'Can you explain that, please, Mrs Helmsley?'

Well, Con went upstairs to get a Christmas present he had for me. I haven't opened it yet. Haven't had the heart. And I stood there in the hall waiting for him to come back down and— Well, you know when you get a feeling someone else is around? It's an old house, I know. You get creaks and such. But I'm convinced. Yes, I'd swear there was someone else there.'

'Where, exactly?'

'At the back of the house. In the back passage or the kitchen.'

'You couldn't have been mistaken?'

'I don't think so. I mean, the hall clock was ticking and the wind was rattling the windows – it was a foul night – but there's a difference between close-up and background sounds and where they're coming from.'

'So who did you think was in the kitchen?'

A shrug. 'At the time, I assumed it was the dogs. But afterwards, I found out that Marian had taken them with her.'

'To a committee meeting?'

'Marian's a law unto herself. You'll soon discover that. So it couldn't have been the dogs, but I didn't realise that until afterwards.' Mrs Helmsley added, as if thinking aloud, 'I've been thinking about this a lot since his death. If there was someone else in the house, Con didn't know it.'

'How do you work that out?'

'Well, I sat outside in the drive after he'd shut the door. The ignition's playing up on my car. You have to give it a couple of pulls and then wait a minute or so before trying again. So I was sitting there waiting and I saw him switch the hall light off and then the landing light before, finally, the light went on in his den. He's a stickler for saving electricity. Always has been. She complains about it. Marian. But he's always been the same since the days when they didn't have two pennies to rub together.' She said, 'He wouldn't have switched the downstairs lights off if he thought anyone else was there, would he?'

'It's a point,' Max said, 'unless he took whoever it was upstairs in the dark with him.'

'You mean he'd got some female tucked away waiting for him?' She shook her head. 'I don't think so. I know my brother.'

'So did you tell the police about the lights?'

'Yes. But they discounted it. They think I'm overwrought. A batty old woman.'

And they might very well be right, Elizabeth thought.

Chapter Three

Another batty old woman was waiting for Elizabeth as she parked the car in the lane by her cottage in the village of South Harptree. Her neighbour, Dottie Marchant, standing in her front porch. 'There you are!' she said. 'You look dreadful!'

If anyone else said it, Elizabeth would scream. She adored the cottage – gabled windows deep into the roof, solid chimneys, incomparable views down over the hills to Bath, three miles away – but she had never before lived in such close confinement to her neighbours.

'Can't sit still and rest. You're like snow in summer,' Dottie said inexplicably.

'Sorry?'

'Snow in summer. The plant. You've seen it. Masses of little white flowers . . . creeps all over the place, takes over walls.'

'I don't see—'

'Spreads itself with abandon, under stones and over. Like you, it's got a runabout habit.' So had Dottie's tongue. 'I've just been on a prayer and study day. Well, it's a day out. You'll never guess who I met. I was just coming to tell you.'

'I've no idea,' Elizabeth said wearily.

'Ernest Crookham.'

'Really?' Elizabeth was none the wiser.

The camellia man. You must have heard of him? He's very

27

well known in the gardening press. One of England's most notable shrub gardeners.'

'You don't say?' Elizabeth wished Dottie would take herself back home. I'm not up to this, she thought.

'He gave a little talk entitled God the Gardener. And then we had tea. And at the end of the afternoon, he sold me one of his latest books.'

'*Sold* you?'

'Well, we all have to make a living. Do you know, he catches rainwater in eighty gallon butts. That's the secret of his success.'

Ah, well, thought Elizabeth. Now we know.

'You look cold. Come in for tea.'

'Can't. Not today. I . . . I've got to go out again in five minutes.'

An hour later she was scoffing apricot tea bread with Ginger in the teashop two doors along from the office. 'Tea and cakes seemed like a good idea,' she said, 'but I couldn't take another hour of Dottie. Not today. I need someone I can have a laugh with.'

'Max will go mad,' Ginger said. 'Shutting up the office like that.'

'Too bad. He shouldn't make you work on a Saturday. Tell him you were on an urgent errand for me.'

'Such as?'

'Such as helping an old woman stay sane.'

'Oh, really!' Ginger took in the silver flecks in Elizabeth's tawny-to-blonde hair, her matronly but trim figure. 'You're the youngest looking sixty-year-old I ever saw.'

'Sixty and some.'

'Even so. You do exaggerate.'

'Maybe I do, but today I need lively company.'

'That bad?'

'That bad.'

'No work talk?'

'No work talk.'

'Do you want to pour?'

'Nope.' She didn't really want to do anything. 'So how was Christmas?'

'Great.'

'Max had a good time with his family up north, I gather?'

'Mmn.' Ginger lifted the pot and poured, frowning a little. 'You noticed anything about Max lately?'

'No. Why?'

'No reason. Only—'

'Only?' Elizabeth sipped her tea and prepared to wait. You needed patience with the young.

'Oh, I don't know.'

'What don't you know?'

'I'm not sure how to take him these days. He's—'

'He's what?'

No reply. The girl chopped her cake into neat little squares.

'You two been hollering at each other again?'

'No. Quite the opposite. It's just that— Well, you know how he usually is?'

Flippant, irreverent, a pain in the butt. 'Yes.'

'You know I can never do anything right?'

'Uh-huh.'

'So he's not like that any more. He's behaving . . . well, impeccably. It's not natural. Take yesterday. Every time I looked up, he was watching me. It's unnerving. Like he's afraid I'll steal the petty cash. He's giving me the creeps. And I sort of miss the sparring. You know? Could you ask him if something's wrong?'

'Ask him yourself, why don't you?' Ginger was usually pretty direct. Not one to suffer fools.

'Not such a good idea. He might tell me.' She gazed across at Elizabeth. 'My work's OK, isn't it?'

'Couldn't be better.'

'So he's not likely to sack me again?'

'Certainly not,' Elizabeth said. How would the office keep running without Ginger? The girl had more sense than Max. Damn it, at times, anybody had more sense than Max.

The following morning, they drove out to the village of Buckland Slade to call on Marian Bartram. Another dark, wet day, sodden and uncomfortable. Rain sweeping in over a deep, narrow valley to the north-east of the city, beating pitilessly against the windscreen. Max drove and talked, Elizabeth sat in the passenger seat and croaked an answer now and again.

He changed gear and threw her a swift, sideways glance. 'I could have done this on my own, you know. Fat use you'll be without any voice.'

'You talk, I'll listen. I just want to be in on it. First impressions and all that.'

'Have it your own way. Just remember I didn't force you to come.'

'It's OK, Max. I won't peg out on you.'

He wasn't so sure. She could see it on his face.

The road – no, the lane – took them past farmsteads grouped around the village much as they would have been a thousand years ago. Past a sweep of fields leading down to the bend in the river that ran a winding course around the valley. A backdrop of trees and water and pollarded willows. Sheep on the hillside beyond. Buckland Slade was very small. No more than half a dozen select properties arranged around a green; the church, a pub called The Gardener's Arms, the village store and a line of stone-built terraced cottages with gardens that would be brimful of flowers in summer. The Old Vicarage – as opposed to the modern (and much smaller) vicarage built across the road from it – stood on the edge of the green, just fifty yards from All Saints Church. A rambling old place, all chimneys and Georgian windows; very desirable, even blurred by rain. Very top drawer.

A plainish-looking woman opened the door. Grey hair parted in the centre and drawn back into a knot at the back of her finely sculpted head. She wore dark trousers and a crew-necked navy sweater with a crisp white shirt underneath. One of the old school, Max thought. He handed her his card, explained the situation.

'My sister-in-law called you in?' Marian Bartram peered through her spectacles at the card, plainly astonished. And furious. 'What on earth for? The police are dealing with the case perfectly adequately.'

'Her main concern seems to be your son, Kit.'

'Oh, yes. Well, it would be.' The blood suddenly rushed to her face. 'Those two are as thick as thieves.'

Max said, 'All this must be an immense strain on you, Mrs Bartram. We realise that. But if we could just have a few minutes—'

'It's Sunday, for heaven's sake.'

'I know. We don't normally work of a weekend, but this is quite urgent.'

She seemed to weigh things up. Then, shortly, she said, 'I'll give you five minutes. That's the limit. You'd better come in.'

They followed her along the hall, past a wonderful staircase, carved and clinging to the wall, and through a door on the right. The drawing-room was comfortably shabby, with barking dogs, a smell of woodsmoke, two lumbering great sofas with rugs thrown over them and several cabinets standing against the walls.

She waited until they were seated. 'What is it that you want to know?'

'First of all, how many people knew that your husband would be alone in the house the evening he was murdered?'

'I've no idea.'

'Could you try and think? It may be important.'

She sat down opposite and began fiddling with the gold watch on her left wrist. 'Myself. Mrs Helmsley, one presumes, since she called in to see him after I left.' A strong reaction, briefly, then it was hidden again. 'Rosie—'

'That's Miss Angel? Your younger son's partner?'

'Yes.' Marian Bartram's face had clammed up.

'Did she call often?'

'Now and then, when she's working in the area.' Her voice was cool and distant.

'And Miss Angel is a midwife, I believe?'

'Yes.'

'That's a bit uncanny,' Max said, 'considering.'

'Considering what?'

'Considering the little package they found across the road on the day your husband died.'

'I suppose you're right.'

'Would you say they were close, Miss Angel and your husband?'

'Close?'

'Friends?'

'I suppose so.' The silence went on and on, but she was giving nothing away.

'So was there any particular reason for her to call that night?'

'You'll have to ask her that.'

Max said calmly, 'We will, in due time. Can you think of anyone, besides Miss Angel and your sister-in-law, who might have called that evening?'

'No.'

She's bloody hard to interview, Elizabeth thought. Nothing comes back. The ball stays permanently and deadly in her court.

Max said, 'You went to a committee meeting that evening, I believe?'

'You've been well briefed. Yes, I left the house at about twenty past seven to attend a parish council meeting. Health and Safety.' She seemed to see no irony in this.

'Did either of your sons visit the house that evening?'

'No. Piers was in the Cotswolds on business and Kit was in a train on the way back from London. He didn't get back to Bath until nine fifteen.'

Convenient, Elizabeth thought.

'And your sons live where?'

'Kit has a cottage near Melksham and Piers a flat on the out-skirts of Bath.'

'I see.' Max moved on. 'So how did your husband seem that evening?'

'Perfectly normal, when I left the house.'

'Mrs Helmsley says your husband died at around ten thirty. But you didn't find the body until next morning.'

'That's right. We . . . He was shut up in his den on the first floor. If he's working, he doesn't like to be disturbed. When I came in, I made myself a cup of coffee, watched the eleven o'clock news and went to bed.'

'You didn't find it odd that he didn't join you?'

'I— We have separate bedrooms. Have done for a while.'

'I see.' Max spoke carefully. 'So you found the body at what time the next morning?'

'Eight o'clock. Eight fifteen. I went to ask him some-thing and discovered that his bed hadn't been slept in. That's when I went into the den. He . . . he was lying on the floor by the fireplace. At first I thought he'd had a stroke. His father went quite suddenly like that. I called the doctor and an ambulance.'

'An ambulance? But you must have known he was dead?'

'You don't act rationally. You think— You hope—' One of the dogs – a chocolate setter – came to life, gave a sudden bark. Mrs Bartram didn't seem to hear. There was a hint of clay in her complexion. Exhaustion in the cool, grey eyes.

'You wanted him to be alive?'

'Of course I did. I thought if we got him to hospital—' She sounded far away, in another place.

Shock, Elizabeth thought. Makes you act irrationally. The

room felt cold and watchful, the floorboards, the furniture, the windows dark with gloom. The dog yapped again. This time Marian Bartram heard it. 'Shut up, Bel.' Her voice was sharp, the strangeness gone out of it.

'How many people had a key to the house, Mrs Bartram?'

'Myself. My husband. The boys.'

'Your sons?'

'I said so, didn't I?'

'I see. Was anything taken from the house that night?' Max asked.

'No.'

'Did you keep much money in the house?'

'No.'

'You're quite certain that your elder son – Kit – didn't call here that night?'

'Positive.'

'But the weapon that killed your husband was one of Kit's chisels?'

'Yes.'

'Do you have any idea what it was doing here? Had your son done any work on the house?'

'No.'

'Did he ever work here?'

'No.'

Taciturn wasn't the word. No emotion now, no anything. It was as if she were reciting a text. And Max was the examiner.

'Were there any signs of a break-in?'

'None.'

'Odd, that.'

No reply.

'So it seems your husband must have let his killer in? Is it possible it was someone he knew?'

'Never! It must all be some hideous mistake.'

'A random break-in, you mean?'

'Or an accident. The killer got the wrong address.'

Bizarre suggestion, but she seemed quite serious. 'Your neighbours didn't hear or see anything untoward that night?'

'Not that I know of.'

'Did you ask them?'

'No. I presume the police did.'

Max looked across at her, his eyes serious. 'Is there anything else you can tell us that might be pertinent?'

'Nothing.'

Elizabeth thought, she knows more. I'd swear it.

'And now, if you'll excuse me— You've had more than your allotted time.'

'I just wondered—' Max kept right on going. 'We wondered if you would allow us to take a very quick look round at your husband's den.'

'There's no need. The police have already been over it.'

'That's fine,' Max said cheerily. 'We'll take their left-overs.'

'No. I'm sorry. It's out of the question.' She said suddenly, 'Do the police know you're poking your noses in?'

'I've really no idea.'

'I shall inform them. You realise that?' She appeared tired and snappy. With reason, perhaps. Her husband had met with more of an adventure than he'd intended. Furthermore, he had met with it not in deepest Africa, not sailing down the Amazon, but at home, in his own house, where these kind of adventures were not supposed to happen.

Max got in one last question. 'Your sister-in-law thinks there was someone here in the back part of the house when she left her brother that night. What would you say to that?'

'I'd say she was trouble-making. She's very good at it. She's been at it ever since I've known her.'

Chapter Four

An odd household, Elizabeth thought, as they were blown by the wind in the direction of the car. But interesting. Brusque, doggy mother on her own for a large part of the year. Of her life. And maybe I can see why. The elder son a stonemason. The younger a bit of a waster, if Ellen Helmsley was to be believed. Must find out who benefited by the will. Must check on that hoax call to the midwife. Max stood by the car watching her with a grin on his face. He said, 'I can hear the old brain ticking over.'

'We need to do house calls, Max. All round the Green.'

'I'll do the calls. You OK?'

'Not really.' She had suddenly flopped.

'Go home and rest.'

'How can I go home?' she croaked irritably. 'There's only one car between us.'

'Then I'll take you home and come back.'

Sometimes – just sometimes – the boy talked sense.

Monday afternoon. Catharine Fletcher, who had spent a sleepless night, stood in the kitchen doorway and watched her rival – her latest rival – heave her bag in through the front door.

This is the first time he's tried to move one of his women in with us.

She felt like a stone. She was hurting, but coldly. There were cavernous, chilly rooms inside her. Whatever was going on out in the hall seemed to Catharine to be happening in another world. A world that she wasn't responsible for, couldn't do anything about. Didn't choose to? No, couldn't. Catharine had accepted a lot in her marriage that many women wouldn't accept, but you had to make your choices and live with the consequences. She had learned to bite her tongue to get what she wanted. Which was what exactly? A social position and a way of life that suited her. OK, she was overworked and under-appreciated, a drudge whose life was selflessly dedicated to running parish groups (her freezer full of fund-raising cakes) and to delivering church magazines. She even had a part-time teaching job to help make ends meet. But she liked being in the vicarage pew, lipsticked and courteous, every Sunday morning. She had been born a vicar's daughter, it was all she knew and she couldn't imagine giving it up for what would be, as Philip's other women had been, a temporary insanity on the part of her husband.

Catharine was a nester – an ecclesiastical nester – but there was a woman of steel underneath the surface. Occasionally it crossed her mind that she was a fool, but she had been married to Philip for a very long time. They had met at university, had married when they were both twenty-three. She had married her first date. Had fallen hook, line and sinker for his combination of compassion and leadership, so she well knew what the women who were attracted to him – by him – were up against. Philip's religious calling was central to their life together, but quite early on she had realised she wasn't the only recipient of his divine aptitude for love. He had persuaded her – it was excruciating, but at the time he was very convincing – that forsaking all others meant making sure that he would father children by no one but his wife.

Children . . . The now familiar pain hit her hard in the stomach. If I had been able to get pregnant, would it have made a difference? Would it have stopped him from straying? Made him less ruthless in the pursuit of other women? He wanted a family as much as I did. And I wanted it so much, it's a wonder I'm not in some nut-house. But he wouldn't come with me to do something about it. Wouldn't even discuss getting medical help.

And so here she was, trapped in her own very peculiar ring of hell. Allowing Philip to persuade her yet one more time that baring more than his soul to selected parishioners was actually part of a glorious vision. He had an answer to all her objections. Catharine's ideas of love were possessive and narrow. His broader capacity for love (mostly in the direction of the young, female members of his congregation) meant development while her more traditional ideas meant their relationship would stagnate.

For almost twenty years, Philip (a vain man who was fond of the showbiz elements of his calling) had persuaded her that she could not object to sharing him with other women. Girls from the youth club, intrigued by what was worn under the cassock, or the ever-present predatory parish helpers. There were times when it almost drove Catharine to distraction. She knew, on the one hand, that it was idiotic to go on putting up with his infidelities, but a clergy marriage was a very public thing. If she were to walk out, there would be one hell of a scandal. The whole parish would know it, her whole world would be shot to pieces. Catharine was too much of a realist to think otherwise. And anyway, if she plucked up her courage and walked out on him, what would she live on? Where would she go? In any other setup, a cheated-on wife would be entitled to her share of the home and of his pension. But they lived in what was virtually a tied cottage.

There would be nothing, not a bean to divide between them.

Not even a stipend, if she were to blow the whistle on him.

Here I am, pale, prim, Catharine Mary Fletcher, forty-five years old, part-time teacher, practically nothing in my bank account. I've never lived on my own, never slept with another man, never really been of much use to anybody. I'm a dab hand at organising a jumble sale, but will that be classed among the world's great achievements on the day of judgement when I'm called to account? I doubt it.

Vivienne McNeil closed the door behind her and stood there in the hall, hesitant about what to do next. One hand moved up to smooth her already smooth hair. In her gentian-blue eyes there were doubts, even if she had allowed herself to be carried away by her knight in shining armour.

And who looks after the knight in shining armour? Catharine asked herself. Who looks after the small child inside the man? The embattled wife. That's who. 'Top of the stairs.' Her voice, she knew, sounded icy. 'Turn left. It's the box room at the end.'

'Thanks. Look – are you sure—?'

'You'll have to carry them up yourself,' Catharine said brusquely. 'The porter's unavailable. It's his Young Wives' afternoon.'

'Of course. I hadn't realised – I didn't expect—' The woman was too thick to see the funny side of the three p.m. appointment in Philip's diary. She was like a cat on hot bricks, desperate to get up out of the line of fire; yet desperate, as well, to throw some sort of ladder over the gulf that separated them. 'What . . . what time does he get back? Get in? Come home?'

'Oh, when it suits him. He's very popular with the ladies, you know.' The disease of irony, she thought. Scoring points is an easy way out. The only drawback being that it makes you refuse to deal with anything.

* * *

Max did as many house calls as was possible on the Monday afternoon. The last – and perhaps the most important – of these was Combe Grove, (Queen Anne house, tall and slim, surrounded by beds all neatly edged with box), owned by a retired doctor and his wife: Fred and Cherry Collinson. A helpful old pair. Dr Collinson was a quiet, self-effacing man with a gentle voice, who happened to be on the Health and Safety Committee and was, therefore, prepared to swear that Mrs Bartram was in the village hall from around seven twenty-five on the night her husband was murdered until they left and walked the few short yards home across the Green together at approximately ten minutes past ten. Mrs Collinson, a bulky old dear in a bright blue woollen cape thing, had seen Ellen Helmsley arrive and leave, but nothing after that.

Both Dr and Mrs Collinson had sort of liked Connor Bartram. A witty fellow. Good company, when he was that way inclined. Some had found him caustic and it wouldn't be hard to imagine. ('But Fred and I never found him anything but charming.') They didn't know him intimately, of course. He was away too much for that. But now and then, Con would pop in and have a beer and tell them about his latest trip. And sometimes Fred would go in there to view Con's curiosities, the little keepsakes he brought back from his travels. There were showcases full of them in his den. No, nothing particularly valuable, well, as far as one could tell. But, then, how would one know? Such peculiar things he hoarded. Why, he'd once come round lugging a great box. ('You'll never guess what was in it, my dear!') A very rare prize, indeed, so it seemed. A keeled horn from a bush-buck, brownish-black and all twisted into spirals. ('No, I've never heard of one either, dear.') The females were hornless apparently, and lighter and redder. Well, of course, they'd had to pretend to admire it, just as Con would feign an interest in the Victorian woodcuts and engravings that Fred collected. No, more than feign, because Con used to bring Fred the odd woodcut he'd come across in London. ('And it wasn't obligatory, you understand. Fred never asked him to. Most kind, when one thinks about it.') The poor man had had contacts all over the world and was just as much a bookman as Fred was, in his own particular way. Why, he'd shut himself up in that den of his and read for hours— sometimes days – at a stretch. Not much fun for Marian! No, I wouldn't say he was ever really much of a companion to her. Fred and I go hunting for pictures together, you see. There's the difference. What kind of books did Con collect? Oh, geographical stuff, mostly. And travel books and anthropological stuff. Books about head-hunters, she shouldn't wonder. He'd once lent Fred a book about some chap who went missing, presumed eaten by a crocodile in the Zambesi.

'So to recap,' Max said, reeling from all this minor detail. 'You didn't see Miss Angel – the midwife – arrive or leave, but you heard Ellen Helmsley leave at around nine o'clock?'

'Exactly so.'

'And after that?'

'After that, nothing. Except—'

'Except?'

'Well, our grand-daughter was staying with us. Flora – she's ten – always sleeps in the little bedroom that looks out over the Bartrams' shrubbery. And I was in there reading to the child and I heard something.'

'Something?'

'I can't tell you what exactly. Just something. A shout, perhaps? It's generally very quiet out there at night – except if the river's high and rushing down at the bottom of the field, but it wasn't that night, so I went to look.'

'And?'

'I concluded that it must have come from the television down below.'

'What time was this?' Max asked.

'Nine fifteen. Nine twenty perhaps.'

42

Max asked her about the lights. 'They went off, definitely, after Mrs Helmsley left. Until just before nine thirty, when the place was suddenly lit up like a Christmas tree. Lights all over. I said to myself, she must have left the meeting early. Marian. The lights always go on when she gets back.'

'But she was still at the meeting with your husband?'

'Yes. It's all very strange.' Mrs Collinson went on, 'You know, it must have been someone young and strong, the person who killed him. Con was quite hardy. He could look after himself. My dear, the scrapes he'd come through over the years. He'd survived a great deal. And for what, one asks oneself? To be murdered in his own house. Poor man. It makes me nervous at night now. There's quite a lot going on during the day – you'd be surprised. But at night it's very silent.'

'So you think the assailant would have come on foot?'

'Unless he parked outside the village and walked up. You'd hear a car and I didn't hear anything after Mrs Helmsley left.'

'Not even Miss Angel's car?'

'I'm sorry. But she may have left it further up by the church where it's better lit. The attacker could have come up the field, of course. Over the wall and into the house by the back way. Daisy says— No, we won't start on that. Daisy's tongue does tend to run away with her. I believe that's why Marian got rid of her.'

Max said, 'I've lost you. Who is Daisy?'

'She's our daily. Well, twice weekly. I have to say that I've never had any trouble with her. You have to keep an eye on her, mind you. She's – well – let's just say she's dependable so long as you give her a sharp nudge now and again.'

'But Mrs Bartram sacked her?'

'I believe so. But don't quote me on that.'

Max made a note of Daisy Pluess's address. 'Anything else you can tell me that might be useful?'

'I don't think so.' She considered for a moment. 'Have you been in touch with the people who are restoring Buckland Mill?'

'Buckland Mill?'

'It's down on the river bank right opposite The Old Vicarage. Actually, I haven't seen the owners for some time. Some sort of trouble with their bridging loan, I believe. They've halted the renovations. But if they were around, they may have seen something.'

'Detectives?' Piers Bartram said offhandedly to his mother. He tried not to let his fear show; merely looked interested, mildly interested. 'Aunt Ellen sent them?'

'As if I haven't got enough to get on with.'

Piers looked across at his mother and managed to laugh. 'Mad old bat.' He went over to pour himself a drink. It was too early, much too early, but he needed something to stop his hands shaking. He tried to get a few simple facts straight in his mind. They knew nothing. They were unlikely to uncover anything. But it was hard to get rid of the clinging feeling that they had known, guessed, suspected . . . something. 'What possessed her?'

'Apparently she's worried about Kit.' There was sarcasm in her voice now.

'Same old story.' Piers gave her one of his smiles.

'Same old story.'

He poured two stiff whiskies and carried one across to her. 'Here. You must need it.'

She did. They stood there sipping whisky for some time. Then, 'Mad old bat,' Piers repeated. 'More money than sense.'

'I don't know how much more I can take. She was here that night. Did you know?'

'Aunt Ellen?' he said. 'Yes, I heard.'

'Delivering Christmas presents.'

'Spreading poison, more like.' He had himself more under control by now. 'Want me to go over there and sort her out?'

'No. No, leave it. I'll sort it myself, if need be.'

Chapter Five

'I'll carry these out to the car for you,' Ginger said, taking charge of the pile of library books and videos.

Elizabeth wasn't having any of it. 'What on earth for?'

'They weigh a ton. You're still wobbly. Why didn't you tell me you were going to the library? I'd have done it for you.'

'Look – I'm not an invalid.' Why were the youth of today so goddamned pushy?

'You will be unless you listen to sense.'

'Neither am I a geriatric.'

'Would I dream of suggesting it?' Ginger was already crashing the door open with her back. That was another thing. All that unnecessary energy they gave out, charging around, lickety-split, like racehorses or trains. 'Keys?'

Elizabeth handed them over.

'Where's your car?'

'Usual place.'

'Right. Look after the office for five minutes. I'll be right back.'

'Where's Max?' Elizabeth croaked as Ginger plunged down the stairs.

'Daisy Pluess,' Ginger yelled inexplicably back up the stairs.

Elizabeth dropped her bag on Max's chair next to the empty crisp packet.

* * *

Daisy Pluess lived in one of the council houses out on Elm Road. 'Yes,' she told Max, 'I did have a falling-out with Mrs Bartram. She said I were too slow. There I was, sweating under the effort of cleaning all them blasted rugs and there's her, Lady Muck, telling me I weren't pulling my weight.'

You'd have a job to do that, Max thought. Some load!

'She had the cheek to say I were malingering. Well, I'm no scholar, but I got the message, like. And I wasn't going to be talked to like that, so I left. Handed in my notice. None of my other ladies has seen fit to find fault.' Daisy was hauling clothes out of the washing machine in the cluttered back scullery – huge, great vests and weird-looking flowered garments as big as a tent. She spent so much of her life looking after other households that her own was in a continual muddle. She had a whole heap of jobs she was always planning to do, but never managed to get round to. Shelves to clear, bins to empty, magazines to sort, sour smelling lavatories to scour. But it was impossible to hop around like a bird when you were Daisy's size. Occasionally she hit a low point and resolved to chuck it all in. But then there would be no money to buy her lottery tickets or treat the grand-daughter. So she went struggling on.

'How many other ladies?' Max asked. In the other room, the television was blaring.

'Let's see now,' Daisy said. 'There's a parcel of Methodist ladies. Plus the vicar and Dr Collinson.'

'You must spend your life tidying up after other people.'

'Too right, I do. Some of them are elderly and infirm, some plain disorganised and others as I could mention are just too grand to keep their houses in order.'

'I was wondering,' Max said, 'did you ever have a key to The Old Vicarage?'

'No, I didn't! Whoever told you that?'

'Nobody told me. I was just enquiring.'

'Well, you can take your enquiries somewhere else.'

Max could see she was flustered. She dragged the last

garment – a pair of men's boxer shorts, surprisingly small – from the machine and slammed the door shut.

'You've been listening to her, haven't you? Marian bloody Bartram. Well, I walked out because I'd had enough of her bossy ways, so you needn't believe anything else you might hear. Trying to drill a body, like you were in the bloody army! Acting as though she didn't trust you. Counting all the food in the cupboard after you'd gone home, I shouldn't wonder. She could never keep paid help. I don't suppose she told you that? Nobody ever stays long in her employment. I was her third in as many years. And she had nannies galore when the boys were younger. Ask Maggie Yelland as used to keep the pub. One or two of them had to pack their bags at a minute's notice. Ask that nice Miss Angel – Rosie. She knows the old cow well enough.'

'You know Miss Angel?'

'She delivered my Vicky's last boy. Lovely girl, but the Bartram woman treats her like dirt. Bloody snob! Or else she's jealous—'

'Why would she be jealous of Miss Angel?'

'Because *he* got too fond of her.'

'Mr Bartram?'

'That's right.'

'And what did you make of Mr Bartram?'

'A dry old stick. The char, that's what he used to call me. "Is it the char's day?" he'd shout down the stairs. Treated you like a hired hand. Now the vicar's wife's exactly the opposite. Embarrassingly grateful for everything. Falls over herself to make you feel at ease, which isn't always what you want.' Her voice changed tenor. 'In some cases, I'd as soon keep my distance, if you take my meaning.'

Max didn't and didn't particularly want to. 'What did you make of Mrs Helmsley? Mr Bartram's sister?'

'She's all right.' Daisy laughed. 'Chalk and cheese, her and Lady Muck. They had a right old barney one morning when I was working there.'

'About what?'

Daisy warmed to her subject. 'Well, I were in the drawing-room polishing the piano. A grand piano that nobody plays, but it still has to be dusted. I'd have got rid of it. It's the same upstairs. Huge great bedrooms. Far too much furniture. A nice old place, but completely impractical—'

Max knew he was in for a long wait. He let her ramble on until at last they got back to the subject in hand. Mrs Helmsley had, apparently, accused her sister-in-law of neglecting Con. 'All them committees! The Youth Club committee, the Village Hall committee, Parks and Recreation, Brownies and Guides, you name it, she's on it. Get a life, Mrs Helmsley told her. Spend an evening with your husband for once instead of sitting round a table with a load of sad old gits as have got nothing else to occupy themselves with. Charity begins at home, she says. Mrs Bartram hit the roof. It made my day, I can tell you—'

The books were useful, Elizabeth found. It had been a good notion to trawl the biography and video sections of the library for anything she could find on Con Bartram. (If there was one thing in her aching, creaky body that still worked – well, more or less – it was her brain.) She leaned, now, against a pile of cushions and watched, on videotape, an interview that he'd done for *The South Bank Show* after returning from a trip to the Gobi desert. Bartram was a small, wiry man with fading red hair and cold blue eyes. There was a look of the kirk or the manse about him. Something thin and distant about his scholarly lowlands voice; something unpleasantly acid, she decided. He wore a buf-fcoloured shirt with a venerable tweed jacket and matching waistcoat with a fob watch tucked into the pocket.

His grandfather had practised at the Bar; his father had been an Edinburgh lawyer and the young Connor had spent his child-hood on Tweedside. A hard, loveless childhood. His mother had died young and his successful and hardworking father had sent the two children away to boarding school, not having the least idea what else to do with them. On leaving school, the young Con had spent two years reading law at university before suddenly getting a bee in his bonnet about crossing British Columbia by river. Abandoning the law, he rented a room in a friend's house, found small-scale sponsorship and spent months studying in libraries in preparation for the trip. After the first expedition had covered itself (just about) financially, he had organised further trips to Borneo and the Brazilian rainforest, this time taking his ideas to a literary agent, to publishers, editors and TV companies, often bluffing his way into the funds and contracts that he so desperately needed.

Marian had entered his life when he bumped into her (literally) in a depressing government office where they were both queuing to collect passports. A year later, they married and his new wife happily (or so it said) accompanied him on his early expeditions. Money inherited from her father (a military man) had helped fund office premises and both had taken odd jobs to keep them afloat. Con had worked as a night porter, a bus driver, a door-to-door salesman, a freelance journalist – anything, in short, that would help him fulfil his ambition. Some called him a ruthless bastard. Cold. Certainly he came across as a man of singleminded determination, as a formidable character with a cool, logical brain that usually served him well. On a Trans-Africa expedition, he had once been held for weeks by local guerrillas; beaten and half-starved, he had still managed to talk and bribe his way out of captivity. On his release, he promptly cashed in on the experience by writing a book about it.

Two more biographies (by this time, Elizabeth was curled up in bed with aspirin, tollhouse cookies and a flask of hot chocolate) revealed a man as deep as the Arctic Ocean; a man who liked living on the edge, who rarely stopped travelling and sometimes found it hard to settle at home. The Arctic, the Antarctic, the Sahara, rapids, avalanches, deserts, swamps, terrorist bullets and faulty parachutes. You name it, he'd braved it, together with a colourful crew of volunteers. He had needed – and indeed, sought – all the publicity he could get.

Driven. That was the word for him. That was the impression that, time and time again, leapt off the page. Driven by what? Curiosity initially; then money, the desire for adventure, a wild ambition.

Flicking back through the notes she had made, Elizabeth drew a circle around a scribbled name. Oliver Lockie. Con's business partner, in the early days. He might be worth tracing. She wound back the videotape and with gritty eyes, began to watch it all over again. He was beginning to intrigue her, the great Wandering Hero who could plan, meticulously, a trans-world expedition, but couldn't handle everyday relationships within his own family.

Chapter Six

'Ask? Why should I?' Kit Bartram said.

'Why? Because I'd really rather like to know,' his wife snapped back. 'You may not have noticed – you never do – but your son's arse is half out of his jeans and Bess needs new shoes. Plus it may have slipped your mind that the telephone bill hasn't been paid—'

'I don't use it.'

'Oh, pardon me for being normal, Mr Michael bloody Angelo, but some of us have friends we like to talk to.'

'Who don't live a million miles away. You don't need to use the phone all day long.' But she always did. She was always walking round the house with the thing wedged between ear and chin, as if by some miraculous feat of medical skill it had been welded to her aristocratic and stupendously determined jaw. Kit tucked the ends of his faded blue shirt into his dusty jeans and grabbed the keys of the pick-up from the dish on the kitchen dresser.

'So why won't you go and see the solicitor?' Serena persisted.

Serena? Anyone less serene he had never met in his life. Even her voice had an edgy rasp to it. She was a tall, skinny woman with bored, blue eyes whose presence in a room did not add much to your peace of mind. Hard to believe now, but once – aeons ago – he had thought her vivid and dynamic. Back in the time when – hard to imagine now – she seduced me beyond my control. I must have been barking. All she does now, Kit thought, is set my teeth on edge. There are times when, let's face it, she's positively scary.

'Why should I?'

'Why? Because we're skint.' She reeled off fast a list of bills for coal, electricity, gas, the village shop, the mail order catalogue from which she'd bought the expensive silk shirt she was wearing; the Barclaycard, her personal overdraft, not to mention the money she still owed her father.

'I told you. I'm not asking. Old Farleigh will let us know in due time.'

'But she knows.'

'Who knows?'

'Oh, for God's sake, your fucking mother. She's bound to know what was in the will.'

'Not necessarily,' Kit said.

'Of course she does. I'll ask her.'

'Go ahead. I know how fond she is of you.' His voice was mocking. It was his only sure defence against her.

'Theo—' her voice rose. 'Will you please stop slopping that stuff all over the table?' Her demeanour was imposing, but her first-born glared back at her with a look that matched it. 'Cheeky little tyke!' she said. 'You'll know if I have to come over there.'

Won't he just? Kit thought; keep your head down, son, if you know what's good for you.

'And don't you egg him on.'

'Who, me?' Kit said in that light, supple voice of his. 'I wouldn't dare.'

'Yes, you would. You scupper all my attempts to discipline them.'

'Discipline isn't what they need.'

'Oh, no? That's not what Theo's teacher says.'

'Theo's teacher is a nice girl, but as thick as that chair.'

Serena said, 'It takes one to know one.' Possibly, she had been born with that supercilious look on her face. Also with a longing for things she didn't have.

When he didn't rise to the bait, she said, 'You're useless. Always were, always will be.'

'Thanks for that vote of confidence,' he said, picking up his toolbag and throwing it, with a familiar gesture, over one shoulder. And he was gone. A man who, in many respects, was closer to his father in nature than he would ever have believed or admitted. A seemingly cold man with hot blood underneath. Prone to sarcasm and to occasional (very occasional) volcanic eruptions touched off by the tiniest spark; almost religious on the subject of his enthusiasms; ascetic in appearance. A man whose head was sometimes an unknown land.

Like his late father, Kit was not brilliant at relationships. Human personalities are passed from generation to generation. Connor Bartram's father, devastated by his wife's death, had buried himself in legal work and virtually ignored his children, so Con had no memory of fathering. Returning from a long expedition, ill-tuned to noticing two small boys, he would get irritable with his sons and bellow at them. Kit, too, was for the most part cool and remote towards his progeny.

And so it goes on. We learn from each other.

Or not, as the case may be.

Starting the pick-up, Kit suddenly remembered something his father had said to him on the morning of the day he died. 'You and I both know how to put ourselves in neutral. It's a handy gift to have. Nurture it.'

Ginger was wearing a plum jersey and a little suede skirt. She dropped a mug of strong, black coffee on Max's desk. 'There you are. Don't say I never do anything for you.'

'Right. Thanks.' He took the coffee and sat there with the phone clamped to his ear. 'Yup,' he said to the person on the other end. 'Nineish. That suit you? Huh? I'll tell you tonight. OK. The Green Bush. See you.' He put the phone down and sat chewing at a fingernail. You would never have guessed he was the brains (or half of them) behind this outfit. His expression was vacant and he seemed entirely at a loss as to what to do next, if anything at all.

'Anybody interesting?' Ginger enquired.

'Andy.'

'Your friend who works for the CID? The one who feeds you off-the-record stuff you shouldn't really know about?'

'Listen – we've been mates a long time. We trust each other.'

'That's nice. So you're going to pick his brains about the Bartram case?'

'We're going to have a jar.'

'Right.' Ginger opened the top drawer of her desk. 'Listen,' she said, swiftly changing the subject, 'if Elizabeth comes in, you're to send her straight home again. OK?'

'OK.' He was giving her that look again. The one that rested an inch or two to the left of her head. And he was agreeing with her, which was even more peculiar. She shook a couple of choc-olate digestives from the packet she kept in the desk drawer and shoved one in his direction. 'I told Caroline to do the same.'

'What's that?'

'Max, didn't you hear anything I said?'

'Of course I did. You're looking after a friend's dog for the week. He got into the fridge.' He waited, expecting affirmation. The way his brown hair flopped over one eye made her want to reach out and shove it back.

'Wrong.'

'You're not looking after a dog? I could swear—'

Was he doing it on purpose? 'Yes, I am dog-sitting, but I told you that yesterday.'

'So?'

'Oh, never mind.' She made an exasperated noise and went back to her keyboard. He'd come out of it – with it – whatever it was, sooner or later. In the meantime, somebody had to keep the show on the road.

'Am I keeping you up?' Max asked. He looked at Andy across the bar table, over the remains of two packets of pork scratchings and two pints of lager. 'Yes, I am, I can see. Look at the state of you. No wonder crime's soaring when they employ crap like you.'

DI Andy Cooper, cautious, prosaic, Somerset born and bred, sat yawning and scratching his stiff, yellow hair. He was used to this particular line of attack. His sleepy appearance and West Country drawl had been a running joke for most of the five years he and Max had known each other. Andy was one of those young men who take a while to get started and rarely look as if they will get out of first gear; but appearances can be deceptive as the criminal fraternity sometimes found to their cost.

Andy lifted his glass. 'It's Lynn. She's in her fifth month and she can't sleep. The new sprog kicks her all night and if she's awake, I'm awake.'

'I thought you said you weren't having any more.'

'Can't stand only children. Spoiled brats.'

'Roly's not spoiled. How old is he now?'

'Two and a half.'

Where did time go? He's a great kid.'

'You wouldn't have said so last night. Only put the cat in the bloody washing machine.'

'Christ. What happened?'

'Lucky it was only on short spin,' Andy said. 'So how's the Bartram thing coming along?'

'Oh, you know. Boring legwork. Too early to say. What did you make of him? Kit Bartram?'

'Weird sort of bloke. Not on the same planet as the rest of us.'

'Think he's guilty?'

'Hard to say, but we didn't have enough hard evidence to charge him.'

'It was his chisel. The murder weapon—'

'He never attempted to deny the fact. Says it should have been in his toolbox with the others, but it went missing a few days before.'

'Any idea where or when?'

'He didn't have a clue. Says he sometimes leaves his tools on the scaffolding on the church tower overnight.'

'Mmn. And he was on a train on his way back from London the night his father was killed?'

'Produced his clipped train ticket to prove it.'

'So what time did he get back to Bath?'

'Nine fifteen, he said. He was due in at eight fifty, but the train was late.'

'And his father was killed at around nine thirty . . . He could have got up there in time. It's only – what? – five miles or so.'

'It's doubtful. We tried it. Anyway, his clothes were clean and the DNA tests we did on him proved negative.'

So—' Andy levered himself to his feet. 'Fancy another?'

Max quickly checked his watch, shrugged. 'I might just force one down.' The same comforting old ritual. 'Yeah, why not?'

Chapter Seven

—————◆◆◆—————

Councillor Sylvia Grey-Wilson listened to Elizabeth's question with a somewhat sly smile. 'Con Bartram? He was a big fish in a little pond. But all the little fish know exactly what's going on, you realise?'

'Meaning what, exactly?'

'Oh, nothing. Nothing at all.'

'Come, Mrs Wilson. You can't leave it at that.'

Which really set the ball rolling. Only Mrs Grey-Wilson, a robust, loud-voiced woman in a grey suit, was left in the hall at the end of the Parish Council meeting. Elizabeth leaned back in the bentwood chair, one of twenty surrounding the heavy oak table in a shabby village hall which was typical Thirties. Wood-panelled, looking out over fields, smelling of chalk dust and bad-minton nets and tea urns and shortbread biscuits.

Elizabeth, bored out of her skull with lying around at home, had come in search of the back story and Mrs Grey-Wilson, the Chairman of the Parish Council, was eager to give it. It seemed there was no love lost between her and Marian Bartram — in fact, they were old rivals. 'That woman blocks every single idea I put to the committee. The trouble with people like the Bartrams is that they think everyone will kow-tow to them because he's on television and such. Well, some of us couldn't give a fig.'

And some of us are as jealous as hell, Elizabeth thought.

'Live by the sword and die by the sword,' Mrs Grey-Wilson said mysteriously.

'Meaning?'

'Meaning he liked the limelight. Publicity. And that attracts misfits. It's my opinion that he was killed by a stalker.'

'You think?'

'It's what comes of attention seeking.'

Elizabeth made her face look interested in what the old harridan was saying. 'OK. So let's see now. You live—' She consulted the plan Max had made of the houses and their occupants. '— at Knowle Cottage, diagonally across from the Bartrams?'

'Yes.'

'So did you notice anything out of the ordinary on the night of the murder?'

'How could I? I was here all evening chairing the meeting.'

Aggressive or what? 'Before or after, then? You didn't see anyone hanging about in the road?'

'That would be difficult. It was pitch dark.'

'Of course.' Elizabeth smiled sweetly instead of spitting in this disgustingly abrupt woman's eye.

'So to recap. All in all, you and Mrs Bartram were neighbours and colleagues on this committee, but you weren't bosom friends?' Go on, disagree with that, you cranky old buzzard.

'It's difficult to be friends with someone who's continually on the make.'

'On the make?'

'I'll give you an example. You may have noticed that we're having the church tower renovated. Of course, Marian Bartram has to have things done her way. She has to tote the services of her son.'

'Which son?'

'The one who works for the undertaker.'

'The undertaker?'

'Barnes and Holden,' Mrs Grey-Wilson said sharply. 'They

carve stones and such.' There was a sniffy pause. 'Oh yes – her precious son has to be commissioned to restore the gargoyle. It's his pocket our money's going into. It didn't go to outside tender . . . oh, no. I protested. I wanted the firm that did the work at St Mary's, but she had the committee eating out of her hand, as per usual. And no doubt he'll charge over the odds.'

A cough from the doorway at the far end of the room. Elizabeth turned her head to see a clergyman standing in the doorway.

'I'm sorry to interrupt. I just wondered—'

'I suppose you want to lock up, Vicar.'

'If nobody minds. Is there a problem? Can I be of any assistance?'

'No. We're about finished.' Elizabeth got to her feet and gathered up her bag. To tell the truth, she would be glad to get away.

'This is Mrs Elizabeth Blair,' Mrs Grey-Wilson announced. 'She's a private detective.'

'A detective?' For a moment, he looked startled.

'For my sins.'

He was a handsome man. Clear, grey eyes, straight gaze, warm smile, chestnut hair turning to silver.

'She's making enquiries about the Bartram murder.'

'Oh. Oh, I see.' Suddenly he relaxed. 'Dreadful business,' he said. 'Dreadful.'

'Isn't it?'

'Right,' Mrs Grey-Wilson said. 'I'll love you and leave you. Other fish to fry.'

The vicar watched her leave. 'Good woman,' he murmured. 'If a little overpowering on occasion.'

'She doesn't get on with Mrs Bartram, I gather?'

He gave a deep sigh. 'Tell me about it. Two powerful women. My greatest achievement to date has been to stop those two murdering each other.' He realised what he'd said and made a rueful face. 'Shouldn't have said that. Inappropriate under the circumstances. The trouble is they're both always right and they're both indestructible.'

'I imagine Mrs Bartram needs to be at the moment.'

'Yes.' He said again. 'Dreadful business.'

'So how long have you been in Buckland Slade?'

'How long have I known the Bartrams?' He was quick. 'Two years. Almost three.'

Perhaps she shouldn't have enquired, but if you don't ask, you don't get. 'Mrs Bartram being such a strong personality . . . You think it's the reason her husband was away so much?'

'No comment.' He showed himself a master of tact.

Oh, well. At least you tried. On the way to the door, she said, 'I hear you had quite a shock yourself on the day of the murder.'

'Sorry?' The startled look had come back.

'The abandoned baby.'

'Oh, that. Yes. I'm afraid you're open to that kind of thing, living in a vicarage. Sanctuary and all that. Open door at all times.'

'Did they find the mother?'

'No. Not yet. I gather the police are still making enquiries. Babies are tough little creatures,' he said consolingly.

'Just as well.' She pictured the poor little scrap in its cardboard box in the rain and cold. Sighed until it caught in her throat and turned into a phlegm-filled cough.

'That's a nasty cold you've got.'

'Sorry.' She dived into her bag for a cough sweet. It tasted foul and it didn't do any good, but it was some sort of a distraction.

'Don't apologise. Half the parish was down with it over Christmas.'

They were out in the porch now. Greener-than-green fields falling away down to the river. Tranquil farm buildings, misty woods on the lower slopes of the valley opposite. 'Superb view,' she said. It reminded her of something. 'Where exactly is Buckland Mill? We should talk to the people who are restoring it.'

'Just there on the bend of the river.' He pointed it out to her. 'You can't see it properly from here . . . the field drops away too steeply. Verey, I think their name is. Nice couple. Two sons, one's a student. Exeter, I think . . .' He rabbited on for a while about the history of the mill. 'Quinlan Cory was born there. The nineteenth-century poet. Friend of Keats. We're having a literary weekend in a couple of weeks in honour of his bicentenary. I must sell you a ticket. I'm sure you'd find it fascinating.'

'You bet,' Elizabeth said. 'I might just wander down there and have a look.'

'Don't stay out in the damp too long with that cold. I'd better get a move on. My wife will wonder where I am.'

'I'm sorry to have kept you. Thanks for your help.'

'It was a pleasure.' He sounded as if he meant it.

The sky was overcast as she went through a stile and down across the field that Philip Fletcher had pointed out to her. The woods on the far side of the valley were washed a deep green. Everything seemed cold and bright and remote. The sun would soon be going down.

Buckland Mill was a hundred yards or so down the valley from The Old Vicarage and almost directly opposite. Conveniently opposite. Elizabeth took a well-tramped footpath that led across a small wooden bridge to the unkempt gardens at the back of the mill. Stood there absorbing every little detail. Situated on two levels, the ancient stone building seemed to be built on both sides of the river. Scaffolding had been erected at one end, where gable windows had been cut into the roof. But work had stopped.

The place seemed deserted – until a noise behind her made her turn. A young man with wiry, chestnut hair and a rucksack slung over one shoulder was coming down the path.

'Hi!' she said. 'I hope I'm not trespassing. I was just admiring the old place.'

'Feel free.' There was nothing to hurt, he told her. The house was as yet uninhabitable. It would take six months at least to get the essential work done. He'd just popped by to make sure there hadn't been any more vandalism.

'You've had trouble?'

'The builders had to be laid off until the bank sorts a bridging loan. So when the cat's away—'

'I see,' Elizabeth said. 'I suppose you heard about the murder across the way?'

'Yes.' He shook his head. 'Couldn't believe it.'

'I don't suppose you saw anything? You or your family?'

'Sorry. We're not here that often.'

'OK, fine.' Elizabeth rubbed her freezing hands together. 'Well, I guess I'll move on. Nice to meet you. Thanks for your help.'

'Any time. Take care on the bridge. Some of the boards are rotten.'

Chapter Eight

On her way back to the cottage, Elizabeth decided to try to locate Rosie Angel. She was in luck. The girl was at home at the address Ellen Helmsley had given her. Saffron Cottage, Batheaston, an unfussy detached cottage with an undulating pan-tiled roof and small, square windows in need of a paint job.

Miss Angel was a good example of a name fitting a face. She was twenty-fiveish, maybe a couple of years older and blessed with peachy skin, clear blue eyes and a swathe of fair hair caught up in a tortoiseshell comb. 'Can I help you?' she said.

'I certainly hope so.' Elizabeth handed over her ID and stood waiting for the fat to hit the fire. But for once it didn't. The girl just stood there in her blue nurse uniform, gazing thoughtfully at the card. She looked like a celestial ballerina with her toes turned out.

'You'd better come in,' she said, her voice all calm and col-lected and as sweet as her face. 'Piers isn't here at the moment, I'm afraid.'

'That's OK. I'll catch him some other time. It was you I wanted to see.'

So there they were suddenly, sitting in a long room that ran the length of the cottage – a flight of stairs at either end, not much furniture, just a couple of easy chairs and a big, round table covered in textbooks and dirty coffee cups – discussing the night Con Bartram had died.

'I'm sorry,' Rosie said, 'I don't remember the exact time I got there. It was probably just after seven thirty, because I'd been running late all day.'

'So you had fixed to be there at what time?'

'I hadn't fixed to be there.'

'No?'

'No. Not really.' A certain vagueness came over the blue gaze.

'But you said you were running late. Which sort of implies that you were expected at a certain time.'

'Not really.' Rosie Angel examined her spotless fingernails, curled one hand inside the other, and said, 'But I did sometimes drop in when I was passing.'

'To see your father-in-law?'

'He's not – wasn't – my father-in-law. I'm not married to Piers.'

'To see Con Bartram, then?'

'Yes.'

'You were friends?'

The wait was interesting. 'I suppose so.'

'You're not sure?'

'I—' Flushed cheeks. The fingernails were being examined again. Minutely. 'Yes, we were friends. He . . . Well, he said I reminded him of the daughter they lost. Apparently I look like her. She . . . she had the same kind of colouring.'

'And did you know that Mrs Bartram would be out that evening?'

Real embarrassment this time. 'Yes. I thought there was a council meeting.'

'Only thought?'

'Most nights she's out on council business.' There was something in the angelic voice.

'You don't approve?'

'It's nothing to do with me.'

'Nevertheless—'

'OK, so I felt sorry for Con. Marian didn't even consider staying home to keep him company. She carried on her life as if he wasn't there.'

'Which he wasn't, by all accounts, all that often?'

'All the more reason to take some notice of him when he was there, wouldn't you say?'

'So you think Con was lonely? That's why you made regular visits when his wife was out?'

'It wasn't like that!' The fingers twitched nervously.

'No?'

'No.'

'So what was it like, Miss Angel?'

'I told you. I dropped in if I happened to be working in the area.'

'Your maternity visits were in the evenings?'

'Quite often, yes. Babies aren't always born in office hours, you know.' For a second or two they gazed at one another. The girl looked defiant and Elizabeth firm but cheerful. Rosie said, 'I came over that evening to see Melanie Gilbert. She lives in the cottage next to the pub. She's nearing her time and she hasn't been well. You can check if you like.'

'I surely will,' Elizabeth said. 'So you just popped in on Con while you were passing?'

'I dropped in because he asked me to, actually.'

'He asked you to?'

'He called me on the mobile.'

'When was this?'

'Late that afternoon.'

'Did he give you a reason?'

'Not exactly. He – seemed a bit low.'

'So he called the nurse?'

Rosie said with some vehemence, 'He wanted someone to talk to. Haven't you ever felt like that?'

'Sure I have.' Every blessed night since Christmas, if you

really want to know. No real reason. It just feels like I've lost the woman I used to be and I can't reinvent her. Inconvenient, but I guess I have to live with it. Keep busy. Try not to panic. 'So what did Mr Bartram want to talk to you about?'

'I didn't really find out. I'd only been there ten minutes when I got a message on my mobile to go round to Anna Healey's. She's expecting twins in February and her husband thought she was going into labour early. But when I got there, it turned out to be a false alarm. He'd panicked and over-reacted.'

'So what did you do when you found you weren't needed?'

'I went home.'

'You didn't go back to The Old Vicarage?'

'No.'

'But if he was low—'

'I – I had a headache. I thought I'd call him later. Only when I did, there was no reply.'

'What time was this?'

'Nine thirty. Maybe just after.'

'So he'd already been attacked?'

'I suppose so.' Rosie Angel sat gazing hard at her hands. 'I wish I had gone back.' Her mouth began to quiver. 'It might all have been different.'

'True enough. But then, you might be dead too.'

Silence. Rosie was seated on a footstool hugging her knees. Elizabeth decided to jump ship to a new subject. It sometimes worked, made new circuits. 'I believe Marian Bartram sacked her cleaning woman a while ago. Any idea why?'

'Marian found her going through Con's desk. She sacked her on the spot.'

Well, now, Elizabeth thought. There's a thing. That was worth coming for. 'I don't suppose this cleaning lady – Mrs—'

'Pluess.'

'Mrs Pluess. I don't suppose she ever had a key to The Old Vicarage?'

'I wouldn't think so.'

'Did you or your partner – Piers – have a key?'

'I don't have one. As for Piers – I'm not sure. I never asked.' She must have sensed Elizabeth's scepticism, because she said, 'He may have done. I just don't know.'

'Did the house have a burglar alarm?'

'No. Con didn't believe in them. He said they advertised the fact that you had something to steal.'

Elizabeth placed him in that den of his, surrounded by rare old volumes and God knows what treasures brought back from his travels and she asked herself in what tone he would have said such a thing? Jokingly? Drily? With some distaste? Once more, she found it hard to get under the guy's skin.

Suddenly, abruptly, Rosie said, 'Is it true that Ellen is paying you to get Kit off the hook?'

'Is he on a hook, then?'

A slight confusion in the blue gaze. 'What I meant was, is Ellen paying you to investigate the murder?'

'She is. Do you think Kit could have killed his father?' The slightest of hesitations. Elizabeth continued, 'They didn't get on too well.'

'No,' the girl said. 'Kit wouldn't do a thing like that.'

'It was his chisel.'

'No.' The girl shook her head hard.

'Not even in extreme anger?'

This time she wasn't so sure. After an agitated silence, she said, 'Not even in anger.'

'And your partner? Piers? How did he get on with his father?'

'They had their ups and downs, but—' Rosie looked at Elizabeth with ill-concealed anxiety. 'Piers isn't capable of murder either. He loved his father.'

'Love sometimes spawns more dangerous emotions.'

'I don't know what you mean.'

'No? But you know what families are like. You try not to resent your parents' criticisms, but tensions spring up. Little arguments that sometimes turn into big fights.'

'Piers couldn't have quarrelled with Con that day. They hadn't spoken for months—' Rosie stopped, realising that she might have said too much.

'Why not?'

'They . . . had a row.'

'About what?'

'I don't really remember. Marian would probably have been involved somewhere along the line. You'll have to ask Piers.'

'OK.' Keeping her voice friendly, Elizabeth said, 'So put yourself in my position, if you will. Who would you choose as the chief suspect?'

'I can't answer that question. All I can tell you is that I didn't kill him.' A burning blush accompanied this statement.

'My dear, would I suggest such a thing?'

She didn't know the answer to that question. She couldn't imagine this delicate young thing going for Con Bartram with a chisel; on the other hand, it was difficult to sum up people when you scarcely knew them. And there were times when Rosie Angel had seemed to act like a suspect. She was quietly edgy, very self-conscious. Almost casually, she went on, 'The baby girl that was left across the road on the day Mr Bartram was murdered. Did they find the mother?'

'No.'

'The village grapevine didn't yield anything?'

'No.'

'I just thought – well, as you were in the business, so to speak, you might have heard something.'

'Mrs Fletcher said the same thing.'

'The vicar's wife?'

'Yes. She seemed very concerned. She made a point of ringing me. All I could tell her was that the mother will be very young and probably pretty desperate.'

'No one on your register, then?'

'Of course not.' I don't lose my mothers, her expression said.

'So where's the child at the moment?'

'She's with a foster mother, temporarily. Why are you interested in all this?'

Why? She hardly knew. And yet she did. A young girl forced to dump her newborn child in a box in the rain and cold. No family she could turn to. Secure, sure, belonging. It just epitomised everything that was wrong with the world today. Makes you despair, she thought. Or is that your depression talking? Maybe, but things *were* different in the old days. Families rallied around. Grandmothers, sisters, aunts. Strong units to fall back on in time of trouble. But that's all crumbling. Going to pot. She sat staring down at an empty coffee cup on the table in front of her and there came into her head suddenly a chilling thought. You're a fine one to talk. You walked away from your family when you came to England to live. Fat lot of support they can expect from you. I'd be there like a shot if they needed anything. Oh, yes? So how would you know from the other side of the Atlantic? There are phones. Airlines. Oh, come on, Betsey, who are you trying to kid? They're on their own and you know it.

'Are you all right?' Rosie Angel broke into this internal monologue.

'What? Yes. Yes, I'm fine.'

'You don't look it. You look pale. Can I get you something? Tea? Coffee?'

'No. Thank you.' Elizabeth snapped out of it, sat up straight, forced herself to extinguish emotion with rationality. 'I'll tell you why I'm interested in the abandoned child. It just occurred to me that the girl who dumped the baby might – just might – have come back later in the evening to check that the little thing had been found. It was a foul night. Raining hard. If it had been me, I couldn't have rested—'

And if the girl had decided to come back? Her agitation subsiding, Elizabeth said, 'And if I'm right – if the mother did return to the vicarage and if we could find her— Who knows? We might have another witness to murder.'

Chapter Nine

———◆◇◆◇◆———

Ginger said, 'What if we rearranged the furniture?'

'Sorry?' Max became aware that she had asked a question and was expecting a reply.

'I knew you weren't listening. I said, do you think it would be a good idea if we did a bit of a refurb?'

'Refurb? In here?'

'Well, I wasn't talking about my flat. I wouldn't consult you about that, would I?' She was growing a little impatient with him. One hand twisting a wedge of auburn hair behind her neat little ear.

'It's fine as it is.'

'It's wasteful.'

'Wasteful?'

'Yes. Whenever you do a first interview with a client, you send me out to the post.'

'So?'

'So there aren't always things to post. You just want me out of the way.'

'That's the way the clients like it. Confidential.'

'Yes, I know.' The smile she used was the one that said, You don't understand what I mean, do you? You're a bit bloody dim. 'But it's a waste of my time and quite often I have to stay on late to finish stuff off.'

'You get paid for it.'

'Granted. But that costs you money.'

'So?'

Her grey eyes just rested on him for a moment. Pebble-shaped, he thought. Smooth, sea-grey, considering eyes. 'So you promised the bank manager you'd be a good boy this month and you can't afford to pay me overtime. How would it be if we moved the filing cabinet into the middle—'

'The middle?'

'—so that it's between my desk and yours and then your client won't see me and I can be sort of hidden away? So I won't have to stop work—'

'No.'

'What do you mean, no?'

'I mean it won't work.'

'How do you know if we don't try it?'

'I'll have to get up and walk round the cabinet every time I want to ask you something.'

'You could just call over it. Raise your voice.' You're quite good at that, her expression said.

'Talk to you over the filing cabinet?'

'Yes.'

'Don't be ridiculous,' he said and that was the end of that.

Ginger leaned back against the wall with her arms folded. She knew she was right, but she wasn't going to let him light her touchpaper. 'So where were you all morning? I kept trying to call you, but your mobile was switched off.'

'I was on a wild goose chase. Daisy Pluess said that Mrs Bartram sacked no end of nannies and for some reason, Elizabeth thought they might be worth talking to. Waste of time, I told her. We're talking thirty years ago, but she wouldn't listen.'

'So it was a waste of time?'

'Yeah. I went round all the agencies, but only one of them was around in the late sixties and they ditch their records every five years.'

'So you got nowhere?'

'I thought I was getting somewhere. The woman that ran the office actually used to be friendly with one of the Bartrams' nannies. They still send Christmas cards, would you believe, so she gave me an address in Chippenham.'

'That was lucky.'

'Not really. It was an empty house that was up for sale, so now I'm going to have to call the estate agent to find out where she moved to.'

'Did you manage to trace the Bartrams' other cleaners?' she asked.

'Yeah.'

'And?'

'Nothing. Marian Bartram's a bossy lady – incredibly fussy about how things are done, but apart from that—' He was looking at her, but he sounded distant.

'Want a coffee?' Ginger asked, more as a way of shaking him out of it than anything else.

'Yeah. Thanks.'

Thanks? From Max? Weird or what?

'Piers Bartram?' Elizabeth said. 'Your partner – Miss Angel – said I'd find you here.'

'She did? Clever girl, Rosie.' He was a tall, confident young man with thick, red-gold hair. The impression he gave was one of complete imperturbability. Bright gaze, flashily charming smile, cocky manner. Life was all a bit of a lark. That was what his expression seemed to convey. Elizabeth found herself wondering how he would make himself look solemn enough to attend his father's funeral.

A street door banged down below. Bartram was ferreting in his briefcase for some papers, while his assistant was talking to someone on the telephone. As for Elizabeth, she was half-standing, half-leaning against the atticky window, admiring the view of the alley three floors beneath. There was an odd little flight of steps, a terrific Venetian window and wet, blue paving slabs running down to a semi-circular courtyard at the bottom.

'Great place you have here,' she said.

'What? Oh – yes. It's a bit poky. One day, when the profits start rolling in, I'll have proper premises. What was it you wanted?'

She told him. Asked all the preliminary questions. Got down, as soon as possible, to the most important one in her book.

'How was it being the son of a famous father?'

The young man stood behind the desk (shabby Victorian with brass handles) and thought about it. 'Bloody awful, as a matter of fact. We got hell knocked out of us at school . . . bullies taking the piss. And it was a boarding school, so there was no escape for weeks and weeks.'

'Did your parents know about the bullying?'

He laughed, 'You've met my mother? Not the type to let you cry on her shoulder. Brace up. Deal with it yourself, she always said. Best way. The sooner you learn, the easier life will be. And dear old Con was off conquering the world, so he wasn't exactly on hand to complain to. I swore if I had sons, they'd go to the local comprehensive. Piece of cake after what I went through.'

Elizabeth gazed at him. 'So you didn't exactly have a good relationship with your father?'

'How could I? I hardly saw him.'

'But when he came home?'

'When he came home, we played him up. I must have been the stroppiest kid in the entire universe. I thought if I gave him enough aggro, he might just notice he had a son. Sons.'

'So did your theory work?'

'Just long enough for him to give me a damned good hiding. Then he'd be off again up the Amazon. So there you go.'

Elizabeth never let her eyes stray from Piers Bartram's face. She noticed that a little nerve was beating fast in his left cheek. 'Then you won't exactly miss your father?'

'Oh, I don't know. Actually I was rather fond of the old sod. In a funny sort of way, I might just about have been coming to appreciate him. Well, as much as you can appreciate a father who calls you a fantasist and manhandles you down the stairs and orders you to get out of his fucking house.'

'He threw you out of his house? When?'

'About three months ago. We had the most almighty row.' He admitted it quite openly. 'I haven't been near the place since.'

Elizabeth waited just a moment, then said, 'That's odd. Ellen Helmsley told me your father was expecting you to drop by the house on Christmas Day.'

He tried to laugh to hide — what? 'Expecting me? You must have got it wrong.'

'That's what she said. I'm certain of it.'

'She must have meant Rosie. Rosie would have gone to see them.'

'Alone?'

'Yeah. Well, I wouldn't have wanted to cause any arguments at Christmas — for Ma's sake.'

'So you weren't anywhere near your father's house the night he died?'

'Nope. I was in the Cotswolds on business. Rosie called me there next morning to tell me what had happened.'

'I see. Do you mind me asking what the row with your father was about?'

'There was something that needed straightening out.'

'Which was?'

'Oh, something concerning my mother. It's of no importance.'

'You might let me be the judge of that.'

For the first time, there was a change in mood. A faint air of disquiet. He started to fidget with the letter knife on the desk top. 'My mother needed some money to pay a bill and he wouldn't give it her. I told him he could afford it and he told me to mind my own bloody business. It all started from there.'

'Was it a hefty bill?'

'Not really. New curtains, I think. Something to do with the house. You'll have to ask her.'

'Was your mother often short of money?'

'Not that I know of. Not really.'

'I'm sorry to ask this, but is she the principal beneficiary of your father's will?'

'Presumably.' He was regaining his poise.

'You don't know?'

'Haven't a clue. We've had enough on our plates without having to deal with old Farleigh.'

'Old Farleigh?'

'The family solicitor. Doddering old fool. His brain's almost as mildewed as his suit. He's the last thing Mother needs fussing round her at the moment, believe you me.'

'Right,' said Elizabeth, permitting herself a puzzled little smile. 'One last thing – your partner – Miss Angel apparently visited your father the night he died?'

'Rosie? Yes.'

'They were close?'

'As close as he'd be to anybody, I suppose. Rosie was quite good with him. He had a soft spot for her. She's got more patience than the rest of us, I expect.'

'And your brother? Was he patient?'

'Kit? He wouldn't know the meaning of the word, except when he's hacking away at a lump of marble.'

'So Kit didn't get on with your father either?'

'Who did? You may have gathered by now that he wasn't marvellous at public relations, my old man.'

Chapter Ten

Catharine Fletcher wiped the oilcloth on the kitchen table and replaced the sugar bowl. She threw the dishcloth into the sink, turned her back on Vivienne McNeil, who was about to start buttering her toast, and switched the radio off. Catharine then dug into the left-hand dresser drawer, brought out the bundle of tablecloths that she kept for her bring-and-buy tables and dropped them into the basket on the chair, together with four cut-glass vases and a packet of teabags.

Bring and Buy. The last Thursday of every month. Funny thing. You do the same thing over and over and never ever tire of it. Routine. It builds up in your bones. Kind of comforting. What would I do without it? She was about to add a packet of ginger nuts to the contents of the basket, when she happened to glance up and see Vivienne looking at her. Dark brown eyelashes over bright blue eyes. Rather a flat face. Emotions skimming over the surface of it and disappearing again before you could catch them.

'They say it's going to clear up,' the younger woman said, nervously reaching for the butter dish (blue spongeware with strutting cockerels). To give Vivienne her due, she was attempting to sound cheery.

'Really?'

'According to the forecast. They said the sun was going to break through.'

'Oh, that'll make us all feel better.' A voice inside her was saying: Mockery. It's a sad weapon. And it was true. But the odd barbed shaft, a certain sardonic tone got results, undermined all the other woman's attempts to be friendly. Vivienne, on shaky ground anyway, could never quite pluck up the courage to return a sarcasm. And you could score points for ages without being accused of stirring up trouble. It almost made the situation bearable. 'Much better.'

Vivienne shot her a scared look, fumbled her hold on the butter dish and the next minute it went clattering down on to the quarry tiles, shattering into a hundred yellow-streaked fragments. She apologised for this mishap. Began, confusedly, to fumble around under the table, gathering the largest fragments up. 'I'm sorry. So sorry.'

Sorry? For what? Catharine wondered, throwing the other woman a withering look. She said, 'Odd how it's always your favourite things that hit the deck.'

'You're angry. I don't blame you.' She was almost embarrassing in her contriteness.

Angry? Oh, no, Catharine thought, I'm way past that.

Her spirits lifted momentarily, as she saw what a mess her rival was getting into with the butter. And then she managed to cut her finger on a sharp edge. The blood started to well up.

'Oops,' Catharine said. 'First aid needed. You'd better go to Philip for that. He's fully trained.'

At which point, Vivienne dumped the bits on the draining board and scarpered.

'Sarcasm is the lowest form of wit,' one of Catharine's aunts had once told her. But it worked and she had no conscience about using a tart tongue in her own defence. It was the only weapon she had left. The thought of Vivienne scuttling back upstairs to her room would fortify her for the rest of the day. It made the corners of her slightly thin mouth twitch. Buoyed her up. She gathered up the broken butter dish and dropped it in the bin. Christian forgiveness? Forget it! The pleasure of being able

to unnerve that woman, of making her run for cover . . .
Catharine had always had good, solid nerves, had never lacked
courage, except in one thing. She had never found the strength
to walk out on her unfaithful husband.

The clergy try to be snow white, but some drift.

It's a fact of life.

Still, I'm hanged if I'll let it get me down. Catharine flipped
on the hot tap and rinsed her sticky fingers. She had promised
to have him for better or for worse and she was the kind of
woman who kept her word – no matter that other people didn't.
She had been strong all this time. Of course she could keep
going. Other people had it tough, too. Marian Bartram, for
instance.

Imagine getting up in the morning and finding your husband
lying dead. Catharine hugged her arms together and gazed down
at the bin. Dead. She closed her eyes and opened them again, but
the vision wouldn't go away. Con Bartram, only just dead,
stretched out on the floor of his den.

Not a likeable man, stiff and almost contemptuous. But
attractive. Certainly that. Blue gaze, drooping eyelids, tough
mouth. Her nails dug into the palms of her hands. If only her
conscience would stop getting at her. If only she could stop
weighing and considering, churning it all up. What was it that
Con had said to her that night, to stop her babbling on? Brisk
and impatient. Hardly able to wait for her to get the question
out.

'Aren't you going to—?'

A knock on the door. Catharine jumped. She had this grinding fear that any day now, she would open the door and find a
constable on the doorstep. She glanced at her watch. Nine
eighteen.

Of course. She opened the door to find Daisy Pluess, puffing
slightly, saying it was cold enough to freeze your socks off. She
dumped her bag inside the door and dragged her elephantine self
in behind it.

* * *

The Jacob's Ladder quilt that had come in to be repaired lay on Elizabeth's lap. A pretty thing in blue printed calico and pink checkered shirting, heavily quilted in leaf patterns, with a hand-loomed silk tape binding.

She had been ferrying it between the cottage and the shop for a week or so and trying to fix it back together in between seeing to the household chores and serving customers. Right now she was fitting tiny scraps into the gaps where you could see plumb through. Catching with thread the frayed, ill-matched pieces in a jagged corner that had been put together by a perhaps over-worked mother or a child being allowed to help for the first time.

Don't ask me why I do it, she told the no-nonsense voice that was having a go at her inside her head. Don't force me to think logically about it. I'm cutting my own throat, I know. Hours of work for not much of a profit. But it is a pleasure putting the old thing back together again. You get a good feeling, and God knows, they're rare at this time of the year. Goodwill. I suppose that's what it's all about. Homage to the fingers that pieced this piece of rare beauty during the days of the Great Depression.

Homage from one great depression to another.

For God's sake, I'll get my violin out—

The other thing was that she could never resist a challenge. And by working on an old quilt, you gained a rare insight into the craft. Take the child (had to be) who stitched away at this crank-sided block . . . Why, her stitches were getting better, shorter. Less awkward all the time. Three more squares of remnant blue and they would be almost as good as her Ma's. Elizabeth's silver thimble (stuffed with cotton lint to keep her finger from getting sore) shifted itself along to another block. And it keeps me going, I guess. It's basic therapy. Better to have something to do in hard times than let things get right on top of you.

A pot of coffee and a quilt to fix. It helps when you're feeling helpless.

And there have been more than a few days, Elizabeth thought, when I've needed my needle and thread. Scratchy days back when we were dirt poor and the kids got on my nerves with their hollering. The lonesome days when they upped and left home, four of them, one after the other. And of course, the blackest days of all after Jim died.

The light outside had nearly gone. Lights were coming on in the village at the far end of the field. Even thinking about those terrible months brought back the anguish and distress. After all this time. Do the kids still feel this bad about losing a dearly loved father? Don't know. Haven't asked them lately. Her mind went back, wretchedly, to the guilty self-analysis touched off by her recent conversation with Rosie Angel. I'm a lousy mother. Shouldn't have deserted them like that. But this time she made up her mind to counter the charge. To marshal a defence speech. OK, so I can't be there to administer to them if they're in need, but there again, they won't have to carry the burden of having to take care of me as I get older. I've relieved them of that. Kate will undoubtedly be glad. Quicksilver Kate, thirty-two years old, a pretty big shot in a newspaper office in New York. As clever as they come, but definitely short on patience. Jim Junior should be grateful to you as well. He's a bag of nerves, a five star worrier. This cough of mine would finish him off. Well, she had saved him from that fate. She bent over the quilt to examine the colour of a home-made blue dye, a most extraordinary colour, probably stewed up in a wash-pot. And the twins, Ed and Holly? Thirty-four years old, lived near each other in Caspian, Michigan. Ed was a doctor and Holly a nurse. Carers, both of them. Nothing they liked better than a lame duck. So here, she told herself, reloading her needle and pressing the quilt real smooth in her lap, the argument begins to falter. It would be great to have the twins on the doorstep when she grew old and decrepit. Oh, come on, Elizabeth! Get a hold on yourself. You're sixty-something, not ninety. You know what? You've been working too hard. Running two businesses. Getting yourself too deep into Max's damned cases. Murders, hostilities, suicides – ugly stuff that you can't leave behind when you go home at night.

It hangs around inside your head. Dourly. Spreading poison, I shouldn't wonder.

As she went on stitching, the slabs of colour on the quilt slowly distracted her from thoughts of doom and gloom. The Jacob's Ladder was one of her favourite patterns, spawned, like so many other quilt designs, from the Old Testament. Easy-to-piece blocks with a multitude of variations: Broken Sugar Bowl; Railroad I; Rocky Road to California; Road to the White House. She had a Sugar Bowl thumbtacked to the wall of the spare bedroom, hiding the damp patch that bubbled up behind the wallpaper at the beginning of November every year without fail.

She stuck the needle into a gaudy magenta triangle. And there must have been something about the shape of it, because suddenly she was a child again, back in Sunday School, stretching her handkerchief as flat on her knees as it would go in order to take away the vision of the fire and brimstone preacher.

The Reverend Aaron Wilkins. Oh, good God. Where did he suddenly pop up from? The Reverend Wilkins, staring at you oddly and shouting at the top of his considerable voice and crying real tears over his Bible as it suited him.

Fifty years had fallen away and she was listening to one of his terrifying sermons. 'And Jacob came to a certain place,' the preacher roared, eyes glittering, 'and stayed there all night, because the sun was set. Have you ever been out there, boys and girls, alone in the darkness? Night noises all around you? Black devils. Creatures with tails and claws?' His words had the quality of being spat out rather than spoken. 'No? Well, Jacob was out there in the DEPTHLESS BLACK. And he had no bed, so he took of the stones of that place and put them for his pillows and lay down on the ground to sleep.' Elizabeth had imagined the young man lying on the hard-scrabble mountaintop road that twisted up the mountain past Turkey Creek, his head on a boulder he'd found in a farm pasture.

'AND HE DREAMED—'

What was it he had dreamed? She dreaded to think.

'And he dreamed—' One shaking fist rose in the air. 'And behold – a ladder set upon the earth. And the top of it reached to heaven: and behold the angels of God ascending and descending.' Tears streaming suddenly from his crazy old eyes. 'Angels! Messengers from God. DARING to climb down to us—'

There was a rap on the door. Elizabeth almost leapt out of her chair. Came out of the past, smartish. 'Yoo-hoo!' Dottie. It was only Dottie.

'Come right in,' Elizabeth said, her heart pounding. Stupid! You stupid woman. How could you possibly have thought it was an angel?

'Sorry to bother you, dear. I just wondered— Oh, that's pretty.'

'Jacob's Ladder,' Elizabeth said, shaking her head at her own stupidity.

'*Polemonium caeruleum.*'

'Sorry?'

'It's the Latin name for the plant called Jacob's Ladder. A pernicious little seeder. Spreads all over the place. A real menace.'

Like some neighbours I know, Elizabeth thought.

'I had it once under the sitting-room window, but I couldn't be doing with it. Had to root it out. Took me several years to be done with it, mind you. Like some men, Mother used to say. There's another kind,' Dottie went on. 'Non-seeding. Long-flowering. Dashed if I can think of the name. *Polemonium* something-or-other. There's a song, too. We used to sing it in the choir.' She stuck her head up in the air and began to sing in a flimsy soprano voice.

> '*We are climbing Jacob's ladder,*
> *We are climbing Jacob's ladd-er,*
> *We are climbing Jacob's ladd-er*
> *Pilgrim, traveller.*'

She stopped, smiled a beatific smile, said with feeling, 'The old songs are the best, don't you find?'

'Oh, I do,' Elizabeth said. Now the goddamned tune would be in her head for the rest of the evening. She vowed to keep the door locked in future. But she had made that vow before.

'So what do you make of him?' Max asked.

'Con Bartram? He had no time for his family, that's for sure.'

'They hardly saw him.' Max sat there staring intently at the dossier of notes Elizabeth had made from the biographies. 'South America, Polar trips, Africa. Plus a couple of years at a time off training for the expeditions.'

Elizabeth took his plate, stashed it in the dishwasher and closed the door on it. They had dined on home-made soup from the freezer and the remains of a quiche. There was a jug of narcissi in the middle of the kitchen table; what a scent they gave out. So powerful, you could imagine being silently gassed by them.

'Small boys shouldn't have families,' she said. 'They aren't equipped to look after them.'

'Small boys? Bartram was sixty.'

'A boy, nevertheless. Obsessive. Able to concentrate on nothing except his next great adventure.'

'You think?'

'I think. Reading that lot makes you feel sorry for his sons.' Who were at present reorganising their lives after a murder; adjusting to the loss of a father.

'And the wife.'

'And the wife, of course.' Though Elizabeth felt a disconcerting lack of sympathy towards Marian Bartram. A hard woman, her mouth beginning to turn down at the corners. 'I wonder,' she said, hit by a sudden thought, 'if he made any enemies while shut up at close quarters on all those trips? Or in the army?'

'Surely if you were out there under pressure together, you'd be mates for life.'

'I'm not so sure. Under pressure, men are the most danger-ous creatures on earth. And the guys he took with him on the transglobe expeditions were a colourful crew.' Volunteers, all, and individualists. She imagined emotions flaring. All sorts of pro-fessional jealousies. Months spent cooped up together in iso-lated camps meant there would be a lot of time to brood on things. 'We should maybe take a look at some of them.'

'Right.' Max lowered his can of beer. 'Tell you what, I would-n't want to have had a go at him.'

'No?'

'No. He was a cool customer.'

Undoubtedly true. Bartram had got himself out of countless dangerous situations. Not a man to frighten easily, Elizabeth thought, or to panic in an emergency.

Max said, 'He got shot in the shoulder six or seven years ago out in Africa.'

'During the political riot? He said it was a random hit. That he just happened to be standing at the back of the crowd when the shots were fired.'

'Do you believe him?'

She wasn't sure. All she knew was that Con Bartram would be a formidable opponent in a fight and that on the face of it, you would need your head seeing to before tangling with him. But somebody had done it and come out on top.

Max said, 'By the way, there's something I meant to tell you. I got a bit of a bonus when I was nosing around Buckland Slade talking to the Bartrams' cleaning ladies.'

'Oh, yes? What's that?'

'Well, I dropped into the post office for a packet of crisps and the postmistress happened to be in the mood for a chat. Guess what she told me.'

'I can't.'

'She said she saw a girl with a big rucksack hanging around

on the Green just an hour before the baby was discovered.'

'Really? Do the police know?'

'She says she told them, but hasn't heard anything since. Anyway, guess who the girl was?'

'No idea, Max.'

'Daisy Pluess's daughter. And I've got her address. She lives in a flat in Bath. I thought I might pay her a call.'

Before Elizabeth could reply, the phone rang. She reached over and picked it up.

'Mrs Blair, this is Ellen Helmsley.'

'Yes.'

'I had a thought today and I've decided to act on it.'

'Oh, yes?' Elizabeth waited, wondering what was coming.

'You know you wanted to take a look around my brother's den?'

'Yes.'

'And Marian wouldn't let you?'

'Yes.'

'Well, I thought we might do a bit of breaking and entering. Care to join me?'

'What — now?'

'Don't be silly. Not tonight. This is just an advance warning. I'll call you when I've found out when the coast is clear.'

Chapter Eleven

Eleven o'clock next morning and Ginger was driving Elizabeth through narrow lanes, across a humpbacked stone bridge and uphill through bare beeches to the converted tithe barn, tucked away inside a foggy wood, that housed Barnes and Holden, Stonemasons.

'I'll stay in the car,' Ginger said when she'd cut the engine. 'I brought a book.'

'Nonsense! You'll come in with me. I need your slant on him.'

'You do?'

'Indulge me. I'm feeling particularly decrepit this morning.'

'You shouldn't be working at all. You know that.'

'I can't sit at home on my own all day. It's getting me down.'

'You know what you're suffering from?' Ginger said. 'Post-viral depression.'

'Is that so? They've got a name for everything these days.'

It was the first time she had ever set foot inside a stone workshop – a lovely, cool, untidy place smelling of wood and stone dust. Great barn doors, soft pools of light underneath the arched roof beams and to cap it all, Frederick Barnes Senior, a sober-looking man with a shock of white hair, who greeted them with a formality Elizabeth hadn't come across in years.

'Private detectives, you say?' He held her business card very close to his tortoiseshell spectacles. 'I don't believe I ever met one in my life. We must find a quiet corner and try and rustle up a little refreshment.'

'As long as it's no trouble,' Elizabeth said.

'No trouble at all, as long as you don't mind a spot of dust.'

Elizabeth explained that she really wanted to talk to Kit Bartram. 'Young Christopher? Then it'll be about his father. Sad affair. We had the police here just after it happened. I told them, that young man is of sound character. He would never have done such a thing.'

'I believe the chisel—'

'The chisel went missing from his toolbag while he was working at All Saints. These things happen. Nothing seems to be safe these days.'

'So the chisel was stolen?'

'Yes. I told the sergeant. Of course his fingerprints were on it. After all, it belonged to him, he'd been working with it.'

'How long has Kit – Christopher – been working for you?'

'Four years almost to the day. When he first came to see me, he was working in a hotel kitchen, would you believe? Dropped all that to become a religious carver. If I can leave half a dozen like Kit behind, I shan't have lived in vain.'

'He's good?'

'The best I've ever had. Staggering technical ability. But that's not all. Sometimes . . . well, they've got it all at their fingertips, but— How can I put it? It's like playing the piano. You can do it all with your fingers, but something else has to come from inside and that's what Kit's got. That extra something. Come on over here. I want to show you something.'

The barn, divided into individual work areas with willow fencing, was a hive of activity, accommodating a team of twenty craftsmen divided, Frederick Barnes explained, into groups in the traditional way. Those with a masonry background prepared the marble, trainee carvers prepared the motifs and his most skilled men worked on the figures. He led them past a line of memorial tablets, past a marble head adorned with a builder's hard hat, past a row of workbenches to a spot at the far end where a great, white chimneypiece stood propped against the stone wall.

'Ten tons of Carrara marble,' the old man said proudly. 'Kit's work. A special piece, commissioned for a country house not far from here. Tell me what you make of it.'

Elizabeth studied the figures that had been carved into the marble: a pair of cherubs, one sitting, one lying in long grass; the smaller cherub offering the other a cup to drink from. Their heads in strong relief; chubby knees and fingers and dimpled elbows; tiny wings sprouting from their backs. The foliage behind was in crisp, lively detail; the face of a satyr peered out — no, leered from behind a corn stook.

'It's magnificent,' she said.

'I'm glad you think so. The boy's mad about his craft. Obsessive, some might say. Always hanging round in the local churches, soaking in the details. Mind you, it shows in his work. I'll tell you something, Mrs Blair — it takes five years to train an apprentice. But the most interesting time will be the next five years when that young man finds out what he can really do. Only then will he know if he's going to be a real craftsman. What you have in this workshop,' the old man went on, 'is two thousand years of knowledge, passed from craftsman to craftsman. Of course, you can get an automatic copying carver now. It'll knock out forty-eight feet all at once, or ninety-six right arms of Christ. But that's not our way of doing things. May I suggest that you see the young man in my office in the farmhouse? I do hope this doesn't mean trouble. I'm very fond of the boy.'

Kit Bartram was dressed that morning in faded jeans, an old woolly jumper that might have come from Oxfam and a worn jacket that had seen better days. A thong around his neck had a chunk of stone threaded on to it. He was tallish and dark, with a face that grabbed your attention. Serious, intense, wintry, subtly reactive. He was not handsome in a boring, hunky, over-rated way, but he had great presence and powerful grey eyes.

'Aunt Ellen sent you?' he said.

'Well, indirectly.'

'What on earth for?'

Elizabeth explained. He leaned against the wall smiling in a disbelieving way. 'She's mad. They let me go. I was in London at a private viewing the night Dad died. There are witnesses.'

'Nevertheless, she's worried about you.'

'No need. Ellen fusses too much. Tell her to save her money.'

'You can tell her yourself. But as we're here' – Elizabeth poured coffee from the jug which an elderly woman (Mrs Frederick?) had brought in on a tray – 'you might tell me how you got on with your father.'

'I didn't. I'm sure you know that already.'

Elizabeth pushed one of the cups in his direction. 'I've gathered a certain amount from your brother.'

'You talked to Piers?' Some kind of alarm – definitely – on his face.

'Start with the family. That's our usual method. Your brother tells me you both had a difficult relationship with your father. Would that be a fair statement?'

A short silence. Elizabeth passed the other cup across to Ginger, took a first sip herself and fixed the young man with her most placid gaze.

'I can't deny it. There were times when I thought he hated me, when I honestly thought I must have been a foundling – somebody else's child – because I seemed to get punished for anything and everything. He took it all out on me.'

'All what?'

'Anything that didn't go right in his life.'

'But I should have thought he was very successful.'

'He didn't think so. There was always more paddling going on underneath the surface than you'd ever imagine.' He sat with his coffee balanced on one knee. 'There's an African mask in my father's den – I can't tell you how much I hated it. It was as ugly as sin. But shall I tell you something? There were times when I used to wish I belonged to a tribe in Africa, because perhaps then he would have noticed me – asked me the odd question – taken some kind of interest in me. He had absolutely no comprehension of my life and my problems. Even when he was at home, he'd shut himself up in his study. We weren't even allowed to knock on the door.'

Elizabeth shook her head in sympathy. 'You mentioned problems. What kind of problems?'

'I wasn't much good at exams, so I used to bunk off from school. I failed all my O-levels because I didn't bother to work. What point was there when nobody seemed interested? So I finished up working as a washer-up in London.'

'What a waste,' said Ginger, her grey gaze full of indignation. 'So how did you become a stone carver?'

'It was my day off and I was walking down this street in Camden and the skies suddenly opened and I ran into this church to get out of the rain. This sounds mad, but it was like a sudden conversion. I was standing in front of one of those carved tombs – you know? – a knight with his little dog at his feet and a chain of acorns all round and I couldn't take my eyes off it. I was moved to tears by it – enraptured. That's the only word. I suddenly knew I had to learn how to carve.'

'So what happened next?' Ginger was fascinated.

'I got a place at art college, but there was no grant and my father refused to fund me.'

Ginger said, 'I don't believe you!'

'He said it was a waste of time and money. I'd never make a living at it. I was determined to show him, so I started this foundation course, but I finished up so broke I couldn't eat. Aunt Ellen offered to help, but I wouldn't let her. It wasn't her responsibility. She called me stubborn, all the names under the sun, but I still wouldn't take her money. So she went to Barnes and Holden and asked them to take me on. Best thing that ever happened to me. I'll always be grateful to her.'

'And you make a good living?' Elizabeth asked. She put her

coffee cup down, listening to the faint tap-tapping sounds coming from the workshop across the way.

'Enough. Why?' Such an expression on his face. A kind of cocktail of vulnerability, aggression, intelligence, all mixed up with a certain inner stillness. 'You think I killed my father because I wanted his money?'

'Did I say that?'

'It was implied.'

'Not really,' Elizabeth said, 'but as we're on the subject, who will benefit from the will?'

Back came the swift reply. 'I haven't the faintest idea.'

'You haven't seen the will?'

'No.'

'Isn't that a little unusual?'

'Not in our family. Mother handles all the business stuff.'

'So she doesn't confide in you either?'

He shook his head. Said lightly, 'Bloody awful family, don't you think? Dysfunctional, I think they call it.'

Elizabeth, for once in her life, was stuck for words. She turned to Ginger. 'Anything you want to ask before we leave?'

'Yes,' said Ginger. 'That stone you're wearing. It's great. Where did you get it?'

He smiled at her. 'My lucky stone. I found it on a beach in Dorset.'

'That wasn't exactly the kind of question I had in mind,' Elizabeth told Ginger as they set off back down the lanes.

'Sorry. I just wanted to know.' Ginger flicked the indicator and turned left almost immediately. 'He was OK. Don't you think? He had a kind of—'

'Wariness?'

'I was going to say integrity.'

'You think?'

'I think. You could imagine him as one of the craftsmen who

built Bath. You know, carving the Greek letters on the front of the Pump Room.'

'What Greek letters?'

'You haven't seen them?'

That was the thing about twenty-year-olds. You knew you had more in your head than they did, but every now and again, when your back was turned, they caught you out. 'Of course I have,' Elizabeth lied. 'I just can't remember what it translates as.'

'The most excellent waters,' Ginger told her. 'I heard a guide in the abbey yard telling one of those—' She stopped.

'One of those what?'

'You won't like it.'

'I'll be the judge of that,' Elizabeth said in her most gravelly voice.

'Well, I was going to say one of those ignorant Yanks.'

'Oh, those!'

'I did warn you.'

'Oh, shut up and find Steeple Warren for me, there's a good girl, before I really get grouchy.'

The foster mother must have thought Elizabeth was selling something. She opened the door and glanced at them in a doubtful way. 'Look – this isn't a good time. The baby's crying.'

'So I hear. She's got a healthy pair of lungs on her.'

'Her? I didn't say—'

'That she's a girl?' Elizabeth smiled. 'I'm sorry. I'd better explain. I got your address from Rosie Angel the midwife.'

'You're a friend of Rosie's?' The woman's face cleared. 'I didn't realise.'

'An acquaintance. We were talking about the vicarage baby and afterwards, I thought—' She shoved a hand into her bag. 'Well, I brought this. It's a gift – for the baby.' She drew out of its tissue paper the Dutch crib quilt. Six leaves on the side

border. Dove hovering above the appliqued crib. A pink
Pennsylvania tulip in either corner.

'It's absolutely beautiful! But I can't – You can't—'

'Please take it. I had it all waiting for the next baby
that came along. And this little mite, well, she's had a bad start.'

'You're very kind.' The woman hesitated. 'Would you like to
come in? Give it to her yourself?'

'Just for a minute then. I mustn't go too close. I've got a cold.
But I'd love to take a peep.'

The nursling lay in a Moses basket on the sofa in the small
back room. She blinked and turned her little face aside from the
sudden winter sunlight. Snuggled and gurgled, nestling in the
depths of her white shawl. She appeared to be in good health.

'Who's a little beauty then?' Ginger whispered, reaching out
to touch the tiny hand. Warm fingers curled round her own.

Comely, Elizabeth thought, her heart touched. It was a
strange fate that had brought this little thing into the world on
the same day that Con Bartram had departed it. 'What's her
name?'

'Rachel, For the moment. They named her after the doctor
who looked after her at the hospital.'

That damned tune struck up again in Elizabeth's head: this
time it was her grandmother singing. A deep contralto, accompanied by the harmonium.

> *Rachel in the land of Canaan,*
> *Rachel in the land of Canaan*
> *Rachel in the land of Canaan*
> *Pilgrim, travller.*

'I'm getting all broody,' Ginger said. 'How about you?'

'Sorry?'

'Wake up!' Ginger said. 'Where were you?'

'I was just thinking, there's no easy way into this world and
no easy way out.'

'Well, on that happy note,' Ginger said, 'I think it's time we were getting you back home.'

Max, meanwhile, was sitting in a dark little flat in the less salubrious part of Bath, talking to a seventeen-year-old girl (skinny, bright blonde hair, wearing jeans and a pink top) cramming soiled sheets into a black polythene bag. A girl with a very stroppy look on her face.

'No, I didn't dump no baby,' she was saying. 'What do you think I am?'

'But you were seen carrying a rucksack near the post office in Buckland Slade a short while before the baby was abandoned.'

'Rucksack? I wouldn't put no baby in a rucksack. I was visiting me mum. Taking home me dirty washing. That all right with you?'

'Your mother being Mrs Daisy Pluess of 13, Elm Road.'

'So? Who sent you? Who's been telling tales? That old cow that runs the post office, I suppose. I had the police here, asking all sorts of questions, because of her!'

'Actually, I found her very pleasant.'

'Yeah, well, you're not on the unemployment.'

'Meaning?'

'Meaning she don't think I should be neither. She reported me.'

'For what?'

'She said I were a prostitute. It's a damned lie. You ask my mum.'

And so he would, all in good time. Back at the office, Max dumped his briefcase on the floor, grabbed a tissue from the box on the desk and blew his nose loudly. Damn it, he was getting Elizabeth's cold. He rang down to Caroline in the shop. 'Any sign of her yet?'

'No.' Caroline sounded woozy, too, but it was only to be expected, as she had only been married a few months (to an embarrassing prat called Rupert) and seemed permanently and desperately transfixed by her new role in life.

'Can you remember what time she said she'd be back?'

'Sorry.' He could practically hear Caroline shaking her head.

Max swore silently. 'I need her signature. Hang on . . .' Someone was coming up the stairs. 'That might be her now.' He dropped the receiver, anticipating tea and buns. He'd been about to put the kettle on himself, but if there were females on the way, decency demanded that you let them get on with it. 'So where were you?' he demanded as the door opened.

'Getting soaked. Nice of you to ask. Bloody awful weather you have down south.' In the doorway stood his sister, Fran.

Chapter Twelve

'Are you sure this is OK?' Elizabeth whispered.

'Positive,' Ellen Helmsley said. 'If anyone catches us, tell them I let you in.'

'You have a key?'

'Of course. I didn't actually intend to break in.'

'Just a spot of trespassing with intent.' Elizabeth stood there shivering. She still wasn't a hundred per cent. Had taken aspirin an hour earlier, but she wasn't sure they were working. There was still this feeling of . . . otherness.

'Look — I told you this afternoon. Marian's out at her Parks meeting. Won't be back till ten thirty.'

'You hope.'

'I don't actually care one way or the other. If she comes back early, I'll tell her why we're here. This is my brother's house—'

'Not any more, it isn't.'

'OK. Technically it's hers now, but there's a lot of stuff here that my brother would have wanted me to have, so I'm helping myself. That's fair, don't you think?' Ellen Helmsley inserted the key into the lock and shoved open the door. 'How are you, anyway?' she enquired.

'Not brilliant.'

'That's to be expected. Flu bugs hang around for months. The den's at the top of the staircase on the right. Follow me.'

Would I dare do otherwise? Elizabeth did as she was told. Only once did Ellen Helmsley pause, halfway up the staircase, to listen. 'Still with me? Good. I like this old house. Perfect proportions. I once tried to persuade Con to sell it to me, but he said it was too big and gloomy. I used to come over and paint the garden, you know. You get the feel of a place, notice things after you've had a few hours of sitting and looking. Changes of light, different plants that stand out or recede. Or die.' The woman had no nerves at all. You had to admire her, though presumably she was at the same time a trifle touched. 'Leaves and petals fall. New things spring out overnight. More than once I've had to run for cover with a rain-spotted notebook.'

Elizabeth said. 'Will your sister-in-law stay on here, do you think?'

'Marian? God knows. Good thing she left the hall light on. There's another small flight of stairs round the corner.' The other woman forged ahead. 'Here we are. Con's den. Two steps down. Watch your feet.'

Every room has a personality as definite as its owner. This one was crammed with all the flotsam and jetsam of a life spent adventuring, with hundreds of objects of ranging sizes in heavy mahogany showcases – books, photographs, manuscripts, saddles, native drums, birds' nests. Indian chests, arrows, ostrich eggs, shields, binoculars, what looked like decaying things – heads? – on the mahogany overmantel. Hoary Turkish rugs covered every inch of the pitch pine floor. There was a tiled grate, a quantity of polished walking sticks. (To beat his sons with? Perish the thought.) A recess containing a desk – a great Victorian thing, leather tooled, with a heavy old inkstand, a six-inch tin globe and some glass paperweights. Several large brown trunks contained tribal masks and what appeared to be a small, stuffed crocodile.

A strange room. A strange man. Where did you begin trying to connect him to ordinary life?

'He died here?' Elizabeth asked. 'In this room?'

'Over there by the window.' Ellen Helmsley was working her way through the books in the shelves under the window, helping herself to the ones she obviously wanted. Elizabeth began opening drawers at random, unearthing headed note-paper, spare light bulbs, telephone directories, file after file of papers (where did you start?), dog training manuals, half a bottle of whisky, a map of Greenland (useful!) . . .

There appeared to be no family photographs. Just a single snap in a silver frame of Con with another man surrounded by huskies in what looked like a white-out blizzard. A photograph familiar to her from Bartram's autobiography.

'Oliver Lockie,' she said aloud.

'Lockie?' Ellen Helmsley took the photograph and peered at it. 'He was second in command on Con's early expeditions. They were very close. Like brothers at one time.'

'At one time?'

'Oh, they fell out. It happens on these long treks. Shut up together for months.'

In one drawer Elizabeth noticed a voluminous green file, labelled: *Domestic*. 'May I borrow this?' she asked.

'Help yourself.'

'And if I want to get it back before anyone finds it's missing?'

'Oh, just bring it over to me,' Ellen said carelessly. 'I'll find some way.' She turned back to the cupboard she was going through. There was such a nervous energy about her, something so frantically impassioned that Elizabeth could suddenly picture her with her derring-do brother; the one as intrepid as the other. Con and Ellen, egging each other on to the next bizarre exploit; comrades in arms; great friends and great rivals.

Mrs Helmsley rammed the cupboard door shut. 'Finished?' she asked.

'Almost.'

'Here – you might find these interesting.' Ellen shoved something at her – a bundle of books bound in green leather. 'I knew they'd be here somewhere.'

'Diaries?'

'Con always kept a diary. Wrote it up every night before he went to bed, even as a child.'

'I'm surprised the police didn't take them.'

'Didn't find them.' She looked across at Elizabeth with a certain amount of satisfaction. 'Didn't know where to look. This cupboard came from our father's house in Edinburgh. There's a secret drawer at the back where we used to hide things. She wouldn't know about it.'

'Marian?'

'Who d'you think?'

You're enjoying this, Elizabeth thought. In some grotesque way, you're having fun. Playing games. You need the thrill of adventure as much as your brother did. The man who could cope with the north face of the Eiger, but not his own family . . .

Ellen was bundling her spoils – an assortment of books, keepsakes, papers – into a polythene bag she had brought for the purpose. Elizabeth stood there watching her. The room felt suddenly cold. 'Don't you think we should—'

'Ssh!' Ellen was about to fasten the bag with a length of string when she stiffened.

'What is it?'

'Sssh! I thought I heard something.'

They stood there listening.

Max, meanwhile, was buying a third round of drinks in his favourite little pub in the middle of town.

'If you'd told me you were coming—' he said to Fran.

She sat on the oak bench, gazing at him with a large grin. Max thought, she's twelve years older than me, in her early forties, must be, but she never changes. Shoulder-length fair hair clipped back with little-girl plastic slides; grey-blue eyes giving you the once-over; baggy old sweater; long legs in denim jeans stuck out in front of her. 'I thought I'd surprise you.'

She'd done that all right. Max planted a glass in front of his sister. 'Get yourself on the outside of that.'

'What is it?'

'Finest scrumpy.'

She was none the wiser.

'Elizabeth calls it bootleg liquor.'

'Right. So is Elizabeth over the flu?' Fran, the oldest of Max's three sisters, was like a second mother to him, making it her business to keep tracks on what was happening in his life and to relay every smallest detail to the rest of his family back home in Manchester. She phoned him regularly (mostly on a Sunday) to interrogate him (Max's word) about every aspect of the week that had passed. Girlfriends, clients, Martha Washington, Caroline's recent wedding, Ginger's new car . . . You name it, Fran knew about it, though this was the first time she had ever turned up to inspect his patch in person.

'Yes, but she's got to the crusty stage. So – how long are you here for?'

'I just thought I'd stay a few days and shop.'

'Right.' There was something on his mind. 'There's nothing wrong at home?'

'No. Why?'

'Oh, nothing.'

'You thought I'd had a bust-up with Charlie. Is that it?'

Charlie was her husband, salt of the earth, the kind of bloke you'd want to have around if you were ever in a tight corner. Steady as a rock. Max said, 'It happens.'

'Not in our family, it doesn't.'

'That's OK, then. Good. Another pint?'

'I haven't finished this one yet.'

'Right.' Max picked up his own pint, drained it and said, 'So where are you stopping?'

'With you, of course.'

'With me?'

'That's what I thought. Isn't it convenient?'

'Yeah. Yeah, of course. Great!'

'You're sure?'

'I said so, didn't I?'

'I'm not interrupting your love life?'

'What love life?'

'Bad as that, is it? So what's wrong with the girls around here?'

'Nothing. Why?'

'I just wondered why they weren't falling for my blue-eyed little brother. It's about time you were settling down.'

'For God's sake, Fran—' The barmaid had heard and was smirking in his direction.

'Thirty-two next birthday. I had two kids when I was that age and another one on the way.'

'It's not like that these days.'

'These days? You suggesting I'm past it?'

'Far from it.' He wouldn't dare.

The door behind them opened and a voice said, 'There you are! I was hoping you'd be here.' It was Ginger. 'I left my house keys at the office. Can you let me back in?'

Max looked at his watch. 'You left the office three hours ago.'

'Yes, I know.'

'You must be Ginger,' Fran said. 'I've spoken to you when I've called the office. I'm Max's sister. No good waiting for him to introduce us.'

'Sorry,' Max said. 'Fran – Ginger. Ginger – Fran. So what have you been doing all this time? Sitting on the doorstep?'

'No. I went round to see a friend. We toasted teacakes and—'

'Excuse me,' Fran said, 'but that's not enough.'

Ginger looked puzzled. 'Actually, I wasn't that hungry.'

Fran said, 'I meant my brother's introduction. He's useless at the finer arts.' She held out her hand. 'Hi! It's great to meet you. How do you stand it?'

'Stand what?'

'Working for Max.'

'It's not easy.'

'I couldn't work for him. Bossy?'

'You're not kidding.'

'Expects you to spoonfeed him?'

'Spot on.'

'Office a bit of a pigsty?'

'Not any more.'

Fran said, 'He lived with us once for six months when he was between flats. One night I wondered what this smell was. I found half a tin of spicy tomato soup rotting away underneath his bed.'

'Excuse me,' Max said with all the dignity he could muster. 'The office keys—'

'Get the girl a drink first,' Fran said. 'Honestly, Max! No wonder you haven't got a girlfriend . . .'

Chapter Thirteen

Elizabeth could hear the noises in the drawing-room from the top of the stairs; someone had put the television on; Marian was home early. She glanced down at her watch. A quarter past nine. What now? There was a tickle in the back of her throat. Swallow hard. Keep the saliva flowing before it turns into a hacking cough.

'Back stairs,' Ellen Helmsley whispered. She gestured towards a passage behind them. 'Get a move on.'

Am I likely to hang about? The woman was a walking pressure cooker. How did I get talked into this crazy caper anyway? I'd have been better off at home with a tumbler of whisky and my electric blanket. Elizabeth followed the torch that had snapped on in front of her. 'Left at the bottom,' Ellen Helmsley hissed. 'Christ!' Something fell clattering in front of her. 'Dogs' bowls—'

Driving away from the village, racketing through the dark lanes, Ellen said, 'Sorry to get you into that. But this afternoon . . . well, I couldn't stand it any longer. The pain of not knowing. Had to do something . . . anything. It makes me feel better. You know?'

Elizabeth understood. After Jim's funeral, she had cleaned the whole house from top to bottom, pulling out chairs, emptying cupboards, scrubbing shelves, polishing every last window pane.

'Ma – you never clean.' JJ, still in shock, bewildered, had watched her.

'I just got converted.' It hadn't lasted, the new religion – cleanliness next to godliness. But at the time it had served its purpose.

Ellen's bony elbows stuck out at an angle from the steering wheel. 'Can't sit around weeping. It's not an option.'

You're right there, Elizabeth thought, still recovering from her fright.

'Leave the breakfast things,' Ginger said. 'I'll do them after work.'

It was eight thirty the following morning and Fran had been persuaded to spend her first night in Bath at Ginger's flat instead of her brother's. Tactfully, Ginger had explained that it would be better to give Max a few hours to sort out his spare room.

Fran dumped the pots in the sink. 'So – what's wrong with Max's spare room?'

'You haven't seen it?'

'I will tonight.'

'Yes, well, he'll have had a bulldozer in by then.'

'That bad?'

'That bad.'

The hot tap went on. Bubbles went in. 'So you've used it?' Fran said casually.

'Used what?'

'Max's spare room.'

'No.' Ginger shoved her mobile and a pack of cheese and pickle sandwiches into her bag. 'I caught sight of it once. It left an indelible impression.'

'He's an idle sod.' Fran swished a busy hand through the bubbles.

'Unless he's interested.'

'That right?'

'Then he really hits the accelerator.'

'You don't say?' A swift, calculating glance in Ginger's direction. 'You know,' Fran said, 'we should have lunch — the three of us. My treat.'

'OK. Can Elizabeth come?'

'Fine.'

'You'll like her. Well, you would under normal circumstances. She's not herself at the moment. But lunch will cheer her up.'

An hour later, Elizabeth was dialling an Edinburgh number. 'I wonder if I could speak with Mr Lockie. Oliver Lockie.'

'One moment.' A bright little voice said, 'I'll put you through. Who's calling?'

'Elizabeth Blair. I'm a private detective.' Among other things.

There was a fair delay. Then a voice said, 'Lockie. How can I help you?'

'Is that Oliver Lockie?'

'Speaking.'

'A Mrs Ellen Helmsley gave me your number. She said you were a close colleague of her brother's.'

'Her brother?'

'Connor Bartram. The explorer.'

'Con? Oh, God, yes. Dreadful business. I read about it in the papers.' An unruffled, well-to-do kind of voice. Intelligent and efficient. 'I spoke to him just a couple of weeks before he died.'

'You did? And how was he?'

'Busy. He practically told me to bugger off.'

'And how did you react to that?'

'I laughed. Good God, we've known each other long enough. Went through some sticky times together.'

'Is it possible there would be people who took offence at his rough and ready manner?'

'Plenty, I should think. For every friend he must have made a dozen enemies.'

'Really? Any capable of murdering him?'

'Maybe. Maybe not. It's hard to say.'

'I've heard him described as ruthless. Would you agree with that?'

'Undoubtedly. He was a strong character. Had to be to achieve what he did. Great guy. Had a gambling streak, mind you. That was how he got on. He gambled that the money would come in for the expeditions even when there was sod all in the kitty. But you didn't cross him if you could help it. Oh, no.'

'Did you ever cross him, Mr Lockie?'

'Once or twice. But that's different. We went back a long way, Con and me. We were at school together in Edinburgh.'

Lockie told her about the group that had run the very early expeditions from a poky third-floor office in south London. He gave Elizabeth the names and addresses (so far as he knew them) of the team members. Marian had been an intrinsic part of it back then, manning the phone, acting as an unpaid secretary, along with Lockie's wife (now ex-wife), Juliet. Marian and Juliet had even gone on Bartram's first polar trip, keeping the log, acting as cooks and bottlewashers. Yes, of course there had been tensions . . . Rivalry and jealousy, among the men, at least. But no real rows.

'Did he have friendships outside work?'

'He had nothing outside work. Nothing else interested him, frankly.'

Elizabeth said, 'There was an incident in Africa. Mr Bartram was shot in the shoulder, I believe?'

'That was just an accident. Con was in the wrong place at the wrong time at a political rally.'

'I just wondered. You hear of African mercenaries.'

Lockie scotched the idea pretty quickly. 'Complete rot.'

Elizabeth said, 'Would you mind if I ask what you're doing at the moment?'

'I run my own business. Why?'

'Just general enquiries. What kind of business?'

'Civil engineering.'

'I see.' Elizabeth said, 'I'd be interested to hear your opinion of Mrs Bartram.'

'Marian.' A short silence. Then, 'Quiet, but arrogant. Between you and me, they didn't always have a happy life. At the very beginning, maybe, there must have been something. But she had a bad childhood. An army childhood. Her father was a major in the Dragoons. The mother followed him all over the world and they dumped Marian with an aunt who abused her. Marian married Con as a form of escape.' A pause. 'Of course, the sick daughter didn't help. Drove them apart. That kind of trauma does. They got over it, but they both suffered.'

'The child was very sick?'

'Pretty bad. Yes. Hole in the heart. They had a nanny in to look after her, but she didn't last long. There was some sort of argument.'

'It's not possible—?' Elizabeth started again. 'There wasn't another man in Marian's life? Someone who wanted Con out of the way?'

'Shouldn't think so.' A quick, barking laugh. 'Have you met her? Not a natural charmer. But persistent. And moody. When she worked in the office, things had to be done her way. Con didn't always agree and then she would sulk. When the children came along, she withdrew and let Con get on with his career.'

'They led separate lives?'

'You'd have said that at times.'

'And the boys? His sons?'

'Closer to their mother than to Con. But that's all I can tell you.'

The second call she made was to Serena Bartram, who seemed to be having a bad hair day. 'You want to see me? About what?'

'I'd rather not discuss that over the phone, if you don't mind.'

'Well, I'm afraid you'll have to.' In the background, a child was yelling.

'OK.' Elizabeth's own voice was misleadingly blank. 'Your father-in-law is Connor Bartram, I believe?'

'Was.'

Hearing that sharp monosyllable made Elizabeth imagine a bird with a vicious beak. 'Was. I do apologise.'

'Are you press?'

'No, I'm a private detective.'

'Oh, shit,' said the delightful Serena and slammed the phone down.

Chapter Fourteen

The baize-lined door banged behind Kit Bartram as he set off up the stone staircase to the top of All Saints tower (dated 1751). Round and round he went, the building silent and deserted beneath him, feeling his way through the half-darkness up to the small door at the top. It was unlocked and the latch lifted with a small click that let him out into a high wind and a thin, wintry, translucent glare that stretched around him, unbroken, for miles. Whole slabs of sky turning a light, gale-force blue as the clouds scudded inland A span of space opening up to him. A span of time as well.

Kit was tired from yet another bloody awful night with Serena, but here, surrounded by all this ancient stonework, reaching out and touching it with his fingers, all the discord dropped away. He felt fulfilled, utterly happy. His wife would say he was mad (and frequently did), but the thought of a full five or six hours lying on his side chipping away, with no interruptions and not a single human voice, was utter bliss. He filled his lungs with fresh air, leaned over the pierced parapet and gazed out at the rural sprawl of cottages, the small farms, the council houses, hidden away on the very edge of the village, the river with the mill – or rather, the ruins of it. In the far distance was the blue haze of the Bristol Channel.

You can see a lot from the top of a church tower. People

scuttling about the village like ants; all those poor bastards down there in the everyday world. The vicar doing his rounds. Daisy Pluess, ditto.

Below, at the foot of the tower, a door slammed.

Daisy Pluess disappeared into Primrose Cottage, on the far side of the Green. Philip Fletcher, clutching a handful of papers, had just passed the lychgate and appeared to be heading for The Old Vicarage. I wouldn't, if I were you, Kit thought. The mood Ma's in this morning, she'll have your balls. He had already called to see how she was and had got his head snapped off for his pains.

On the other hand, he thought, let the bastard walk right into it. He deserves it. Damn it. The tension was coming back.

He took his eyes away, to a point on the far horizon. He could still feel it, though, the house and everything that it held inside it. The panic, the crowding of unreal events, the gut-wrenching events on the day of his father's death. The rising apprehension whenever he thought about Piers. Kit was very fond of his younger brother, in an offhanded sort of way. They were chalk and cheese, of course, always had been, always would be. Piers was an absolute plonker. A schemer, who told lies, then deluded himself that they were the truth. I can't deny it, Kit thought, but blood is thicker than water. And Piers was fragile, in spite of his looks and his superficially outgoing personality. Insecure? Surely, but guess who made him so? Got it in one. Our dear father. Piers, chronically thin-skinned and overly reliant on their father's good opinion, had never managed to win it.

I gave up on that elusive prize years ago. Grew a tougher skin.

But Piers would keep on trying, no matter what the cost. Until . . . Kit stood gazing down past the round-headed window with Y tracery to the buttress from which he had removed the weather-worn gargoyle. Until he had created problems for himself that were almost insuperable. There must be something I can do. (Kit had always taken his brother's problems on himself.) A bank loan? You are joking? Aunt Ellen? No. That wouldn't be fair. There was always Ma. She held the reins now, financially speaking.

Catharine Fletcher owes you. Don't be daft. They're as poor as church mice. Common knowledge. Might be worth a try, though.

Kit stood searching the greener-than-green landscape spread beneath him as if something down there might just offer a solution to his problem. So absorbed was he in his thoughts that he failed to realise that he himself was being watched . . .

The last person Marian Bartram wanted to see that morning was the bloody vicar. She had been up since four o'clock, walking round the silent house, her head buzzing with memories of the early days of her marriage. Stupid? Of course, under the circumstances, but that grotty basement flat near the tube station would keep popping back into her head. Their first home together as newlyweds. The only meal she could cook – or they could afford – was bean casserole. No, that was a lie. She'd learned how to make onion soup from an old book that had belonged to her mother, so that was what they'd survived on for months, but neither of them had cared. Too ecstatically happy. Too busy having fun under the blankets on that ratty old double mattress. How long ago it was!

The elation had still been there at the end of the first year, in spite of the unpaid bills, the first arguments (mostly about money) and the thousands of hours Con had spent on the phone trying to drum up sponsorship for a hair-raising trek around the borders of Peru. Marian had gone with him on those first few trips and had taken a largeish part in the proceedings.

When he was younger, she thought, it was different. We were different. Life was different. But then the children had come along. Impossible to drag them halfway round the world, so she had built herself a base at home and that was when the real resentment had kicked in. Once Con was planning an expedition, he forgot completely about anything – anyone – else. His career had been like a disease taking a stronger and stronger hold on him. Only a madman would think of living such a life. When he was away at the bottom end of the earth, Marian had carried the whole burden of their home life. And there were times – she had to admit it – when the strain had become too much.

You can love a husband, she thought, but not know him at all.

How had she survived? By bringing up the family. And yes, if anyone was asking, she was disappointed in how her boys had turned out. She'd had such plans for them and mostly they'd let her down. It's a terrible thing to be disappointed in your children. Worse than losing a husband. Worse by far.

'The funeral tomorrow . . .' Philip Fletcher was saying in that confidential voice he used when concentrating hard on being compassionate. 'I forgot to ask whether you wanted the reading to be from King James or the modern version? I almost telephoned, but then I thought, no . . . there's more comfort in a pastoral visit.'

Claptrap, Marian thought. She had little faith in the church, didn't believe in the existence of its God. 'Use whichever you wish,' she said. 'It makes no difference to me.'

Philip Fletcher made an entry in the notebook he was carrying. He said, 'There was one other thing I thought of. You called me to make an appointment—'

'I did?' There was blankness in her voice.

'Most certainly. On the morning of the day your husband sadly—'

'Met his demise.' She brought the term into use before he could. 'Yes. Yes, I'd forgotten.'

'Not at all surprising. Events . . . overtook you.' He waited. A long silence.

'So . . . was there anything urgent? Anything I could help you with?'

'I remember now. I wanted you to have a word with Mrs

Grey-Wilson about her attitude towards my son, Kit. I was sick and tired of the barbed remarks she was making at council meetings – her one-woman smear campaign.' Her tone was abrupt. 'I thought you might remind her that Barnes and Holden won the contract for the tower renovation in a perfectly fair manner.'

'I could have a word, certainly.'

'But leave it now until after the funeral. I can't think of anything else at the moment.'

'Of course. I quite understand.' The reverend gentleman was wearing brand-new suede shoes and a whiff of some kind of musky aftershave had come into the room with him. Not a holy man, Marian decided, though the parish hadn't been so well run in years. No, something quite different. A particularly smooth personnel officer? A business executive. Yes, that was it. A forceful personality determined to be a success in his chosen career, to rise in the church hierarchy. Conceit, she thought, is God's gift to little men.

She moved across to the window. Philip Fletcher now looked at her with an expression of particularly tender sanctity. 'With your permission, I should like to say a prayer before I leave.'

A quizzical eyebrow went up. 'Oh, no. Nothing like that.'

'It will help, though you might not believe me.'

'I don't believe you.'

'Nevertheless—' He launched himself straight into the prayer, eyes closed, head down, before she could stop him. 'Dear Lord, Help us here now as we feel ourselves to be stumbling through darkness—'

Marian stood with haughty dignity by the drawing-room window, from where she could see the great sweep of the gravelled drive and the wrought-iron gates at the end of it. How could she have been so stupid as to let him in? Outside the window it was beginning to rain,

'Heal our pain, fill our emptiness. And help us to know what to do for the best in these troublous times. In the name of the Father and the Son and the Holy Ghost. Amen.'

The room was quiet. For a moment, Marian almost had a sense of comfort. But then, as a single word resounded in her head, the vision faded out. She was simply a woman in a dark room, waiting for an unwelcome visitor to get out of her house.

'Remember, if you need anything, night or day—' he said unctuously.

'Thank you,' she said crisply, 'but that won't be necessary.'

Chapter Fifteen

—————◦∞◦—————

'Didn't get far with young Mrs Bartram then?' Max sat studying the menu.

'She wasn't a mouse, that's for sure.' Elizabeth clutched her gin and tonic as the door opened. It was a raw, uncomfortable day. Cold, easterly winds and a pinching chill.

Ginger said, 'I'll have the aubergine bake. Funny how lovely men always marry bitches. Kit Bartram would make a good priest, don't you think? There's something almost religious about him. Perhaps not religious in the traditional way. He's just mad about churches. The buildings—'

'They say he's a peeping Tom.' Max tried to attract the waitress's attention.

'Who says?'

'The woman in the bread shop. Apparently he spies on couples from the top of the church tower.'

'Oh, come on!'

Elizabeth said, 'He's certainly a loner.'

'There's just something unworldly about him. Did you notice his hands?' Ginger asked Elizabeth. 'Those long fingers. And his eyes . . . Know what? He'd make a good angel—'

'Bloody hell!' Max sat shaking his head in disbelief.

'A stone angel come to life—'

'Gorgeous shops here,' Fran said to nobody in particular. 'Expensive, though.'

Max told Ginger, 'I hope you're not going to turn into a religious freak like Elizabeth.'

'Who's a religious freak?' Elizabeth glowered at him.

'Elizabeth has a thing about vicars,' Max told Fran.

'I like a man of the cloth. I can't deny it.'

'What was the name of that bloke you used to go to tea with?'

'Bloke?'

'The vicar of St Bartholomew's.'

'Richard Timms. Nice man. A honey, in fact.'

'Toy boy if you ask me.' Max winked at Fran.

Ginger came out of her thoughts to tell him to have some respect.

'Respect?' Fran said. 'You're talking to the boy who asked the Reverend Father if he was wearing a wig.'

'You're a Catholic?' Elizabeth was stunned. 'I didn't know that.'

'Lapsed,' Max said.

'Very lapsed,' Fran said. 'Are we going to eat or what? I'm starving.'

They ate. The restaurant filled up. Fran told them what she'd bought that morning (a shirt for Charlie, an ancient Roman towel for the dog, some candles from a stall and a skinny black frock). Max ordered coffee and asked what the file from Elizabeth's break-in had yielded.

'Break-in?' Fran looked startled.

'Not exactly. Well, almost.' The papers had revealed very little that was useful. Paid bills, insurance policies, tax forms, share certificates. 'The only interesting thing was an estate agency leaflet about a property in Scotland. Pretty recent by the look of it.'

'He was moving house? Nobody told us.'

'Might just have been something he picked up. On the

other hand, his sister said he was mysteriously moody of late. People get the urge to move when they're depressed.' Me for one, she thought. 'I'll call the agency and find out.'

'What about the diaries?'

'Pretty terse. One or two sentences each day. Where he went. What he did.'

'Sent sherpas up mountains? That kind of stuff?'

'That's about it. I can't say there was much that's useful, except—'

'Except?'

'Except that one of the set was missing. We seem to have lost a year of his life.'

'What part of his life?'

'Mid-twenties.'

'Interesting.'

'Mmn.'

'So where was he living at the time?'

'In Paddington in a basement flat. I called Mrs Helmsley.'

'Was this before or after his marriage?'

'A couple of years after.'

Max said, 'I talked to some of the people on Lockie's list. Not a lot that was interesting really.' He sat there thinking. 'So who would destroy a diary? His wife?'

'You tell me. Ellen says Marian didn't know about the secret drawer. Never went into the den.'

'Oh, come on! When he was away so much?'

'Wives pry, you mean?'

'Of course they do.'

'Not necessarily,' Ginger said.

Max reached for another chocolate mint. 'If you believe that, you'll believe anything.'

'You're so cynical.'

'It goes with the job. Elizabeth will agree with me. Ask her.'

Elizabeth didn't want to agree with him, but she had to

acknowledge that while men are out there in society being powerful, women have control of the secret places in the home. They
were surreptitious and clandestine. Subversive. Sometimes had to
be in order to survive.

Max said, 'I tried to check out the family who bought the
mill — the Vereys. The house they're trying to sell is near
Bridgewater, but they're in Australia until next week. Family
wedding. What about the Pluess girl?'

'On the game, if you ask me. I don't think she's our runaway
mother, but I think we should see Daisy again if Marian sacked
her for going through Con's desk.'

'So how did Marian know, if she never went into the den?'
Max grinned when he saw Ginger's expression. 'I knew I was
right to be cynical.'

'Not necessarily.' All Elizabeth would say was that people's
little frauds were interesting; they revealed character or the lack
of it; little weaknesses that led to bigger ones.

Monday morning. A different kind of a day. Mist steaming off
frost on the fields. Max drove past the posh end of Buckland
Slade, past the shop and the pub and parked his car just short
of the council houses at the far end of the village. Can't be too
careful, he told himself, not even when the council estate had
patches of gentility: a mock Georgian front door (No. 5); a pair
of carefully clipped cedars (No. 10); a set of diamond leaded
windows and bloomer blinds (No. 12).

Daisy Pluess lived at No. 13 (straggly privet hedge and
windows that could do with a good scrub). Max banged on the
front door. No one came. He thumped harder. No wonder they
couldn't hear. Julie Andrews was warbling at top volume. It was
only when he thumped a third time that the music snapped off
and Daisy opened the door. 'Yes?' She was wearing mangy
bedroom slippers and a voluminous red dressing-gown.

Christ! Max thought. Who's having a fat day?

'Not you again,' she said. 'What is it this time?'

Max stood there, hands in pockets. 'More questions, I'm afraid.'

'I haven't got time for questions. Anyway, you upset my Lou.'

'Lou?'

'My youngest. She said you went round there accusing her of dumping that baby. Cheek!'

'Is it?'

'Yes, it bloody well is! My Louise knows too much to get caught like that and even if she did fall pregnant, she'd come straight home to her mum. She may be a bit wild, but she's a good girl underneath.'

'Is that so? The postmistress seems to have accused her of being a prostitute.'

'Well, that's a lie as well and I'll bloody tell her so!'

Max didn't doubt it for one minute. He said, 'So your daughter's rucksack held nothing but dirty washing that afternoon?'

'That's God's truth. She brings it home with her every Friday. Now, if you've quite finished—' She was about to shut the door but Max forestalled her by shoving his foot in.

'Look – what is this? I told you last time—'

'I know what you told me. Trouble is, I was stupid enough to believe you.'

'I don't know what you're on about.'

Max knew Daisy Pluess's type. She would get away with what you allowed her to. Not a bright woman, but one who knew when to grab an opportunity if it came along. Given an inch, she would take five miles. 'Oh, I think you do, Mrs Pluess. Now, shall we go inside or would you rather I called the police?'

She wasn't keen on that idea, so she let him in. The house felt clammy and smelled like – what? Stale onions. She led the way into the living-room. On every available radiator and chair-back there was something drying. Towels, underpants, socks. On the table lay a Catherine Cookson novel, a mail order catalogue and the *Daily Mirror* open at the horoscope page.

She let out a wheezy cough. Thirty a day, at least, Max thought. She stood by the window, one plump hand resting on the table. Her face was hard and defensive. 'So?' she said, facing him out.

'So why don't you tell me the real reason Marian Bartram gave you the push?'

Momentarily Daisy Pluess lost her couldn't-care-less air. Struggling to find it again, she said, 'You suggesting I'm a liar?'

'I know you're a liar. Mrs Bartram found you going through her husband's desk.'

'Who told you that?'

'Never mind. What were you looking for? Money? Something you could sell?'

'It wasn't like that!'

'No?'

'No. I'm not a thief, though she accused me of pinching stuff. I told her, I never stole anything in my life.'

'So why were you going through the desk?'

Defiance changed to sullenness. 'I . . . found this letter one day and I got curious.'

'Letter?'

'To his nibs.'

'Mr Bartram?'

'Who else?'

'And what did the letter say?'

'I can't rightly tell you.'

'Why not? You read it, I take it?'

'Yes.' Her eyes were more evasive than ever. 'I couldn't help it. It was in the wastepaper basket.'

'Which, no doubt, you always go through?'

'Not always. No.'

'But sometimes.'

'If there's anything lying on top that looks interesting. Like—'

124

'Like what, Mrs Pluess?' He could well imagine. Bank state-ments, old bills . . . Her mind would be a daws' nest of secrets gleaned from village rubbish baskets.

'Anything that looks interesting. You don't read stuff on purpose. It's just – well, you can't help it. Your eye gets – well, sort of caught.'

'Really?'

'It's no good looking like that. You wouldn't be able to resist it either.'

'Resist what exactly?'

'Cards . . . old letters that got chucked away,' Mrs Pluess said, her face filling with life. 'He got letters from cranks – all sorts of nutters that wanted to get in on trips with him. Or they'd want signed photographs. Or money—'

'Money? Did he cough up?'

'How the hell would I know?'

'You might have read his bank statements.'

'Yes, well, they don't exactly tell you much, do they? It's just lists—' She stopped, realising what she'd said. 'I didn't read no bank statements.'

'And I'm an Indian rajah.'

'I didn't,' Daisy said in her high-and-mighty voice.

'Oh, go on. You can tell me. How much was he worth?'

'Not so much as you'd think.' Daisy couldn't resist letting that slip out.

'Really?' Max decided to bring out his superduper smile, the one he kept for best, the one that usually floored them.

'You'd be surprised.'

'I expect I would.' He kept the smile burning. Daisy was no match for it. She named a sum.

Max whistled. 'That all?'

'Mind you, he had stocks and shares.' Daisy knew it all and she let most of it out. But it wasn't the money so much that Max was interested in.

'The letter you found in the wastepaper basket . . . The

one that got you looking for more—'

'I didn't say that.' Her guard was coming back up.

'I know.' Watch it, Max. 'It just sounded – intriguing.' This time he let the silence sit in the air and waited.

At last, Daisy got reckless. 'Playing games, somebody was.'

'Games?'

'That's what I said.' She nodded emphatically.

'What kind of games? What did the letter say?'

'Note. It was a note. I can't remember the exact words, but it was something like: "Take a risk. It's what you do for a living, isn't it? Just give me a chance." '

Max stood there thinking. 'Were there any more letters besides that one?'

'Nothing. Well, she came in while I was looking and that was the end of that.'

'Did you tell the police about the note in the waste bin?'

'What do you think? I wasn't going to get involved. Incriminated, thank you very much.' A sly expression came into her eyes. 'Anyway, I'm not the only one as does things they shouldn't. There's others in this village— You should knock at the vicarage door one morning. Ask him what he gets up to in his spare time.'

Elizabeth, pouring herself another cup of Earl Grey from the pot on the shop counter, wedged the phone into her neck and said, 'Well, if you insist, I shan't deny it. I have a nasty cough.'

'So what are you eating?' her son asked.

'Tonight? I bought a fishcake. I shall stick it under the grill.'

'Mom – you have to eat properly. You know that?'

'JJ – it's only a cough.'

'That's not a cough – it's a hack! You've got an infection. What happens if you're taken ill in the night? If you collapse or something?'

Good old JJ. He could always be relied on to think you into

the hospital Emergency Room. He'd be standing there with a look of drama written all over his face.

'I'll bang on the wall for Dottie next door.'

'Fat use she'll be. What you need is one of those things.'

'Things?'

'One of those panic-button efforts. You wear it round your neck.'

'Oh, for God's sake, I'm not that old!' She put the phone down on him.

Outside the window in tourist-land, people were still drifting through the alley. The stones of the city were a soft nutmeg colour. The sky above the rooftops a dark blue-grey, starkly beautiful.

Caroline, stylish, Dettol-fresh, leisured and leisurely, surfaced from the tiny kitchen-cum-storeroom. 'Problems?' she asked.

'My son thinks I'm in the departure lounge.'

'Oh, right.' Caroline didn't get the allusion, but this was nothing new. Besides, she was eyeing the clock and longing to run off home to concoct a tasty little supper for her Rupert.

'You run along,' Elizabeth said. 'I expect you've got things to do.'

Caroline patted her wide, curving hair. 'Are you sure?'

'Sure I'm sure.' All that yearning. Cruel to stand in its way any longer.

No sooner had Caroline gone out of the door than the phone rang. Max said, 'It's me.'

'Hello, me.'

'I checked on Anna Healey.'

'Who's Anna Healey?'

'The pregnant mum who's expecting twins. The one Rosie Angel visited the night of the murder.'

'And?'

'And her husband did call Rosie's mobile number on the night of the murder. He says it was about ten to eight. She arrived at their house at eight fifteen and left at a quarter to ten.'

'That's a long stay for a false alarm.'

'She wanted to be quite sure everything was OK. And he felt so guilty for calling her out for nothing that he made her stay for supper.'

'So how far is the Healeys' place from The Old Vicarage?'

'Eight or ten miles.'

So there was no way that Rosie could have got back to Buckland Slade before Connor Bartram was killed. Nevertheless she was hiding something from them; Elizabeth was sure of it. We'll wait a while, she thought, and come right back to her.

Chapter Sixteen

After deciding not to attend Connor Bartram's funeral on the grounds that it wouldn't do much to lift her spirits, Elizabeth changed her mind and turned up at All Saints Church ten minutes before the service was due to begin. The churchyard, newly trimmed for the occasion, was buzzing with photographers; some on stepladders propped against ancient memorial stones, others on the scaffolding that shrouded the tower. Dottie, who had chosen to keep Elizabeth company because she liked a good funeral, thought it scandalous. A shocking invasion of privacy. Yet why shouldn't people be interested? Elizabeth thought as she studied the printed sheet handed out with her prayer book. Connor Bartram had spent much of his life seeking publicity in order to fund expeditions and sell his books, so that particular bandwagon was bound to roll on. Live by TV exposure, die in its glare . . . Or was that uncharitable? She turned the page and examined the hymns. *The Lord's my Shepherd* and *The Day Thou Gavest, Lord, is Ended.* Usual trite old stuff. Couldn't they have found anything more distinctive? Oh, shut up, she told herself. You're turning into a sourpuss.

'I am the resurrection and the life,' Philip Fletcher's voice intoned from the church doorway. 'He that believeth in me, though he were dead, yet shall he live.'

Marian Bartram, her face expressionless, followed the coffin down the aisle, her sons, both in dark suits, one step behind her, Kit stony-faced, Piers barely holding back tears.

Every rung a generation,
Every rung a generation,
Every rung a generation,
Pilgrim, traveller.

The coffin came to a halt by the altar steps. 'His last journey,' Dottie said in a stage whisper. 'I should like to have seen more of the world. Not that I didn't gad about in my younger days. Mother and I went to Rome once, just after the war. It was most interesting.'

Catharine Fletcher sat in the vicarage pew listening to her husband's voice reading the psalm. A most beautiful voice, she had to admit, speaking to two or three hundred people as if to one person, using all the skills of the professional actor he very nearly became.

'Lord, let me know mine end, and the number of my days: that I may be certified how long I have to live.'

They have no idea, Catharine told herself. All they see is a figure in white in the pulpit, lifting his outstretched hands. A glimpse of magic, the oldest kind of magic, the kind that Donne and Wesley performed . . . The only difference being that they were men of the utmost integrity.

'Behold, thou hast made my days as it were a span long . . . For man walketh in a vain shadow, and disquieteth himself in vain: he heapeth up riches, and cannot tell who shall gather them.'

Such a voice . . . It makes you melt when you don't feel like melting. God, the impact of it the first time we met. The thrill of being singled out for attention by the most charismatic man in the room. A man who made ripples. No, bloody great waves.

Mustn't swear in church. Why not? Being good hasn't got me very far. Sorry, Lord, she said, not really repenting. There are thousands of women worse off than me. Must be. It just doesn't feel like it, that's all.

'And now, Lord, what is my hope: truly my hope is even in thee.'

He used to say that to me. 'You're my only hope, Catharine.' His mother having died when he was eight, his father a few years later. The Church and I, we gave his life a structure. Security. In some odd way, perhaps I still do. No act(s) of unfaithfulness can change that. Catharine moved in the pew, caught a glimpse of the back of Kit Bartram's head and felt a burst of sympathy. He looks scrupulously clean for once; unnaturally so. Poor Kit. Poor Con. If only I'd stayed, that last night—

'Thou with rebukes dost chasten man for sin, thou makest his beauty to consume away, like as it were a moth fretting a garment—'

Her mind flickered back to the words of the psalm. Making his beauty to consume away? Is that aimed at me? Possibly. Philip was always slipping little hidden messages – pep talks – into his sermons. He never once doubts that he will get his way. Panic starts up somewhere deep inside her. What am I going to do? Improvise, as always. What else is there?

The coffin processed down the church path to the waiting hearse. The Green, a hundred yards away, was dotted with bystanders. The line of cottages beside it stood meticulously tidy.

One of the photographers was so frantic to get the right angle on Marian Bartram that he wobbled sideways on his stepladder. Behind him, a woman in green stepped back, alarmed. Marian, her hair carefully parted, looked up, flustered and hurried by the commotion. Only Ellen Helmsley, walking behind with her favourite nephew, seemed deaf and blind to it all, a lonely, red-eyed figure in a voluminous woollen coat.

It was a cold day. Fog hung all around in the lanes. A small group of locals moved off down a side path, among them a young man whom Elizabeth recognised – the wiry boy she had spoken to at Buckland Mill. What was his name? Verey. They were back from Oz then. The funeral procession moved through the lychgate.

'There's Mrs Fletcher,' Dottie said, adjusting her gloves. 'I must just have a word. Charming girl. She officiated at the St Swithin's Antiques Road Show. Mrs Fletcher—!' She jumped forward to grab the vicar's wife by the hand. 'Dorothy Marchant. You may remember me. South Harptree Antiques Show back in April. I brought along my father's racing flask and some curling tongs.'

The lady looked briefly startled, but rose to the occasion. 'Yes, of course. Nice to see you again.'

'If on a sad occasion. This is my neighbour, Mrs Blair. She keeps a quilt shop in town, when she's not tracking down criminals.'

'Criminals?'

'It's not as bad as it sounds.' Elizabeth felt Mrs Fletcher gazing at her with apprehension. 'I'm a private detective, but part-time.' A smell of diesel wafted towards them as the hearse started up.

'I see.' Not true. She didn't understand at all.

'I was talking to your husband the other day.'

Now that she did understand. A look of disquiet crossed her face and stayed there in spite of a deft attempt at a smile. She looked younger than her husband. And rather unhappy. Or was that reading too much into the other woman's colourless face?

'He was telling me about the baby in your porch?'

'Oh, that. Yes.'

'She's a beautiful child. But such a tiny scrap. I popped in to see her.'

'Yes. Look – I'm sorry. I have to go—'

Something I said? Elizabeth wondered. Her clear green gaze watched Mrs Fletcher bolt through the lychgate. Why so jumpy? And what was it that Max had gleaned from the Pluess woman about the vicar being no better than he should be? Perhaps we should pay a return visit to the Fletchers . . .

These cracklings of curiosity take you up many a back alley.

As soon as she got home, she rang Max for a chat about the Fletchers. But she didn't get the chance, because Max had other fish to fry.

'Listen – I finally got hold of the Bartrams' ex-nanny. The one whose house was for sale in Chippenham. Only it turned out not to be her house at all. She was renting a room from the woman who owned the house. Anyway, Allison Jackson – that's the nanny – is now working in a school for the mentally handicapped down in Exeter, if you want me to go and see her.'

Chapter Seventeen

At eleven fifteen the following morning Elizabeth called on Serena Bartram, a young woman in her mid thirties; short brown hair, a baldly unmade-up face, thin brown arms, thin everything really.

'Yes?' she said when she opened the front door.

'I'm Elizabeth Blair. You slammed the phone down on me.'

'Christ, you're persistent. Look — is this strictly necessary? Only the baby's asleep and you're cutting into my coffee break.'

'Sorry about that. I won't keep you long.'

'So what's it about?'

'Well, if I could come in—'

The tumbling family cottage was a shambles inside and out. A dark little sitting-room to the right of the front door was littered with children's toys. Where the damp had penetrated one wall and a corner of the ceiling, paint was flaking. There was one hell of a whiff from a bucket of dirty nappies.

She must have seen Elizabeth's face. 'Yes, I know it's a tip, but there's no point in doing up a sodding rented cottage.'

'Rented?'

'You thought that because of my husband's illustrious family, we'd be rolling in money. Well, I'm sorry to disappoint you, but I married a pig in a poke.'

'Is that so?' Forthright wasn't the word. 'You didn't get what you thought you were going to get out of the marriage?'

'You can say that again. I thought I was marrying a trainee chef, but twelve months after the wedding, Kit changed lanes. I found myself married to a stonemason. And it's no fucking fun, believe you me. There's no money — well, only what I can drum up from my people — little prestige and even less laughs.' She sat down and began rolling herself a cigarette. An unpleasant young woman. A sour-tempered bossy boots who might have been branded a witch in the old days.

'So you're disappointed with your lot?'

'I thought I'd made that clear.'

'And your husband?'

'What about him?'

'Is he happy?'

'When he's working. Have you met him?'

'Yes, I did. I called at the workshop.'

'Then you'll know what I mean, Kit has no time for anything except his lumps of stone.' Two children, a boy of about four and a two-year-old girl were having fun on a broken rocking horse behind their mother, jumping up and down on it, making the thing creak like blazes. 'Theo — Bess — stop that for God's sake!' She lit the cigarette. 'No time for any of us. It pisses me off.'

'I suppose it would,' Elizabeth said in a voice laced with disapproval that such language should be used in front of the children.

Serena didn't even notice. 'I've threatened to leave.'

'Then why don't you?'

'And do what?'

'Get a job?'

'With three children under five? You are joking?' She took a long pull at the cigarette. Changed tack. 'So Ellen Helmsley sent you here to grill me — is that right?' She glared at Elizabeth with an expression that verged on derision.

'Mrs Helmsley was concerned about your husband. Yes. Tell

me something, Mrs Bartram. How did you feel about your father-in-law?'

'Con?' A smile almost touched the thin mouth. 'I couldn't stand him and he couldn't stand me. I think that would just about describe it.'

'Really? Why didn't you get on?'

'Why? He knew he couldn't push me around like he did the rest of them. I stood up to him. I told him exactly what I thought of him.'

'Which was?'

'Con was another selfish bastard. Singleminded. I can see where Kit gets it from.'

'So when was the last time you saw your father-in-law?'

A shrug. 'Three months ago. I called round there to drop off the children. He was in the garden.'

'And?'

'And we had a slight altercation.'

'About what?'

'About dear little Rosie.'

'Miss Angel?'

'Who else?' She gazed at Elizabeth as if inviting her to go further. A young woman who looked as if she had left the womb bitching and biting and belittling.

'So what was the row about?'

'I asked him if he was having an affair with Rosie and he hit the roof.' Serena, still holding the cigarette, smiled. The memory amused her. There was an unmistakable whiff of jealousy in the air.

'He denied it?'

'Well, he would, wouldn't he? He said she was like a daughter to him.' Malice now in the pale eyes.

'But you thought he was lying?'

'Of course he was. Marian knew. Everybody knew.'

'Even Piers?'

'Oh, Piers laughed it off, but that's Piers.'

'And your husband? What did he think?'

'No good asking him. Rosie wraps Kit round her little finger, as she does most men.'

Elizabeth sat there watching the children. The little girl was crayoning on the wall; the boy, Theo, spitting on his fingers and rubbing the marks in. He was the image of his father – light-boned, dark, a look of intense concentration about him. 'Daisy Pluess,' she said. 'I gather your mother-in-law dismissed her for going through the drawers in Mr Bartram's desk. Would that be correct?'

'Marian got rid of Daisy because all sorts of things had disappeared from the house.'

'Such as?'

'Small antiques. A piece of Staffordshire. A Regency brooch Marian was particularly fond of. One or two other bits.'

'I see. So who does she employ now?'

'Some girl the vicar recommended, I think. You better ask Kit.' That mocking tone again. 'He did a sketch of her. Says it's for work, but if you believe that, you'll believe anything.'

Allison Jackson, meanwhile, was looking at Max oddly, uncertain what to make of his questions. 'Yes, I worked for the Bartrams when they lived at Lavender Cottage. That was before they bought The Old Vicarage. I was their nanny for a while. But this was twenty-odd years ago. What's it got to do with his murder?'

'Just background enquiries,' Max explained. Driving down to Exeter had taken a couple of hours. The rest room at St Joseph's School for the Blind was quite spartan. Green painted walls, a long coffee table. Leaden skies over the park beyond the balcony. Loud voices now and again passing the door. The room smelled of burnt herrings, was toasty warm but there was no sign of any food. He had grabbed a sandwich at the motorway services, but already he was hungry again, could murder a big fat slice of chocolate cake. Or a jam doughnut or a jacket potato with chili topping.

Allison Jackson was friendly, but she wasn't a goer. Fortyish, floppy dark hair dragged up to the top of her hefty head with a stretchy band. There was more than a hint of Aberdeen Angus in that heavy face as she asked, 'Did she do it? Marian?'

'Kill her husband?'

'What else?'

'Do you think she's capable of it?'

'Shouldn't be surprised. If you'd seen the fights they used to have. She could be pretty . . . abrasive, Marian, but she had a lot of problems at the time. The little girl was in a bad way.'

'So she was always losing her rag?'

'Understandable, I suppose, given the circumstances. You should have heard the things they used to say to each other.'

'Like what, for instance?'

It was hard to remember the details, she said. They just seemed to hate each other's guts, spent half of their time – when he was there, which wasn't often – trading insults.

'You must remember something?' Max said.

She sat looking at him for a moment and then, irritatingly, went off at a tangent. 'That was the worst job I ever had. I loved the baby – Millie – she was a dear little thing in spite of her problems. And the boys were OK, I suppose. But Mr and Mrs Bartram – I'm not kidding, they were like a couple of spoilt brats. It was bloody awful. And then when the other one started causing trouble—'

'The other one?'

'The woman he was carrying on with.'

Max felt the hairs on the back of his neck start to prickle. 'Are you sure of this?'

'Positive. I'd answer the phone and she always asked for him. Mr Bartram.'

'Can you tell me her name?'

'Sorry.' A bovine stare out of the window. 'It might have been somebody that worked in his office. You could hear voices in the background. Another phone ringing.'

'So how do you know it wasn't just business? His secretary or something?'

'Because she always rang when Marian was out.'

'Did Mrs Bartram know about the affair?'

'Definitely.'

'What makes you say that?'

'Because she used to scream at him about it.' Allison picked up a toy monkey in a gingham skirt that lay on the window sill. Sat holding it in her ample lap. 'I think, in the end, he gave her the push.'

'The other woman?'

'That's right.'

'What makes you say that?'

'Well, she turned up at the house one day. Knocked on the door and asked if he was there. I recognised her voice.'

'So was he there?'

'Yes. I was giving the boys their lunch in the kitchen. He shut the door in between, but you could hear it all going on.'

'All?'

'She accused him of dumping her. That's all I heard before he shut the door.'

Max swore to himself. 'So what happened in the end?'

'He got rid of her somehow. He could be very sharp. I was quite scared of him, to tell the truth.'

'And the boys? His sons?'

'The boys were terrified of him. He was a disciplinarian. I left because I couldn't stand him beating them.'

'With what?'

'This strap he had. I remember one time poor little Kit couldn't sit down for a week. I threatened to report him.'

'But you didn't?'

'No. He was getting well-known. I didn't think they'd believe me.'

'And Marian didn't stop him?'

She tried, but he was as tough as old boots. He said he'd been beaten as a child and it hadn't done him any harm.'

No? Max thought. I wouldn't bet on it. 'You didn't hear the woman's name?' he said. 'The one who came to the house?'

'Juliet. That's what he called her. "For God's sake, Juliet" – that's all I heard before he shut the door.'

'So The Old Vicarage is on your books?' Elizabeth put a big tick opposite the last name on her list.

'Was,' the estate agent corrected her. 'Mrs Bartram rang last week to ask us to take it off. It's no longer on the market.'

'That's a shame. It was just the kind of property I'm looking for.' You'll never go to heaven, she told herself.

'We have many other properties, madam. If you'd like to pop in, I'm sure we could help you.'

'I may just do that. Thanks anyway.' Elizabeth put the receiver down and sat there thinking. Marian Bartram hadn't said anything about the house being on the market. Now maybe she'd just forgotten to say.

'But if not—' she murmured. 'If Con Bartram intended to sell the place and Marian was against the idea – then, we may just possibly have a motive for murder.'

Chapter Eighteen

Marian Bartram said, 'Why didn't I tell you he'd put the house on the market? Because it was none of your business.' There was great fortitude of character in her face. She was very pale, very intense. Shocked, perhaps, by her husband's death but not broken-hearted. None of them are, Elizabeth thought. Nobody much liked the man, his family least of all. How was she readjusting to life without her husband? Maybe without too much difficulty. After all, she's been living on her own, virtually, for years.

'*He* put the house on the market? It wasn't a joint decision?'

'It was in his name. He wanted to leave and I didn't.'

'So he was going to sell it over your head?'

'He . . . hoped I'd come round to the idea in due course.'

'And if you didn't?'

A shrug. 'As it happened, I didn't have to.'

'Convenient.' It came out before Elizabeth could stop the thought. 'I'm sorry. That sounds harsh. But you must see—'

'It gives me a considerable motive for murder.'

'If he was going to sell the house and force you to move—'

'That's true. But I didn't kill my husband.' There was a pause. Marian rose from her chair, looking calm and collected. It wasn't difficult to imagine her as ruthless as her dead husband.

'OK. Why did he want to move house, by the way? Any particular reason?'

'He took it into his head that he wanted to buy a farmhouse in Scotland. I can't tell you any more than that. He didn't have any rational reason.'

'It was just a whim?'

'If you like.'

'There's something else I have to ask you. I've been told that your husband had an affair when your children were small. That when he broke it off, this woman came to your house and caused a rumpus.'

'Who told you this?'

'I can't tell you. It's confidential.'

'It's also utter nonsense.'

'Then you're denying it?'

'Absolutely.'

'Your marriage was perfectly happy at that stage?'

'No marriage is ever perfectly happy. We had our problems. Tantrums of early marriage. Doesn't everybody?'

'But there was no other woman that you knew of.'

'I told you. No.'

But do I believe you? That's the question. 'Of course, the life he lived must have put a strain on you both?'

'I won't deny that.'

'And you lost a daughter in infancy, I believe?'

'I hope Ellen's paying you well for all this snooping?' Marian's brown eyes were sharp, alert, icy.

'It's in your son's best interests, Mrs Bartram.'

'My son doesn't need her so-called help. The police have accepted that he had nothing to do with his father's death.'

'He has no witnesses to prove that he was in London all that evening. I'd say he's still pretty vulnerable. Look,' she said after a pause. 'My snooping, as you call it, isn't very pleasant for you. I realise that. But if it helps catch your husband's killer— All I'm trying to get is a clear picture of his life.'

'All right.' Suddenly she gave in. Waved a weary hand. 'The marriage wasn't easy. Wasn't perhaps the happiest. Con was away half the year, but it didn't do any good dwelling on the fact. I didn't sit around getting bitter. I diverted my energies elsewhere. Committee work and such. And I had the children.'

'Who didn't see much of their father?'

'They wouldn't have done anyway. They were away at school for a lot of the year. But — yes — there was a space between them and their father and I regret that. I think Con did, too, deep down.'

Elizabeth waited a little before asking the next question. 'Did your husband keep a diary, Mrs Bartram?'

'Not that I know of.' Her gaze seemed steady enough.

'Only Mrs Helmsley says that he did, that he's done so since he was a child. That there was a whole series of them tucked away in his den — and one of them is missing.'

'Missing?' Marian's face remained blank, but she seemed dazed by the information. 'How would she know that?'

'You'll have to ask her, I'm afraid.'

'I most certainly will.' She was furious, but trying to hide the fact. Her voice sounded as if it had been dunked in an ice-bucket. Then, quite suddenly, she leaned forward and said, 'You can tell her this from me. If I find she's responsible for the latest break-ins at my house, I shall inform the police immediately.'

'Other break-ins?' Elizabeth had gone weak around the knees.

'Yes. Piers almost caught an intruder last week.'

'Really?' Get a hold on yourself, Elizabeth. 'Which day last week?'

'Friday.'

The day after Ellen Helmsley had organised her own little break-in. Elizabeth relaxed. 'So what time of day was this?'

'Late afternoon. Piers brought me back from a shopping trip to Bath and we heard someone in the kitchen.'

'Can he describe the intruder?'

'No. He didn't see him.'

'Him?'

'He can't prove it was a man – he only saw a shape disappearing into the dusk – but he thought it was a man. I had to have all the locks changed.'

'I'm sorry to hear that. You must feel uneasy at night.'

'Not really. I don't scare easily.'

I bet you don't. 'One last question. I don't suppose you'd like to disclose the contents of your husband's will?'

'No. I wouldn't.' She rose, glared. 'I'd like you to leave now.'

'Okey-dokey. Thanks for your help,' Elizabeth said, doling out a cheery professional smile. It was only when she got outside that a thought came to her. Mrs Bartram didn't ask which particular diary was missing. Now that's odd, isn't it? Not to be curious about such a thing.

Her next port of call was the other vicarage. The modern, custom-built variety. Crossing the road, she glanced at her watch. Eleven-thirty a.m. Would she find anyone in? Let's hope so. It's just the kind of morning to sit in your study and write a good sermon. Sunny blue sky, almost a glittering light behind the bare beeches. Such a tidy little detached house, though, for a clerical gentleman. It has an empty look. Hard to say why. The bald morning light? The taut blinds at the upper windows? Not to Elizabeth's taste. But there, why should it be? Not everybody went for twig beds and puckered quilts. She rang the bell and waited for someone to answer it. 'Hi! Remember me?' she said when Philip Fletcher opened the door.

'Mrs . . . er—'

'Blair. We met at the village hall.'

'Of course.' Today he was wearing a green sweater over his dog collar. It made him look younger. Also, he seemed to be less biblical. She detected a whiff of aftershave.

'This is my day off.'

'I'm sorry. If I'd known—'

'No, that's fine. Come on in.' The hair at the back of his head was quite curly. She shut the door behind her and a hoover started whining at the back of the house. He led her into a small room halfway down the hall. One wall was lined with books. A chair was drawn up in front of a portable gas fire. A table by the window held a lot more books and a small computer.

'You're still investigating the murder?'

'Among other things.' She threw that in, sneakily, to see what effect it would have. Not a lot, as it happened. He looked mildly, vicarishly interested, but no more than that.

'You were at the funeral,' he said.

'I'm surprised you noticed. The place was packed.'

'You'd be surprised how much you can see from the pulpit. It's a good vantage point.'

'I'm sure.' In the silence of the house, the Hoover went on humming.

'So how can I help?'

'Your doorstep babe – I wondered if you'd have any notions as to the identity of the mother?'

'Goodness, what a question.'

'I just thought – well, you must know everybody in the parish.'

'Not everybody.' He waved her to the chair by the fire and remained standing by the window. 'Not these days.'

'But a good number? Any problem families, for instance?'

'The police asked the same question.' The hoover had stopped now. The house was extremely quiet. 'I told them, Buckland Slade isn't that kind of a place.'

'I don't believe you. There's a council estate tucked away on the outskirts of the village.'

'A very sedate council estate. Pretty tame, I'm afraid.'

'Mind you—' Elizabeth was thinking aloud. 'Dysfunctional families don't necessarily live in council houses.'

'That's true.'

'The Bartrams, for example.' She put out a hand to smooth the cat that was curled up asleep in front of the fire.

'You may be right.'

'I know I'm right.' She brushed the warm fur once more, very lightly, and the cat stirred in its sleep. 'You have a youth club attached to the church? Is that right?'

'Yes, but—'

'Any young girls there who might get pregnant?'

'Mrs Blair – the police did a house-to-house. I hardly think—'

'I know. But I'm being paid to go over it all again.'

'Very well. I'll give you names and addresses. But it'll be a waste of your time.'

'Fine by me. One other thing – I was told that you recommended a young girl for a cleaning job with the Bartrams.'

'Who told you that?'

'Sorry. It's confidential.'

'I just don't see the connection.'

'You don't have to. Is it true?'

'Yes.' He seemed rattled.

'Then I'd like her name.'

'I don't see why.'

'She may have been a witness. May have seen something the day Mr Bartram died.'

'She doesn't work there on a Friday.'

'Oh?'

'Well, I can't say for sure, of course.' He was backtracking. 'But I think she works there on Monday and Wednesday.'

'Really?' Very precise.

'The thing is, in a small place we know what's going on across the way.' He smoothed the curls at the back of his head and smiled past her, his voice larded with ecclesiastical charm.

'Same all over the world.' Elizabeth sat there gazing out at the greyish morning. 'Do you have a family, Mr Fletcher? Children?'

'No. I'm afraid not. We . . . wanted them, but it hasn't happened. Catharine – that's my wife – gets uptight about it at times.'

'Especially when an unwanted child is dumped on your doorstep?'

'Yes, well. She was upset that day.' There was a loud thump outside in the hall. The Reverend Fletcher's gaze went to the door.

'I can imagine.'

'Such a dreadful afternoon. Wet and blowy. My wife nursed the little thing until the police arrived.'

'I see,' said Elizabeth. 'Beats me how anyone can do that?'

'Sorry?'

'Leave a newborn in the dark and cold.'

'She must have been desperate, poor thing.'

'I guess so.'

'If I'd only known – I mean, if I'd opened the door just a fraction sooner – I could have done something. Had a chance to talk to the poor girl—'

Wouldn't want you counselling me in an emergency, Elizabeth mused. The thought came popping out. Why don't you like the guy? Too sure of himself? Vain? I think so. Seems to me he's all voice and no depth. A bit of a poser. She'd met a few in her time.

At 8.10 p.m. Piers Bartram came out of The Gardener's Arms with a pack of cigarettes in his hand. He shoved the change that the landlord had given him in his jacket pocket, pulled the seal off the packet and stood quite still for a moment, thinking about the phone call he was to make in an hour's time. What was he going to say when it came to the crunch? He was scared to death, to be honest. His fingers, shaking a little, delved into the packet and drew out a cigarette. It'll be all right. You'll think of something. Who are you kidding? It won't be all right. How can it be?

A voice behind him said, 'Excuse me, please.'

'Sorry.' Even when he was in dire straits, his manners were

impeccable. That was Piers. Polite, even when out of his mind with worry. He stood aside to let the woman pass.

Across at the church, there was a movement, a flash of yellow. Somewhere near the top of the floodlit scaffolding. He looked up and saw someone stepping back into the shadow of the tower, someone carrying a tool bag. Kit, he thought, feeling pathetically grateful that his brother should still be up there working. He stuck the fag in his mouth, lit it and inhaled deeply. Better already. Kit would know what to do. No trouble so big that Kit couldn't solve it. At that bloody awful school when the morons were after him and he couldn't cope (so what's new?), Kit had sorted them. Piers took a deep, steadying breath and stepped out of the porch. He'll think of something, he told himself, crossing the Green. It was damp underfoot. The moon was trying to come out. He said, 'It'll be OK,' and flipped his jacket collar up.

A car drove past as he went up the church path. He turned right at the locked porch and approached the ladder. Took a last drag on the cigarette and threw it away. Grabbed the ladder and began to climb.

Chapter Nineteen

The body of Piers Bartram was found lying at the foot of All Saints tower at seven thirty the following morning by a woman out walking her dog. He had fallen from a ladder on the fifth level of scaffolding, his foot having gone through a rung that had been half sawn through. It had snapped beneath his weight, he had lost his balance and hit the gravel path sixty feet below.

'He was pronounced dead at the scene by a police doctor,' Max told Elizabeth when he phoned her at nine o'clock. 'Andy rang me as soon as he heard. Nature of the injuries not yet revealed.'

Elizabeth was stunned by this new tragedy. 'But what on earth was Piers doing climbing up there at night?'

'No idea. Andy says they've pulled Kit in again. Apparently the pub landlord noticed a man near the top of the tower at about seven-thirty last night. He couldn't be sure who it was, but he recognised Kit's hard hat – the one he wears when he's working up there.' There was a pause, then he said, 'Fancy meeting us up there later on? We could lunch at the village pub. Listen in to the local gossip. Might pick up something useful – you never know.'

It appeared that half the inhabitants of Buckland Slade had had the same idea. By twelve-thirty, The Gardener's Arms was packed out with both locals and ghouls who had driven over to get a sniff of the action. Two murders in the same village within the space of a couple of weeks. Father and son, to boot. The place was humming with it. They had been lucky to get a table.

'Poor old Piers.'

Ginger said, 'Poor Mrs Bartram.'

'So who was it intended for?' Elizabeth puzzled.

'Kit, I should think. He's the one always up there.'

'But how did Kit get up there, if the ladder was sabotaged?'

'According to Andy, Kit says he wasn't there at all that night. Says it must have been somebody else. He swears he was in Bath having a drink with a mate.'

'Can he prove it?'

'They're checking on it now. I just spoke to Andy again.'

Ginger said, 'Kit Bartram wouldn't kill his brother. He's not the type.'

'It's not always that simple.' Max selected a crisp (salt and vinegar) from the packet and prepared to give her the benefit of his knowledge. 'Anyone can kill given enough provocation.'

'That's rubbish. Anyway, even if Kit did plan to kill Piers, he's not going to do it in a place where the burden of suspicion falls straight on him. His place of work. That would be just plain stupid.'

'So maybe he is.' Delicately, Max bit the crisp in half.

'He is not! And brother doesn't easily kill brother. You might want to at times. My brother drives me up the wall, but I couldn't ever do that to him.'

'I didn't know you had a brother. You didn't say.'

'You never asked.'

'The Verey boy mentioned vandals,' Elizabeth pointed out.

'That's true,' Max said. 'I just had a chat to the landlord. Apparently Piers came in here last night to buy cigarettes.'

'He didn't tell anyone he was intending to climb the tower?' Elizabeth had her eyes on a group of girls who were playing the quiz machine.

'Nope. And he wouldn't stop for a pint, either, though some-

body offered him one. Apparently, he was quite popular, old
Piers. They liked him, though occasionally they laughed at him
behind his back.'

'Why would they do that?'

'Oh, he'd sound off about how he was going to make himself
a fortune in property. But at least he'd talk to you, the landlord
said, which was more than the other one would. Kit.' He shot a
glance in Ginger's direction. 'They'll grant he's a good craftsman.
He renovated the village pump and the war memorial. Spent
weeks working on them. Off in his own world . . .'

Everyone needs another country, Elizabeth thought. Kit has
his carving. Con Bartram his trips up the Amazon. And Marian?
Where does she go? Not sure yet.

'Piers had his daydreams of succeeding wildly somewhere,
but never wanted to work too hard.' Max gathered up the glasses.
'Same again?'

'I don't mind,' Elizabeth said. 'So where's your sister this
evening?'

'Gone back to her old man.'

'She have a good time?'

'Seemed to.'

While he was gone, Elizabeth told Ginger about her last interview with Marian Bartram. Ginger said, 'Do you think she's lying
about the diaries?'

'I suspect so.'

'So who do you think pinched it? The one that's missing?'

'Could be the murderer.'

'There was something from that period that may have given
the police a clue as to his identity?'

'It's a possibility.'

Ginger was thinking hard. 'But the police didn't find the
diaries.'

'The murderer wasn't to know that.'

'I suppose not.' Ginger's mind was wandering back to the sa
of the house. 'I can understand that Marian wouldn't want t
move out of that house. What if he planned to move to Scotlan
on his own?'

'If he was planning to divorce her? I thought of that.'

'If he left her, divorced her, she'd only get a part of the valu
of The Old Vicarage.'

'Which wouldn't suit. Whatever else went wrong in her life
she's always been lady of the manor. Mrs Bartram of The Old
Vicarage.'

Ginger fiddled with the bracelet on her slender wrist. 'But it
still doesn't explain who'd want to kill Kit. Or Piers.'

Elizabeth said, 'I know someone who hates Kit enough to kill
him.'

'Who's that?'

'His wife.'

'You're kidding!'

'Oh, it's not a serious theory. But it's a fact.'

'There we go.' Max placed three brimming glasses on the
table.

Ginger took her pint. 'I hate people who say that.'

'Say what?'

'There you go. What does it mean? Nothing.'

'It's just an expression. Everybody says it.'

'Every waitress that ever serves you,' Elizabeth said. 'Damn
that music. They've turned it up.'

'Sign of old age,' Max told her, then winced as Ginger kicked
him under the table. 'What was that for?'

'Tactlessness.'

'Don't mind me,' Elizabeth said, taking a swig out of her gin
and tonic.

'She knows I don't mean it.'

'Then why say it?'

'All right. All right.'

'Listen,' said Elizabeth, 'I'm an old broad. Who's denying it?'

'I am,' Ginger said.

'Nice try, kid. Thanks a bunch, but take a look around you. I'm the oldest here by years.' Elizabeth found the thought profoundly depressing.

'My granny got like you,' Max said. 'Dead miserable. They blamed it on the change.'

'For God's sake, Max!' Ginger glared at him across the table.

But Elizabeth's mind was racing ahead. She had remembered something. 'The baby case.' She dipped into her coat pocket and passed him a slip of paper. 'Would you check this girl for me? A Nina Harrison. She took over Daisy Pluess's job at The Old Vicarage.'

'No problem.'

'Thank you.' She was brisk now, all business. 'And we should talk to Oliver Lockie's ex-wife. She worked in Bartram's office in the early days. And her name is Juliet.'

' You'd better do that. I'm booked up for a couple of days.'

'Doing what?'

'The Sweet case. A female high-flyer who wants us to do a pre-marital check on her boyfriend's bank balance.'

'That's grotesque,' Ginger said.

'Possibly, but she thinks he might be a fortune hunter. Wants us to check his assets and sexual history for a big, fat fee.'

'Yuk!'

'You may scoff. It pays the bills.'

'So what does she do, this high-flyer?'

'Financial adviser. She met this bloke at a business convention. In his forties. Claims to run his own business, drives a BMW—'

'So what's the problem?'

'Well, he's wined and dined her, bought her lingerie, showed her photographs of his London flat. But she's suspicious because he always pays for meals and such in cash, won't give her his phone number and never invites her home.'

'So how will you find out about him?'

'Checks at Companies House for a start.'

'Sad though.'

'That's what life's about these days. Women climbing the ladder, putting their emotional lives on hold while they establish themselves in their profession. By the time they're looking for marriage, they're in their thirties with a lot of savings. Vulnerable to the odd scavenging rat. Better watch it doesn't happen to you,' he said.

'On what you pay me? No chance! Anyway, I'm not old enough.'

'That's true.' His eyes lingered on her for a moment. Not joking, not teasing, not brash, not even very appreciative. The kind of glance that didn't say very much at all. Unless you knew the boy very well. As Elizabeth did. Well, well, she thought. Who'd have thought it? Now there's a thing.

Chapter Twenty

Thursday. Four-thirty p.m. A pretty little terraced house at the bottom of Winchcombe Hill on the outskirts of the city. I've seen you before, thought Elizabeth, taking in the poised, slim-boned figure of Juliet Hughes (formerly Lockie). At Connor Bartram's funeral. The woman in green who was almost felled by the photographer. You look tired. Dark rings about the undoubtedly fine hazel eyes. Nice haircut, though. Expensive. And the skirt is quite something. A blue-grey silk crêpe affair, beautifully cut on the bias.

'What can I do for you, Mrs . . . Blair?'

'I'm making enquiries into a murder.'

She looked startled. 'Oh, really?'

'And I believe you knew the victim? A man called Connor Bartram.'

One level glance and she looked away again. The silence that followed hung heavily in the air. You hate my guts for coming here and involving you in this, Elizabeth thought. I've ruined your afternoon. Ruined your husband's afternoon, too, by the look of it. A stocky little Welshman in a green body warmer. Retired draughtsman. He likes the simple life. Has that look about him. Polished shoes, (brown leather), neat little moustache, impeccable cufflinks. He's all ready to drive off to the golf course, clubs stacked in the car outside, keys in his hand and what happens? An American weirdo waltzes in, drops a bomb-shell, ruins everything. But what the hell. I feel like upsetting applecarts.

'Listen — you don't have to go,' Max had said before she left. 'Leave it until I'm free.'

'It needs doing.' She had enjoyed the show of stubbornness, pitting her will against his and winning.

'OK. OK. Just don't say I forced you. And don't go in there like a whirling dervish. Don't go overboard.'

She hadn't the least idea what he meant by that. Overboard indeed. As if. She turned her attention back to Juliet Hughes. 'I believe you once worked in his office in west London?'

'Years and years ago.' One hand went down to smooth a wrinkle out of the skirt. 'When I was in my twenties. I'm sorry — I don't see what that has to do with—'

'With the murder?' Elizabeth's eyes were wide, clear, intensely green. 'Anyone who knew Connor Bartram well will have some-thing to add to the file we're putting together on him.'

'But I didn't—'

'You didn't know him well? That's not what I've been told.'

'I don't know what you mean.'

'This is very difficult.' Elizabeth threw an overtly apologetic glance in the husband's direction. 'But I have to ask. We have a witness who says you had an affair with Mr Bartram.'

'Don't be ridiculous!'

'It's not true?'

'Of course it's not true.' A note of panic in her voice. 'Who on earth told you such a lie?'

'A nanny who used to look after the Bartram boys.'

'What's her name?'

'Allison Jackson.'

'And she says she knows me?'

'That's right.'

'I'm sorry, but she's lying. I never met anyone by that name in my life.'

'Well, perhaps you could tell me where you were on the night Connor Bartram died?'

'Where? Let's see now. What date would that be?'

'December twenty-second. A Friday. Three days before Christmas.'

She thought hard. Too hard. 'Oh, yes. I was here. We had some friends in. Christmas drinks.'

'That was the Friday before,' her husband reminded her.

'Was it?'

'Of course it was. The twenty-second was the Golf Club dinner. I had to go on my own. You had a migraine.'

'Yes, of course. Silly me.' Her eyes were wide with some kind of tension. 'But you're wrong if you think I was ever close to Con Bartram. I worked in his office when Olly — that's my first husband — was part of his team. But that's all. I just worked there—'

The door opened and someone else entered the room. A young man with reddish hair. Not overly tall, thin, late twenties, blank expression. 'What's going on?' he asked, standing in the doorway, his coat half unzipped.

'It's nothing,' Juliet said quickly. 'Just business. Nothing that need concern you. Good day?'

'All right. What kind of business?'

'I'm a private detective,' Elizabeth told him. 'And this is?'

'This is our son, Michael,' Juliet said quickly.

'What's this about?' Michael Hughes asked.

'We're making enquiries about a murder.'

'Murder?' His face revealed no emotion.

'Connor Bartram. The explorer. Heard of him?'

'Vaguely.'

'And his son, Piers.'

'So what's it got to do with us?'

'Nothing, dear. Nothing at all.' Juliet Hughes got up, braced herself, smiled at them, then said, 'I'm sorry. There's nothing else we . . . I can tell you about this matter.'

And before Elizabeth knew it, she was being shown the door.

How come this place always looks a mess, Elizabeth thought as she walked into the office a half hour later. Ginger tidies, I pick things up, we have a cleaner, but there are still yukky coffee cups on my desk and a stepladder leaning against the piano and a stain that looks like baked bean juice on my desk diary.

'It's a tip in here,' she growled. 'And cramped. Ever thought about getting a new office?'

'Ever thought about minding your own business?' It was out before Max could stop himself.

'It is my business. Well, half of it.'

'Half?' He aimed a scrunched up stick-it note at the wastepaper basket and missed. 'Is that all?'

'Meaning what?'

'Meaning that sometimes you act like you're the big boss and I'm the office boy.'

'You know something? Maybe we'd get along better that way.'

'Know something? I'm fed up with you being so snotty all the time. I heard you niggling at Caroline yesterday. Without any reason.'

Suddenly it was wartime. 'Listen, buster, I won't tell you how to run your business and you don't tell me how to run mine!'

Max said, 'That's a laugh.'

'What's a laugh?'

'You're always sticking your oar in.'

'If I didn't, this place would fold inside six months.'

'It was running perfectly well until you came along.'

'Oh, yes?' Elizabeth's head was pounding. She stood there glaring at him across the desk. 'Shall we call the bank manager and ask him to confirm that?'

'Money's not the most important thing in the world, you know.'

'No, but we might make a bit more if you took your feet off the desk and lifted a finger now and again.'

Ginger said, 'Don't you think—'

'No, I don't,' Elizabeth told her. 'So butt out.'

Max said, 'You're suggesting I don't pull my weight?'

'I'm suggesting you don't often get yourself into a muck sweat.'

'Delicate term.'

'I may not be delicate like you Brits, but I sure know how to put in a day's work. You sit glued to that damned chair. Or a bar stool.' Suddenly she was enjoying getting it off her chest.

'Running round like a headless chicken isn't everything. I prefer to use my grey matter.'

Elizabeth barked out a laugh. 'What grey matter?'

'Of course, I realise my brain could never match up to yours,' he said. 'How could it? You know everything.'

'I know more than you do. But that wouldn't be difficult.'

'Well, stuff you! If you dislike it all so much, why don't you just sod off back to Uncle Sam?'

'Max!' Ginger stood by the filing cabinet looking absolutely horrified.

'So maybe I will. Maybe you should go back to doing everything yourself and see how you get on.'

'Done!'

'OK. So I'll keep out from now on.'

'Fine by me.'

Ginger looked even more horrified. 'Elizabeth – you don't mean that?'

'She does.'

'Yeah. I do.'

'Oh, well done!' said Ginger when Elizabeth had clumped off down the stairs.

'Oh, bugger off,' said Max.

'You want me to?'

A long sigh. 'No. OK, you're right. I fucked up. She was getting on my nerves.'

'She's—'

'I know. She's not well. She wants to be alone. Well, let her.'

'We can't.'

'Why not?'

'Because we're her family.'

'Oh, bollocks. We're not her family. She's got this weird lot back home in Turkey County.'

'Turkey Creek.'

'Now you're doing it.'

'Doing what?'

'Picking at me.'

'Well, you should get your facts right.'

'Why?'

'Because — well, it's obvious. Facts are facts.'

Max swung his feet off the desk. He straightened up, drummed his fingers on the desk and said, 'You know what? She needs a man.'

'Max, a good shag isn't the answer to everything.'

'No?'

'God!'

'What?'

'You're so—'

'What?'

'You're a dinosaur.'

'Is that a compliment?'

'No.'

'Didn't think so. I'm just practical. That's how it all works.'

'The world and all that's in it?'

He thought hard. 'Yes.'

'Well, I've got news for you,' Ginger said. 'Sex isn't that high on most women's priorities. Certainly not Elizabeth's.'

'So you're saying she's too old for it?' He swivelled his chair so as to reach a chocolate bar that lay on the window-sill.

'No. Yes.' She sounded exasperated.

'So which is it?'

'It's just – well— Oh, never mind. You wouldn't understand.'

'Try me.'

'Look – Max – maybe she does need someone special, but for God's sake, don't try telling her so.'

'Not even if I take her out for a meal and break the subject gently?'

'Max – don't even think of it.'

Chapter Twenty-one

Resign from the case? Walk out on it all before it was decently over and done with? No way, Elizabeth told herself. When she took something on, she made a proper job of it. So although she was mad as hell with Max (damn him, damn him) and she had steam coming out of her ears and could have kicked him to kingdom come, she still drove round to Ellen Helmsley's house the following morning. And as a matter of fact, it did her good. Put her own petty little problems (and colleagues) into perspective.

'Dreadful business! Dreadful.' Ellen Helmsley was very upset. And possibly frightened, underneath the tough exterior. She poured herself more coffee. Her kitchen smelled of kippers and toast. There was a jug of daffodils in the middle of the pine table next to a Greek head in marble (its features as smooth as the passing of time), and the bowl of candles and a crooked pile of paperback novels that looked enormously tempting.

'So what do you make of it?' Elizabeth said.

'If you ask me, Piers was in financial trouble. I didn't mention this before, but Con told me the boy had asked to borrow a large sum back before Christmas. He refused. Not that he didn't have it, but Con was always very stiff about lending them money. They had to learn to stand on their own feet, he said. No good bailing them out all the time.'

Elizabeth reached for her bag, drew out a man-sized tissue and blew her nose. 'Your sister-in-law must be devastated. Will you call and see her?'

'No.' The answer was unequivocal.

'But—'

'It wouldn't do any good. Only make things worse.' There was a sudden hardening of her voice. 'Anyway, to my mind a lot of this is her fault. It's of her own making. Piers was her spoiled baby. If she'd brought him up more sensibly—'

It was a harsh judgement. 'You can't say that when we don't know how or why the boy died.'

'I am saying it.' Outside, the sun suddenly came out, flooding the garden with a peculiar winter light. 'Just look at that grass,' Ellen said abstractedly. 'I should catch it now before it changes.' She stared out into space. 'Green isn't the easiest of colours, especially in July and August. Leaves get dusty. Trees get darker.' A silence. Then 'You got me into hot water,' she said.

'I did?'

'Yes, Marian accused me of breaking into her house and going through Con's things.'

'Well, so you did.'

'I know that. You know that. She didn't have to.'

'I'm sorry. I just needed to see her reaction.'

'And?'

'And – I'm not sure. I wondered – do you happen to know the contents of your brother's will?'

'Pretty straightforward really. There's a small legacy to me, plus my choice of keepsakes from his personal effects. The rest goes to Marian and after that to the boys.'

'But only after their mother's death?'

'That's right.'

'And the house?'

'To Marian, of course.'

'I see.' Elizabeth sat there thinking. 'Did you know he'd put the house on the market?'

'Yes, I did. He told me a few weeks ago.'

'And the reason?'

'He was bored. That's the most I could get out of him. He just wanted to live alone back in Scotland.'

'Alone? You didn't tell me that before.'

'Didn't I?'

'You certainly didn't. So he was asking Marian for a divorce?'

'Not in so many words.'

What did that mean? Elizabeth waited. 'Con told her he wanted some space.'

That old thing.

'He wanted to explore how it felt to live alone.'

Not a lot of fun, buster, I can tell you. Not in the dead of winter when your friends shoot you down and jokes are not funny any more and you're holding confessional conversations with yourself in the still of the night. 'So how did the boys feel about their home being sold?'

'Well, it wasn't their home any more, strictly speaking.'

'Nevertheless?'

'Piers was hopping mad. I don't think Kit cared much. He's not into bricks and mortar. He lives very happily – that bitch of a wife apart – in a rented cottage.'

Elizabeth shoved the sodden tissue back into her bag and went off on another tack. 'Tell me something – did you ever meet a man called Oliver Lockie? Or his wife?'

'The Lockies? Yes, I met them once or twice. Nice man. They were as thick as thieves in the early days, the four of them. Juliet. That's her name. Juliet Lockie. I once thought there might have been something between her and Con.'

'What makes you say that?'

'I've got eyes. The way he looked at her. The way she avoided looking at him.'

Elizabeth told her what Max had heard from the ex-nanny. 'Would she be a reliable witness, do you think?'

'Oh, God, yes. Dull as ditchwater, but a steady girl. More

coffee? I'll tell you something else. Marian had a crush on Lockie. Quite exuberant she used to get when he was around.'

Marian? Exuberant? It was hard to imagine. But people change, honey. One minute you're young and thrusting, living your life with furious intensity and the next it's all gone quiet and you're as much fun as a funeral wake. People have histories as long as from here to Virginia and back. Which makes this whole business harder. You can't label them because the goods change. What you see is not necessarily what you got.

Max, meanwhile, was dealing as gently as he could with Rosie Angel. 'You have no idea what Piers was doing up there?'

She shook her head. She stood by the window staring out. Silent and gentle, yet hard at the same time. She had scarcely moved since he entered the room.

'Was he in any kind of trouble?'

'No.' Her voice shivering a little, though the rest of her seemed frozen solid.

'There's something we didn't ask last time. Did you know that The Old Vicarage was up for sale?'

'Yes. Piers told me.'

'You didn't mention it before.'

'I—' She was distressed, very pale. 'He said I wasn't to tell anybody. It hadn't got round in the village and he thought it would look bad for his mother if the police found out Con was trying to sell the place over her head.'

'I don't know, but I'd guess that Piers must have been angry with his father?'

'Furious. That was what the row was really about. He was really bitter that his mother was being forced to move against her will. Actually – he offered to buy the house from his father.'

'And?'

'Con laughed in his face. With what? he asked. Buttons?'

'So he didn't even consider it as an option, even though Piers was in the property business?'

'He just laughed. He didn't think much of Piers's business abilities. He didn't think Piers had the money.'

'And did he?'

'No. Not at the time. But he might have raised it.'

No need now, Max thought. That's a godsend to Marian Bartram.

'So how did Kit feel about his father selling the house?'

'I've no idea. You'll have to ask Kit. But I imagine he'd have been as angry as Piers about it.'

'I'm sorry to ask this, Miss Angel, but what kind of state were your partner's finances in before he died?'

'I don't know. I have no idea. Piers never told me anything.' Suddenly, in what appeared to be a flare of anger, she turned to face him. An angel with a strop on, head tilted high, tears streaming freely down over her face. 'I'd like you to leave now. I'd like you to get out of my house and leave me alone.'

Max did as she asked, but he wasn't satisfied. She knows more, he thought as he climbed back into his car. Much more than she'll admit to.

Chapter Twenty-two

And Kit Bartram? Where is Kit at this most terrible time in his life? Simple. Absolutely predictable. Kit is seeking solace in the Abbey Church, in the heart of Bath – this city of fashion and elegance that has adapted itself to augment all the little comforts and luxuries of life. The church that stands on the same spot where a temple to Minerva once stood. In fact, the temple was converted into a Christian church – St Mary de Stalls – the niches in the former temple being called stalls. Kit often wanders down to the Roman Baths to gaze intently at the Gorgon shield from the portico of Minerva's temple and the female bronze depicting the goddess of intelligence and of the arts and crafts.

But today he is not in gorgon mood.

Today he has come to see the angels. He is greatly in need of them.

He has this ritual when he comes to worship the Abbey. He likes to sit (an incongruous figure: torn jumper, dusty boots, mildly mad brown eyes) on a low wall in the Abbey Yard and to imagine St Mary de Stalls at the end of the fifteenth-century a forlorn ruin shamefully neglected by a community of monks decimated by the Black Death. He likes to take himself back to a point in time just before his favourite story begins to unfold. He stands just behind the starting line, so to speak, and anticipates the moment to come with a delicious quiver of anticipation.

We all do it. Own up. We relive – rekindle – favourite events, memories, myths in order to bring a momentary glow to a dim day.

A fanfare of trumpets (inside Kit's head) and up pops Bishop Oliver King, the newly elected Bishop of Bath and Wells. Let the story begin. The good bishop had a dream. Lying one night in Bath, praying hard for the prosperity of Henry VII (the wisest and most peaceable king in all Europe) and his heirs, he saw a vision of the Holy Trinity with angels ascending and descending by a ladder, near the foot of which was a fair olive tree, supporting a crown. And a voice said, 'Let an olive establish the crown and let a king restore the church.' The dream wouldn't go away (sometimes they don't) and so the good bishop began to build a new church and on the great west front he had stonemasons carve his vision of the angels and the ladder.

At this point, a smile touches Kit's face. He lets his eyes go up to the octagonal towers, to the angels (much mutilated now, some of them) ascending and descending ladders. He gazes at the dove, the figure representing God the father and a whole host of cherubim and seraphim. At the top of each ladder is a defaced figure, one standing for heaven and the other– the one with two eyes, an open mouth and large teeth – hell.

Kit's smile dies. His hand, trembling slightly, touches the side of his head. He knows all about hell . . . He has been living it ever since Piers . . . since Piers . . . He can't bring himself to say it. Can't even think it. He almost sways as he sits there on the wall. Is this real? Is it happening? He stares up at the carved man asleep under the carved olive tree. The shape of the branches makes him think of another tree, a long time back. Of a woman shouting so loudly that his father threatened to call the police. A woman in a pink gauzy dress. He hadn't thought about it for years until the funeral brought it back.

What had she been shouting? Something about money. About payments. A flame springs up in Kit's brain when he thinks of it.

The angels – quick. Keep the story flowing.

Bishop King's dream project . . . Unfortunately, he didn't live to see it finished. After the Dissolution, the monastic buildings were sold and demolished. (The bells fetched £98.) Only the Abbey church, still roofless and unglazed, and the Prior's lodging, on the south side, remained, until the first Queen Elizabeth, on a visit to the city, was so shocked by its ruinous state that she sponsored a nationwide fund for its restoration. George Rivers, Warden of New College, Oxford, gave a goodly oak, (Kit likes that phrase) grown on his manor of Cullerne, one that yielded almost five tons of prime good timber. Other private donations, left in wills, reglazed the windows, paid for the vaulting, repaved the floors . . .

Time to move. He slides off the wall, dodges a tour party, pushes his way through a side door into the Abbey and through a group of Japanese dutifully waiting to pay the entrance fee. He ignores their scandalised frowns, feels not the slightest rush of guilt. 'Churches are for high and low times,' he had once told the upper-class lady cashier. 'For meditation and for prayer. They have nothing whatsoever to do with money and you are shitting on holy ground by standing there collecting it.'

His face shuttered and blank, he makes his way into the centre aisle. The inner narrative that is shoring him up begins again, at a faster pace. The Abbey is small, compared to Wells or York or Lincoln, but it appears bold and commanding. Called the lantern of England, it is of a peculiarly light interior, thanks to the fifty-two windows (one for each week of the year) and the whiteness of the glass in them. The choir is unusually long and bears all the proportions of a Noah's Ark. It was the last great church to be built before the break with Rome. The first English church for which fan vaulting was included in the original plans. Groined vaulting, fanlike lace in stone . . .

Practically the whole of the interior surface — wall, floor and columns — is lined with slabs and tablets, at least four hundred and fifty of them, in all forms, sizes and colours. In this strange world of brass, copper, stone, slate, marble and wood, Kit feels at home. He drifts from tablet to tablet, pausing to read (with empty heart) the memorials to the famous and the obscure who came to Bath for healing and came in vain. Many of them doctors, for Bath, being the crowded resort of the sick and super-annuated, as well as of the healthy, necessarily had among its residents a large proportion of medical men.

Physician, heal thyself. As if. Kit forces his feet to move on. Thomas Litchfield, lutist to the first Queen Elizabeth. Beau Nash, 1674–1762, Director of Festivities in the Georgian city. James Quin, the actor, (obit 1766), whose epitaph was provided by Garrick, no less:

> *That tongue which set the table in a roar,*
> *And charmed the publick ear, is heard no more . . .*
> *Here lies James Quin! — Deign, reader, to be taught,*
> *Whate'er thy strength of body, force of thought,*
> *In Nature's happiest mould however cast,*
> *To this complexion thou must come at last.*

But not at the age of thirty-one with so much living still to do. Piers. Piers . . . Little brother. If I told you how much I'll miss you, if you could hear me, you'd laugh. Bollocks, you'd say. Did I ever actually tell you I loved you? Never. Oh, God, if only — I can't stand much more.

On to Rebecca Leybourne, 'Interr'd at the foot of this pillar.' Not too clever, really, Kit decides, burying all these bodies underneath a church. Bad for the stability of the building, repugnant to think about — the whole earth beneath the flooring consisting of putrid human remains. The dead underneath where the living congregate.

Deceased Feb 18, 1756. Rector's wife. Stepney, London and Oxford:
Who never saw her once ruffed with anger,
Or heard her utter even a peevish word.

Bollocks to that as well, thought Kit. You should try living in my house some time.

Resigned, gentle, courteous, affable;
Without passion, though not without sense,
She took offence as little as she gave it.
She never was, or made an enemy.

Then she's lucky. Or else someone is lying through his teeth. My father was the one who made enemies. But Piers? It's mind-blowing. Why? Who? A sudden stab of anger sends him moving on to the next slab.

Here under lyes all that was mortal of Colonel Ambrose Norton. He
served the crowne of England above forty years . . . He was a branch
of the ancient family of the Nortons in Somersetshire. Expecting a
blessed resurrection.

And my father? What did he expect? I hope he rots in hell for the way he treated Piers. All of us. That's not fair. Isn't it? Pretty damned fair, I'd have said. Hard, selfish, cruel. He deserved all he got. Kit thinks of him lying in the ground in the bit of field that is the new cemetery next to All Saints churchyard. I'm glad he's dead. I'm glad he's not here, contaminating this place.

Piers should be here.

And what epitaph would you carve for him? Gone, in all the strength of his youth. There was no sin in him. And if there was, it has passed away.

He will be avenged. Someone will suffer for this. Oh, God, yes.

I promise you, Piers.

Chapter Twenty-three

'So I'm cynical,' said Max, lying back in his swivel chair and clasping his hands behind his head.

'Damn!' In forcing a file back on to the shelf, Ginger had torn a nail. 'Sorry? What was that?'

'You called me cynical.' He shoved a printed sheet across the desk to her.

'What's this?'

'Report on that prenuptial case.'

'The girl who wanted you to check out her new boyfriend?'

'That's the one. Stuart Manfred Evans. No connection whatsoever with the limited company he's supposed to be running. And he doesn't own the flat he's supposed to be living in. All he showed her was the estate agent's particulars.'

'He's an undischarged bankrupt.' Ginger was scanning the page.

'And a chauffeur. Hence his expensive car. Now apologise.'

She sat chewing at her nail and thinking about it.

'So she was right to check on him. Career women get targeted at clubs these days, particularly in London. Some blokes do it virtually as a career. They meet a woman with money who clubs, they're charming, they pick their victim and then they make sure they meet them accidentally. It goes on from there.'

'Better to find out now than later, I suppose.' Ginger had to concede that. 'So she'll be giving him the big elbow?'

'Not necessarily.'

'You are joking?'

He gave a shrug. 'Let's face it, by the time the women get to our office, they're usually well on their way to the truth. What they do with it is their own business.' He picked up a pencil and twiddled it in his fingers. He was thinking of something else. Ostentatiously he cleared his throat. 'I was wondering. You doing anything tomorrow night?'

'I'm not working late,' she told him.

'Did I ask you to?' He swung his gaze away from the pencil. 'It's just—'

'And you can't borrow my car.'

'Would I dare?'

'After the last time, no.' She hadn't forgotten the occasion when he'd put it off the road by absentmindedly filling the tank with diesel.

'I just thought . . . Well, I had an idea.'

'What kind of idea?' Ginger looked at him warily.

'A surprise.'

'For whom?'

'Well—' He was about to enlighten her when the telephone rang. He picked it up. 'Shepard Agency.' He listened for a few seconds. 'I'm afraid Mrs Blair isn't here at the moment. This is her business partner, Max Shepard. Would you care to talk to me instead?' He flicked the pencil round and waited. Then jotted down an address. 'That's before the second crossroads? Right. I'll be with you in' – he jerked up his wrist – 'say half an hour.'

'What was that all about?' Ginger asked.

'Juliet Hughes. She wants to talk to us.' He picked up his mobile and car keys. 'I've got to meet her in a lay-by on the Frome road. So tomorrow night's OK? Yes?'

'Yes, but—'

'Give you the details later. Can't stop now.'

* * *

Juliet Hughes said, 'It went on for about eighteen months. I couldn't tell you this in front of Brian. He wouldn't have liked it. He's very strait-laced about that kind of thing. He's an elder in the Baptist church.'

Max could see her point. 'And then? Con broke it off?'

'Yes.'

'Why?'

'He got bored with it. He was like that.' A wry twist of the mouth that was almost a smile. 'Always after some new adventure.'

'And this was how long ago?'

'Just over thirty years ago. I was in my mid-twenties.'

'And he decided he'd had enough? Why? Was there another woman to take your place?'

'Not that I know of. I told you. He just got bored.'

'And how did you feel about that?'

'I was heartbroken.'

'You were still in love with him?'

'I still wanted him . . . yes.'

'So what did you do about it?'

'I went round there one afternoon and made a scene, like the nanny said. Stupid of me, I know, but I couldn't help myself.' A nerve was pulsing in her throat. The back of her hand was pressed against her lips.

'How did he react to that?'

'He just stonewalled me. He was cold. Treated me as if I was some madwoman. He said I was upsetting the children, that he'd call the police if I didn't leave.'

Max stretched his legs and tried to think. 'Tell me about your first husband. Oliver Lockie. Did he know about the affair?'

'I think so.'

'You're not sure?'

'Yes, he did know, towards the end.'

'You told him?'

'No. Someone else did. Someone in the office.'

'And?'

'It broke up our marriage. Broke up Con's team. Oliver walked out on both of us. Went back to Scotland. Started his own business.'

'Do you have regrets about the affair?'

'Now? Yes, of course I do. Oliver was a good man. A good husband. I shouldn't have done it to him, but—' She sat there biting her lip. 'But you do these things and there's no going back.'

'Do you think your first husband could have borne a grudge all these years?'

'Against Con?'

'Yes.'

'You think he might have—'

She shook her head vehemently. 'No. He might have been jealous, but he's not capable of such a thing. Anyway, he's happily married again.' Her eyes dipped away from his. She regrets that, Max thought.

'And Marian Bartram? Did she know about the affair?'

'Yes.'

'And she was a friend of yours. How did she react?'

'She never spoke to me again.'

'And you left the office?'

'My services were no longer required.' A wry smile. 'Take it from me, Con Bartram was a complete bastard.'

The fields and roads were swishing wet, but Max enjoyed the drive back down to Bath. There was a blur of rain down over the city, an air of wet peace over the woody landscape on either side. I liked her, he thought. Juliet Lockie/Hughes. Intelligent, undramatic, a little vulnerable. Elizabeth wasn't sure about her new husband. Or the son. They might bear looking into.

His phone bleeped. He pulled into the side of the road to answer it. Andy's voice said, 'Do you want the good news or the bad news?'

'Your choice, mate.'

'OK. The good news. Thought you might like to know we went over the Bartram house again and found something we missed before.'

'What's that?'

'A new print.'

'So what's the bad news?'

'It's not family and it doesn't belong to anybody we've got on the files.'

'Well, that's great. So we're dealing with a random burglar?'

'Your guess is as good as mine.'

'Well, thanks for nothing,' Max said.

'Any time, mate. Have a nice day.'

Chapter Twenty-four

Juliet Hughes, mechanically taking a biscuit from the tin, bit into it and stared at the photograph in front of her. A print of a small boy with the sun on his hair and a sullen look on his face. The symptoms were already there, she thought, in the moody stare, the expression of permanent bolshiness. Could I have done anything to prevent all this happening? Probably not. You don't hear the alarm bells ringing until it's far too late.

The house was quiet. The clock ticked hollowly. Both Brian and Michael were out. Brian was on the golf course and Michael, as usual, had gone out without telling her where. Why couldn't she pluck up the courage to ask any more? What's the matter with me? Us? Once we were friends. Once Michael would come home and talk to me, pour things out, but lately— Her stomach contracted as she remembered how coldly he'd spoken to her (no, at her) the last time she tried to get him to open up. God, what a mess my life has become. Why can't children stay children for ever? Small and cheerful. She picked up the photograph again. Not that you were ever cheerful. More pliable, perhaps, but never easy. Such a tense little face. All broken up with worry. Stop fretting over him like a dog over a bone, Brian had said. Stop overcompensating. Let him stand on his own two feet. But that's what Brian would say. If you didn't bring a child up his way, the fire and brimstone way— How she sometimes hated him and his outdated outlook on life. Methodical, self-satisfied, suppressing all the natural instincts, using the rod and not sparing the child. Well, it hadn't worked, had it? The boy had turned into a practised liar who'd neglected his studies and was fast turning into a wastrel.

You're scared of him. Your own son. Own up to it, why don't you? Because I'm his mother and I don't want to, that's why. Then you're a coward as well as a fool.

The phone shrilled. She reached out and picked it up. A woman's voice said, 'Juliet? It's me. Eve. You free for lunch?'

'I don't know.' Suddenly, without warning, Juliet's eyes filled with tears. Her voice broke. 'Oh, God, I don't know.'

'Juliet — what's wrong?'

She put the phone back on the hook, sobbing now, totally out of control. What's wrong? Where do you start? Life was one long nightmare.

Anne Verey (dark hair, dark complexion, friendly eyes and a blue cashmere sweater) was an English lecturer at a sixth-form college near Bridgewater. She squeezed Max in between lectures and was happy to answer as many questions as she could fit in. 'Yes, we bought — or are attempting to buy — Buckland Mill, though sometimes I think we must be quite mad. What do I know about Connor Bartram? Practically nothing, I'm afraid. My husband and I stayed at the pub in Buckland Slade once or twice in the early days when we met the planning people and such on site. But you don't get to know your neighbours until you move in and I'm afraid we're a long way from that. Our sons? Stephen, the elder one is reading medicine at Exeter and James — he's seventeen — is still at school.'

'I think my colleague met one of them at the mill.'

'That would have been Stephen. He was in Bath a couple of weeks back staying with a friend.'

'You've had trouble with vandals, I believe?'

'Nothing serious. Just kids with nothing else to do. Happens a lot these days.'

At two o'clock, back in the office, Elizabeth picked up the phone and heard a slow Somerset drawl, a voice made for loafing around. It was Daisy Pluess. 'Is that the lady detective?'

'It is.'

'Well, I thought of something.'

Now there's a thing. 'You did? In connection with what?'

'With the vicarage babby. That day it got dumped—'

Charming way of putting things. Elizabeth hit a key on the computer, which duly delivered her into the wrong file. She swore silently. To err is human, she thought, but to really foul things up, you need a computer. 'Yes—'

'Well, I just remembered, the day it got dumped, I saw this girl go past, carrying a bundle.'

'A bundle of what?'

'Hard to tell. A big parcel of some sort.'

'So how big was the parcel?'

'Difficult to say exactly. The light was bad and it was raining. Three foot by two maybe?'

'Now I want you to think very carefully, Mrs Pluess. This parcel the girl was carrying – could it possibly have been a cardboard box?'

'I can't say for sure. Brown paper round it. That's all I can swear to.'

'I see. So what time was this?'

'Four o'clock. I was settling down with a cup of tea and I thought, I'll draw the curtains and shut the rain out. And I was hitching at the blasted thing – we need a new track, but he never gets around to it – I was hitching at it and I looked out and saw her. Young Kirsty Andrews. She was in the same class at school as our Vicky.'

Elizabeth made a note of the name. 'You didn't think to mention this before?'

'It came back to me, like.'

But in your own good time. 'So where does this Kirsty Andrews live?'

'No idea. She moved into Bath when she got married. That's all I know.'

'So Andrews isn't now her surname?'

'Wouldn't be, would it?'

'Can you remember who she married?'

'Some young chap that works in computers.'

Well, that really narrows it down, Elizabeth thought. 'But you don't know his name?'

'Sorry. All I know is that Kirsty works in the Blind Shop in Broad Street.'

'The Blind Shop.' Another quick scribble. 'OK. Thanks. Did you let the police know about this?'

'No. I only just thought of it and your card was on the table next to the toilet roll. Damn it all, there's somebody at the door. Got to go.'

Elizabeth left the screen as it was and checked in the telephone directory for the Royal Society for the Blind. Nothing. There was the Magdalene Trust for the Blind in Brock Street. Daisy must have got it wrong. Damn. Now she would have to check both streets. More trudging around. For some inexplicable reason, her wrists ached and her head felt as if somebody had stuck it on with Sellotape. She was about to close the file when the phone rang again. She picked it up. This time someone said, 'Just calling to say I got home safely. By the way, I found your shaving brush in my washbag. Do you want me to post it back to you?'

'Do you have the right number?' Elizabeth enquired.

'You're not Max.'

'Not at the latest count, no.'

'It's Elizabeth — right?'

'Right.'

'Well, this is Fran. Max's sister. I'm back in Manchester. Is he there?'

'Sorry, no.'

'Ginger?'

'Ginger isn't here either. She had to go home. Something about a dog she's looking after.'

'Oh, God, that thing.'

Elizabeth, faintly curious, said, 'So what kind of dog is it?'

'A bloody awful brown boxer. Answers to the name of Henrik. When I was there – God, the smells that were coming out of him! I said, what have you been feeding him on? She said she doesn't feed him, he grabs anything that's going and just wolfs it down. Cake, boxes of chocolates, sugar, coffee, washing-up liquid—'

'Washing-up liquid?'

'Yeah. I said, no wonder he's letting out noises like Vesuvius. So – you're on your own in the office?'

'Yes, I am.' Thank the lord.

'Good. Then we can talk.'

'About what exactly?'

'About Ginger and Max.'

'What about them?'

'Oh, come on, Elizabeth, you must have noticed?'

'Noticed what?'

'You're not dumb. You must have noticed the way he looks at her?'

Elizabeth made a sort of uncommitted noise that almost qualified as an answer.

'You do realise that this is the only girl Max has shown an interest in that I have actually liked. And there have been dozens of the other kind, believe you me. We have to try and help it along a little.'

'Look – I'm not sure what you're suggesting, but I don't think we ought to interfere. It might have the opposite—'

'Oh, come on, Elizabeth! Americans are good at this kind of thing.'

'What kind of thing?'

'Getting stuck in. Driving things along. I thought maybe you could talk to Max.'

'Max and I had a row. Things are a bit dodgy at the moment.' Though it seemed he was trying to apologise in his own inimitable way. Ginger had informed her that Max had booked a table at Guillaume's that evening by way of an apology and she was to join them there – no arguments – at eight that evening and it was his treat.

'Then here's your chance to make it up. Listen, you're fond of him, too. I'm not blind. Do you want him to settle down like a normal human being or not?'

'Well, of course I do—'

'Then get in there. Help things along if you can and keep me in touch with what's happening. Have you got my number? No? Well, write it down. I'll give you time to get a pen.'

Seven p.m. Elizabeth took a couple of aspirin and got herself into the bath. Stared out over a darkening landscape of fields and woods. I've had enough for one day, she thought. Charladies, dogs, heavy sisters. I've a good mind to call Max and tell him I can't make it tonight. Too much effort. Oh, I know he's trying to make it up to me and so he should. But there's a March gale getting up and the spirit's not very willing, let alone the flesh, and I'd just as soon stay here and soak as have to get into my glad rags.

What glad rags? What are you going to wear if you do go? Something you're comfortable in, that's for sure. Whatever suits your mood. So what would that be? The light went streaming out on to the windswept trees while she pondered. Not the blue. It's pretty but the label sticks into my neck like a scaggy needle. The red's too bright. Can't take it at the moment. The green

silk's cold and the black makes me look putty-coloured. So . . .
it'll have to be the brown jersey. You'd rather look like a game
warden? You should go shopping some time, extend your
wardrobe. Yeah, yeah. When I stop looking as white as a hospital pillow. When my spirits pop back up. If ever.

She was careful not to get to the restaurant too early. Max
was always late and he was picking up Ginger and she didn't want
to be sitting at the table like a lemon, all on her own. Anyway,
there was the fire to make up and the breakfast dishes to wash
(disgraceful, but there had been no time that morning) and the
bin to empty . . .

Candles were burning on the tables at Guillaume's when she
walked in through the door. Max was there – good – at a table
in the window, looking unexpectedly dressed up in collar and tie.
What was going on? Ginger, too, was looking pretty, all formal
in a velvet top and silver ear-rings.

Elizabeth wound her way round a clump of potted palms
and through the tables to the one in the window. The place was
humming already. High jinks over at the bar, where somebody
was evidently celebrating a birthday. It was a nice place in a run-
of-the-mill street just behind the Abbey. She felt almost a fizz of
pleasure as she circumvented the last table. More cheerful than
she had been for some time, hungry; she prepared to greet Max
with a smile. But hang on. There was someone else with them at
the table. Someone she hadn't seen in ages.

The Reverend Richard Timms . . .

Chapter Twenty-five

Hell was let loose in the office next morning. 'Don't you *ever* do that again,' Elizabeth exploded.

Max said, 'Do what?'

'Try to set me up on a blind date. I have never been so embarrassed in all my life!'

'I thought you liked Richard Timms.'

'I do like him. That's exactly the point.'

'I don't see—'

'You do see. The man is thoroughly decent. You embarrassed him as much as you embarrassed me.'

'How do you work that out?'

'I used my eyes, Max.' She ripped into him again. 'What on earth did you tell him to get him there?'

'I said we were having a little celebration.'

'And what exactly were we celebrating?'

'Well, I sort of hinted you'd just had a birthday.'

'I did. Three months ago.'

'Well, I said it was a belated party and that you—'

She waited.

'That you'd been a bit down and that—'

'Yes?'

'Well, that you needed some . . . er . . . spiritual guidance.'

'In a restaurant?'

'I told him I thought it would break the ice. That you were embarrassed about asking him.'

Oh, brother.

'Well, I didn't exactly tell him. It was more a case of . . . gentle hints.'

'Max — you wouldn't know a gentle hint if one hit you between the teeth.'

Max said, 'Ginger thought it was a good idea.'

'I did not!' Ginger glared at him 'You didn't even tell me until we got to the restaurant.'

'You said she needed a bit of fun for a change.'

'I didn't.'

'You said it wasn't too late for her to find a new relationship.'

'Who's "she"?' Elizabeth asked. 'The cat's mother?'

Max put the milk carton he'd just taken a swig out of back on the desk. 'So you didn't enjoy yourself?'

'How could I?'

'He enjoyed himself.'

'Richard? He's just very polite. And a good actor.'

'Comes with the surplice,' said Max. 'You know, I think you're being a bit unfair to the Reverend Timms. He's lonely, too.'

'And how, may one ask, did you come to that conclusion?'

'He told me.'

'Like hell he did.'

'Well, he told me he's a widower.'

'You asked?'

'I led him round to it. His wife died eleven years ago and he sometimes gets tired of living on his own.'

'So when exactly did you extract this information from him?'

'I rang him up. Look — vicars are blokes, too, you know.'

'I'm surprised you don't have it blazoned on a hoarding outside his church. God give me patience! I've had enough. I'm going home. And don't follow me,' she said as she stomped off out of the room, 'or I might just slug you one.'

* * *

'Well done,' said Ginger in the silence after Elizabeth's footsteps had walloped down the stairs.

'She'll be OK tomorrow.'

'I wouldn't bet on it.'

He was still thinking, quite deeply, it seemed. 'You liked old Richard, didn't you?'

'Of course I did. He's really nice.'

'Well, then.'

'Well, then, what?'

'You can see why I did it.'

'Max – you can't just shove people together like that.'

'Sometimes people need a shove.'

'Granted, but it's still not wise to do it.'

'Why not?'

'Because life doesn't work that way. It'll backfire on you.'

'Bet?'

'I wouldn't take your money,' Ginger said.

'Big talk.'

'Must be catching.' She stood there eyeing him with a reluctant smile on her face.

'What?' Max asked.

'I was just thinking. You really are a prat.'

The way she said it – straight shot but with a quick, sweet smile – it sounded halfway to a compliment. Max thought about it when he got home that evening, over a beer and a tuna pizza. Funny thing, that. She tore her eyes away as if she'd hit a hot spot and wasn't sure if she liked it, if she wanted to keep the spark going or not.

He went to bed thinking about her and fell asleep feeling that, the cock-up with Elizabeth apart, things might – just might – be going right for once.

Elizabeth was still good and mad when she got home. Little bursts of anger kept bubbling to the surface and sputtering back down again. She took the iron out, then the ironing board (banging and clanking it up the deep stone step from the scullery) and set into the pile of linen that had been gathering in the basket for months.

She only ironed when she was worried or hopping mad. There was something about the activity, the pulling out of creased linen, shaking it hard, clomping the hot iron down on it (wish it was Max's head) ramming it to and fro ad infinitum, that dispersed frustration. Frenzied activity. Static electricity both inside and out. Can't fell the little so-and-so with an axe, but I can brand him with a hot iron.

The indignity of it! What possible good had he thought it was going to do? What must Richard Timms think of me? How will I ever be able to look him in the eye again?

The phone rang. She ignored it, waited until it had stopped and then clocked the number. Ellen Helmsley. What did she want at this hour of the night? Eleven twenty? Forget it. Let her call during working hours. But curiosity in the end got the better of the cat. She hit the recall number and waited.

'Hello?'

'Mrs Helmsley. Elizabeth Blair. You called.'

'I did.' The other woman sounded hurried. 'I hope you weren't in bed? Only—'

'No. I'm still up.' And how! 'What did you want?'

'Just to tell you something odd. Con's solicitor rang me tonight. Apparently, he's had a peculiar phone call. A man's voice, asking what will happen to Piers's share of his father's will now that he's dead.'

'So what will happen to Piers's share?'

'It will go to Kit.' She sounded hurried. 'On his mother's demise. They refused to tell whoever it was that, of course. Look – I've got to turn the light off. Splitting head. I can't think why I called you, actually. What possible use the information will be to you.'

Neither can I, Elizabeth thought after she'd put the phone down. But you never know. Sometime, somewhere, it might come in handy.

Chapter Twenty-six

Marian Bartram sits in the chair, half alert and half in a drugs-induced stupor. Thinking — or trying not to think. Remembering as if through a fog their raised voices. Con and Kit. Kit has been odd lately — odder even than normal — but he won't tell her what it is, what's wrong. Only the two of us now, she says to herself. How will that be? Unimaginable. God, how I miss Piers. She opens her eyes, or tries to. Winces suddenly as a little mini-explosion goes off in her right ear. The sound takes her back to the early days with Con. That trek we made to the South Pole. Sudden unexplained noises sounding in the valleys, and rebounding on ice walls as the sun climbed higher. Avalanches? Imploding crevasses? The crevasse has infinite depth. Like my husband. My murdered husband . . .

Repeat after me. You won't think about it. Hurts too much.

Her eyes move slowly, very slowly, to the lilies in the jug on the window-sill. Who sent them? No idea, but the room is filled with their sweet, almost sickly scent. Almost a seasidey smell, almost salty. Love is an essence, a powerful essence like that. Shut your eyes and it's still here. No words needed. Not even a presence. Open them again and there's a glossy yellow ribbon; curling petals; thick, creamy-white spirals with raised flecks, like white rain. Like spots on your tongue. Marian can almost feel them. The centre of each lily is deep green with a long stamen, like —

What like? Like long-life light bulbs. There's a touch of brown at the end of one of the petals. Already dying. But it will take its time about it. Like me. Sitting here in black but with no tears.

'Are you all right?' a voice said.

'As right as I shall ever be.' A wry joke had escaped from somewhere deep inside her.

'I won't stay long,' the voice told her. American. That woman. 'Are you sure you're OK?'

'Fine. Sedative. Don't like it, but the doctor insisted.'

'That's understandable. I was so sorry to hear about your son.'

Silence. Then, 'Which son?'

'Piers.'

'Ah, Piers.' The two syllables dropped into the silence surrounding them.

'We'd like to help. To find out who tampered with the ladder.'

'The ladder. Yes.'

I shouldn't be here, Elizabeth thought. Certainly shouldn't be interviewing her. She's not fit. She's a mess. And with reason. But if anything comes out of it . . . Slowly, very clearly, she said, 'Your husband had an affair, Mrs Bartram, many years ago. I'm sorry to hark back to it, but it may be important.'

'Yes, there were other women. Affairs.'

'Long-term affairs?'

'I never asked.'

'But you suspected it?' No reply. 'How did you know about the other women?'

A long pause. Marian Bartram said, putting her words out with great precision, 'Just impressions I gleaned.'

'Can we talk about Juliet Lockie?'

'Juliet?'

'Yes. Your husband had a long relationship with her.'

'Juliet was my friend. We worked together.'

'But she betrayed that friendship.'

A long silence.

'Your husband had an affair with Mrs Lockie. You did know about it. There's no point in trying to deny it.'

Grey eyes, looking through Elizabeth: detached, far away. 'He was a locked door. Yes, that's it. A locked door. I wasn't allowed in any more.'

Elizabeth leaned forward slightly in her chair. 'Mrs Lockie told me they had an affair. That it lasted several years.'

Marian no longer seemed to be listening. She was far away. Running the tips of her fingers over the linen of the chair arm. 'At first,' she said slowly, 'he was like some god come down to earth. Adonis.'

'Your husband?'

'At first we were happy, but then he went away from me and I didn't love him any more. Once maybe, but not now. Not for years. He made himself unlovable. This house took his place. It means more to me than—' Her gaze moved across to the window. 'I'm not often away, but if I go to London to visit my sister – if I go and I come back – the sight of this house makes my heart miss a beat. I love it so much.'

'But he was going to sell it?'

Mrs Bartram pursed her lips.

'And you couldn't bear the thought?'

After a minute, Marian said, 'It looks dark at this time of the year – gloomy – but you should see the place in summer. All the doors and windows open to the garden. It was a bit of a ruin, you know, when we moved in. A lovely old ruin with useless plumbing. No heating, dry rot, green mould, rising damp . . .' Her voice quickened. 'The roof leaked. But bit by bit, I pulled it together. I did it. Not Con. Ask Tommy Jewell, the local builder. Ask him how many hours he's spent here, bringing the place back to life. And Con was going to sell it.' A snap of her bony fingers. 'Just like that. I was so angry. The great man had decided. I asked him where I was supposed to live and he said I could find a bungalow. Much more suitable . . . At my age. On the money I'd have.'

'So your husband put the house on the market and was moving to Scotland. You didn't fancy that?'

'Oh, no. Over my dead body—'

'Or his?' Elizabeth said quietly.

'His?' Marian's head slowly came round.

'His death intervened. It saved you.'

'The house is no longer for sale,' was all that Marian would say. 'Piers wanted to buy it from him. Did I tell you?'

'I did hear. Yes.'

'Piers offered to buy it and let me live in it, but Con laughed at him. He didn't believe the boy could find the money. Maybe he was right, but Piers was a good son. He cared about me. None of the others do.' She suddenly burst into tears, covering her face with her hands. Elizabeth let her cry for a while, touched her arm, waited for the storm to abate. 'I'm sorry,' she said after a few minutes.

'No need,' Elizabeth said. 'Can I ask you one last question? Oliver Lockie. What did you make of him?'

'Oliver? Nice man. Always so very kind.' She was exhausted now, wiping her face with a sodden tissue. 'Came here once years ago to see Con, but he'd just left. My husband treated this house like a hotel. Did I tell you? This has been my home for thirty-five years. Only now can I arrange a bowl of flowers and know that I'm safe here.' Her arm came out. 'But I didn't kill him, if that's what you think.'

Elizabeth sat stitching away at the Jacob's Ladder. Thinking didn't require your hands. She frowned at a large block of linsey that was on its last legs. The quilt (a summer-weight, hand-pieced and tufted in Vermont around 1880) was fragile, unravelling in all sorts of places. Always happens when there's linen in the warp thread. You can fix the flaws, but it won't stand up to wear and tear. Display purposes only from now on for you, old thing. Colourful but puckered around the edges. We make a good pair.

It was one o'clock and the shop was beginning to empty; one single customer poking around in the scrap basket.

'All right if I go for lunch?' asked Caroline.

'Fine. You run along.' Elizabeth intended to lunch on a cheese pie and an apple. They sat under the counter waiting until her appetite heaved into view. In the meantime, her fingers kept busy and her mind rippled away on a course of its own, going over and over the fine detail of the Bartram murders. Con Bartram had been low, according to his sister. Stressed out? I wouldn't have thought so. He's not the kind of guy to go under. He didn't get on with his sons but that never seemed to bother him. Those boys . . . Piers unsafe with money. Kit as poor as a church mouse. Might he have killed his father for a stash of dough? Hard to imagine. His wife, however – Serena, that sharp, unattractive lady – she's a different kettle of fish. Could see her doing it. No real point, though. Kit won't get a penny until his mother's gone. Could be another forty years.

Patterns. Combinations. None of them making much sense.

Let's start again. Shuffle the material around a bit. We have two murders on our hands. Con and Piers Bartram. Father and son. The two deaths are connected, I'm sure of that. But how? There's something – I can't think what. Something that's just itching to leap out at me, but can't quite make it.

Solving a crime is like piecing blocks. You fill bits in here and there. It takes an age before you see the whole design. She lifted the quilt, turned it round, chose a new square to work on. She drove the needle through and caught a loose thread. Jacob's Ladder. Her thoughts went back to the story of Jacob and Esau. The Reverend Wilkins. 'Jacob the deceiver, boys and girls! Think of that. Jacob tricked his father into handing over his brother's birthright. Jacob stole from his own brother!' Brothers yet enemies. Rivals for their father's favours. What if there had been such sibling jealousy in Marian's house? Suppose Piers—?

Her thought processes were interrupted by a rap on the shop door. Elizabeth swivelled round in her chair. Her customers didn't usually knock. She pulled off her spectacles and then and only then realised that there was something else that was unusual about the newcomer. He was a man. Not many of those to be found in your average quilt shop.

'Mrs Blair. I hope you don't mind me dropping in on you?' He came on into the shop, closing the door behind him. Richard Timms. Elizabeth for a moment couldn't think of anything to say except, 'Not at all. You're very welcome.'

Chapter Twenty-seven

'Actually, it was quite funny,' Richard Timms said, trying to put her at her ease.

'Toe-curling,' Elizabeth suggested. Her own voice, like his, much too hearty. 'I don't know what possessed him. Really.'

'I gather he's quite worried about you.'

'The boy acts first and thinks later. Always did.'

'There are worse things.'

He was right, of course, but she wasn't going to admit the fact.

'I expect you gave him what for?' Richard Timms's dark eyes were twinkling under his bushy brows.

'I certainly did. I'm afraid I uttered some not very Christian sentiments.'

'Most of us do on occasion.' He grinned and poured himself more coffee. 'It occurred to me that I might ask him to sort out one or two members of my congregation. He could start a luncheon club. Pair them all off in a twinkling.'

She tried to banish the feeling that his soothing tone was the same that he would use to a parishioner with problems. And yet there was a look about him that was genuinely genial and sort of interesting. He was very tall, fifty-something perhaps, dark receding hair, with a charming smile. 'He'd do that all right. Though I'm not sure they'd thank him for it.'

There was a momentary pause. Then he said, 'Forgive me, but

Max was quite right to worry about you. You don't look well.'

She struggled not to show her irritation. 'After-effects of flu, that's all.'

'Flu. It can knock you back.'

'Surely can.'

'You'd think they could find a cure for it.'

'If only.'

A silence fell. He let it go on, lie in the air, hover there, almost defying her to break it. 'There's nothing else wrong?' he asked after a moment or two had gone by. 'Nothing you'd like to talk about?'

'Not really. Look—' she said, 'this is very kind of you, but I don't need a pastoral call.'

'I didn't intend that for one minute.'

Holy liar.

'It's just—' He hesitated. 'It's just that the problems of the body and the soul often go hand in hand.'

He was too damned astute. Practised, no doubt, at diagnosing the ills of the soul. 'I feel down. I won't deny it, but I wouldn't tell anybody else that.'

'So who else is there?'

Damn it, there he goes again, like a doctor putting his finger on the bit that hurts first time. 'No one. My husband died in a car crash back in the States.'

'I'm sorry. You must miss him dreadfully.'

'Every goddamned day of my life. Sorry, Vicar.'

'Richard, please.'

'Richard, then. Yes, I miss him. Jim was one of the best. We lived for each other.'

He quoted:

> '*I am in your clay*
> *You are in my clay.*
> *In life we share a single quilt.*
> *In death we will share one coffin.*'

'That's exactly it.' She was touched by the lines.

'The thirteenth-century poet, Tao-Sheng. It seems apt. So — how long ago did your husband die?'

'Ten years, almost to the month.'

'Ah, well.' The two monosyllables said it all.

'There's something else,' she heard herself saying in an abrupt way, almost violent. 'I lost a child. A miscarriage. It was around this time of the year. The dead time, I always think of it. I was forty-two years old, I had four happy, healthy children already, so to everyone else, it was soon forgotten. God didn't intend it, my mother said. Rationally, I know she was probably right. Emotionally I was a mess for a while. Maybe I still am.'

'Because you still mourn the loss of a child?'

'Briefly. At times. Yes. Is that stupid after all this time?'

'Quite normal, I should think,' he said gently. 'Losing a child is the worst thing in the world.'

'Some mothers don't think so. The ones who dump babies on doorsteps.' She looked at him. OK, she thought, maybe we're now getting down to the nitty-gritty. This is what I've been brooding over, what has been eating into me. Why didn't I see it before?

Another silence. Richard Timms said, 'I can't agree with you, I'm afraid. This poor girl who abandoned her child — I imagine she's going through hell at this moment.' He looked at her, enquiring. Willing her to agree.

And Elizabeth, gazing into the fire, sighed and said at last, 'You may be right.'

Richard said, 'If I've learned one thing in life, it's that there are no tidy answers in such situations.' A pause. 'How long had you been married? Do you mind me asking?'

'Not at all. Thirty five years, give or take a month or two.'

'Half a lifetime.'

'Uh-huh.'

'And now you're wondering what to do with the other half?'

'I had decided. There's the shop. And the business I seem to have gotten into with young Max.'

'But it's not enough?'

'It was until a couple of months ago. And then—'

He waited.

'And then—' How to explain the sudden malaise, the hopelessness that had dropped over her? 'It just doesn't feel right any more. Am I nuts or what?'

'You seem perfectly sane to me.'

'Well, I'm not or else I'd be happy.'

Richard Timms sat there looking at her. 'Not necessarily. Happiness can be an elusive substance. So how often do you get back home to see your family?'

'I was over there for Thanksgiving. Family reunion. Everybody trying to catch up with everybody else's news. Talking like maniacs, racing to get it all out before we all take off again. Hopeless trying to have a good, long chat with any of them—' She stopped. For God's sake. Why was she telling him all this? He was sitting leaning back in the chair with the coffee mug balanced on his knee. How can I get this conversation back on an everyday footing? she asked herself. Then found the answer. 'There is one way you could help me. It's not personal. It's to do with a case we're working on at the moment.'

'Fire away.'

'Well, there's a Reverend Fletcher . . . Philip Fletcher.'

'Buckland Slade.'

'That's it. You know him?'

'Not terribly well, but we bump into each other occasionally in the line of duty.'

'What kind of man is he? What do you make of him?'

'He does a perfectly adequate job.'

Adequate? What kind of word was that? Guarded, she thought. Non-committal. Wary even. 'You're not keen on him?'

'I hardly know him.'

And you wouldn't say if you didn't care for him, Elizabeth thought. Too much of the English gentleman in you as well as the parson. But there's something . . . a drawing back, a hesitation. Something that you don't particularly want to say. Don't know me well enough. I should like to know you better. This last thought was out before she could stifle it.

'I should go.' Almost awkwardly, he stood up and put the mug down on the table. 'I have an appointment at two.'

'Sure. Well, thanks for coming to—' To what? She wasn't sure.

'I just didn't want you worrying about it.'

As you knew I would. 'You're very kind,' she said gruffly. 'Thanks.'

It was some time before she forgave Max and let him off the hook. She had to visit the office later that afternoon to dictate some letters for Ginger, but repulsed all his efforts to butter her up.

'I hope you're listening,' he said as soon as she got inside the door, 'because I'm about to apologise.'

'That so?'

'I'm very sorry if I did anything to upset you. I didn't think.'

'Seems in character,' she said.

'No – I mean it. I'm not just saying it.' He dropped something on her desk. A cream envelope.

'What's this?'

'Peace offering. A ticket for the Buckland Slade literary weekend. I thought it might be up your street. Thought it might—'

'Yes?'

'Take you out of yourself.'

Elizabeth snorted. Went on sorting her mail in disdainful silence. Ginger took refuge behind her filing cabinet and sat tapping away on her machine.

'Coffee?' he asked with a hint of desperation.

'No, thanks.'

'I tried to get hold of Nina Harrison. The house seemed shut up. Andy says he'll check on the Lockie son. See if he has any previous.'

'The Hughes son.'

'The Hughes son, then. Plus I asked about the vicarage baby. They checked all suspect families in the village.'

'And?'

'Nothing. Nobody in the village saw anything that night. Nobody knows anything. The village is quiet enough at the best of times, but it was a filthy night – rain sheeting down – so nobody was hanging around.'

'Kirsty Andrews was hanging around,' she said, stopping him in his tracks.

'Who's Kirsty Andrews?'

'You mean you don't know? It's up to me to ferret out all the new witnesses?' Unfair of her, but it served him right and she fully enjoyed being one up on him. Petty, but satisfying.

Pride cometh before a fall, isn't that what they say? Half an hour later, standing in front of a disordered counter in the charity shop in Brock Street run by the Magdalene Trust for the Blind, Elizabeth discovered that no one by the name of Kirsty Andrews had ever been employed there.

'Are you sure?' she asked.

'Quite sure.' The woman with the neat, white perm gazed right back at her. 'I've worked here for the last ten years and I know every single person we've employed, even on a casual basis.'

'Are there any other charity shops for the blind in the city?'

'There's the Torch Fellowship for the Blind in Bathampton.'

They didn't employ anyone by the name of Kirsty Andrews there either. Elizabeth checked, but to no avail. Damn it, she said to herself, that Pluess woman is a pain in the butt and I shall tell her so when I get hold of her.

Chapter Twenty-eight

Michael Hughes walked straight across the back lawn to the little summer house that stood in the far corner of the garden. At the back of it, there was another small, wooden structure, a rectangular shed set at right angles to it, half hidden by a couple of sprawling rhododendron bushes. It was 11.30 a.m. A cold day and getting colder. Michael unlocked the door and put the padlock in his pocket. Inside, it was musty and dim. There were tools on the bench to the right of him, the same bench on which, ten years ago on summer evenings, he used to do his homework to get away from the constraints of the house; from his father's constant questions about how far he'd got with his reading; (His father the church-goer, the preacher, the saintly snooper.) and from his mother's depression, her moods and headaches.

Michael loved them both, but at the same time, he couldn't stand them.

He found them maddening, baffling, particularly his father, with his stiff grey hair, his heavy face, his permanently sober lifestyle. Sometimes he even thought— There was a pull and a rip as he caught the leg of his trousers on a nail sticking out of the bench end. Michael cursed. Kicked the thing hard, as if it had stuck itself out and snagged him on purpose. His mood, that day, was as changeable as his mother's. Malaise moving into a kind of vicious emptiness. A pointless anger.

His nerves were strung up. That's what she says. Control yourself. Calm down. There were two high shelves above his head. He stretched up and, with his fingers, reached to the very back of the top shelf. Nothing there. He felt again. Still nothing. Michael brushed the dust from his fingers, brought them down again and looked out through the tiny window without seeing anything. His face was as pale as paper, his breath uneven. He sat down on an empty packing case and put his head in his hands. Remained there, staring at his feet for some minutes more.

Catharine Fletcher was in a bit of a state, too. She had a tense headache and she was tired of being a perfect Christian with a perfect home and a perfect temper at all times. Especially when her husband, who had all the time in the world for needy strangers, was as capable as anyone else of storming out of the house in a huff.

She said to the person on the other end of the phone, 'I cleaned the brasses in church with one of Vivienne's designer tops. I pretended it had got mixed up with the dusters in the airing cupboard. She was furious. Philip said it was a vindictive act. I was forced to agree with him and then I asked if he had any special prayers that would help get me back on the straight and narrow. The awful thing is that I found myself enjoying it. God will punish me, I expect.'

'Nothing to do with God. You're punishing yourself.'

'Isn't that the pot calling the kettle?'

'Probably.'

'Are you all right?'

'Surviving.'

'Can we meet?' Catharine asked. 'I have to get out, even if it's only an hour.'

'Call me tomorrow.'

'If I can. I've got W.I. until nine thirty, but I could sneak off early. Are you sure you're all right?' She pressed her cheek against the cold glass. Her reflection gazed back at her, sideways on, the lips too pale, the eyes looking sad but fierce. 'You don't sound it.'

'I feel like somebody stamped on me.'

'It wasn't your fault, you know.'

'It was my fault.'

What a pair we are, Catharine thought. Tired, guilt-ridden, needing each other to survive. She heard a door slam. 'He's just come back in,' she said hurriedly. 'I'll call you tomorrow.'

'Listen, Catharine – I've told you before – you don't have to stay there. All you have to do is walk out on him. Tell somebody. Then the shit will hit the fan.'

It's more complicated than that, she thought, putting down the receiver. Or is it? She felt herself filled with a kind of frustrated energy. Footsteps came along the hall. Catharine looked up. Philip stood in the doorway. She picked up the teapot. An amber stream flowed from the spout into the waiting cup. 'Got over your temper tantrum?' she asked.

He declined to reply.

'Suit yourself,' she said with a shrug.

Twice Elizabeth telephoned Daisy Pluess and twice she was out. Damn the woman, she thought. Wasting my time and shoe leather, not to mention my energy. And then there was Max, who was still trying to get back on the right side of her. The more Elizabeth ignored him, the more he followed her around the office like a penitent dog. 'Any luck with the new witness?' he asked.

Elizabeth pretended she hadn't heard him.

'The baby's doing well, anyway. I suppose it was lucky the vicar and his wife were at home. Lucky the baby yelled and made itself heard.'

'They reckon they're programmed to survive, you know. Babies. I was watching a programme about it.'

'A lot didn't in the old days.' Elizabeth deliberately raised her voice and addressed it, over the top of the filing cabinet, to

Ginger. 'I remember a story my mother told me. There was a baby born up in the mountains during a winter's blizzard. The hired woman who was to have assisted with the birth didn't turn up and the father had to do it.'

Under the circumstances, Max didn't dare to interrupt her.

'The baby died. Only the ground was too hard to bury it.'

He fell into an irritated silence.

'They dressed the poor little thing and put him in the casket. The father built a fire and let it burn for hours on the frozen ground in the cemetery, so that he could dig a grave.'

Ginger, inside her den, gave a silent shudder. Max shoved his desk drawer in hard so that it shut with a bang.

'There were no ministers to call on for assistance and they couldn't bear to just let him be carted away and buried, so they arranged the funeral and conducted the service themselves.'

Max said, 'For Christ's sake, Elizabeth, will you stop being so bloody maudlin!'

'The mother read a chapter from St John.'

'You're doing it on purpose now. It's just play-acting.'

'She lined the casket with an alphabet quilt she had made for—'

'It's boring with a capital B.'

This last, at least, seemed to have got through to her. She swung round to face him. 'Of course!' she said, suddenly delighted. On the boil again, the old brain really working. 'Capital B. Broad Street. I'm a complete idiot!'

Chapter Twenty-nine

Kit Bartram bent his knees to take the full weight of the stone sea stag (it was the weight of a sack of spuds), before heaving it into the back of his pick-up truck. The original seventeenth-century version had come from a coat of arms above the door at Halchards Hall five miles away. This replacement that Kit had carved had taken five weeks to create. He had been working on it when they put the scaffolding on the tower, when his father died, when Piers—

He pushed the thought away before it got to him. Disconnected it entirely. This was the only way he could cope. After a while, the pain, the anguish deep inside him would burn off. But in the meantime, the memories would keep rising to the surface. *That day we went off and got drunk together on my birthday.* Kit dumped the original sea stag (flattened, polluted, wiped out by time) into the truck beside the new one. *Last year, was it? Bottles, glasses, good-natured joshing, a slap on the back – no more, ever – when we met. A touch on the back from a brother. 'God, I'm pissed,' as he fell out of the mini-cab at midnight. Fell all loose and relaxed. The light sound of his voice. 'Cheers. See you.' His face – Piers – say his name – all aglow.* Kit started to throw a canvas sheet over the carvings. *'Night, you silly sod. Got your key? God knows how you'll get it into the lock.' 'Rosie's there.' Rosie Angel. Daft* name, but apt. Why the hell didn't he marry her? Scared of marriage. Don't blame him. Wish I'd never done it. Why did you do it? Why do you do anything when you're young and stupid? He lashed a rope over the canvas and knotted it tight. You make your bed and you lie on it. Oh, really? Even if it's bloody uncomfortable?

'Kit!'

He looked up and saw her racing down the path after him. Serena, thin as a whippet; moved like one, too. Swift, snappy, mercurial.

'You're not going?'

'Some of us have to work.'

She said, 'What's that supposed to mean?'

'Whatever you like. I don't give a shit.'

'Oh, very clever. Very caring.' She stood there in her bathrobe, a silk-embroidered kimono tied with a green sash. Hard eyes, one elbow stuck out, cigarette between her fingers. 'Running away again, are we? Afraid to face me?'

'Go to hell.'

'Like your precious brother?'

He swung round to face her, eyes blazing. 'Leave Piers out of this.'

'How can I? He's the cause of it all.'

'You don't ever listen, do you?'

'That's probably because you rarely open your mouth. I'm sick and tired of your moods and your silences.'

He swung his tool bag out of the back of the truck, dropped it with a clink and a thud on the path. 'And I'm sick of your tongue.'

'If you'd listened to me—'

'Listened to you? When do I do anything else?'

'If you'd listened to me— But, no, you had to go and borrow money from Fred Barnes to help your rotten brother pay off his debts. And what happened? He put it on a horse and bloody well lost it!'

'He needed a hell of a lot more. He was desperate—'

'That's right. Stick up for the useless prat. Your brother was a cheat and a liar.'

He clenched a fist.

'That's right. Go on. Hit me. It won't be the first time.'

With a sudden move which took her (both of them, perhaps) by surprise, he reached down into the bag; with one swift movement, whipped something our of it. A chisel. One hand grabbed her by the shoulder, the other took the sharp edge to her throat.

'Don't you ever mention my brother's name again. Do you hear?'

Silenced for once in her life, she shook him off. Whereupon Kit flung the chisel hard against the wall. 'Bitch!' he said.

Max sat sharing a lunchtime pint with Andy. 'I checked the Verey lads,' he said.

'And?'

'Nothing. Neither of them was in Bath the day Bartram died. It was Christmas – well, almost. One was at a party in London with his girlfriend – bags of witnesses – and the other – the younger boy – was at home in bed with the flu.'

Andy slouched over the bar as he studied the sports page of *The Chronicle*. 'Bloody rubbish, that,' he said.

'What?'

'Getting hammered by Wasps.'

'Right. Yeah.' For once, Max's mind wasn't on the rugby. 'Anything new on the damaged ladder?'

A shrug. 'Nothing important. We're working on the theory that it was meant for the other brother, the one who was working on the tower. Nobody could have foreseen Piers climbing up there. He never had before.'

'Did you get round to see the Hughes lad?'

'He's clear. He was out with his mates the night of both

murders and anyway, the print didn't match the one found in Bartram's den.'

'Did he have any previous? Hughes?'

'Nope.'

But Elizabeth had sensed something, she'd said something about a look Hughes had given her, and Elizabeth (though he hated to admit the fact) was often right. 'Fancy another?'

'Can't, mate. I've got to go home and shift some furniture.'

'Can't it wait?'

'Wish it could. But the new babby's going to have to sleep in the little office room, so the desk's got to go down to the cellar. And I'm back on duty tomorrow so it's got to be today. Fancy lending a hand?'

'Oh, great! Just what I need.'

'Come on. Buy you a curry later.'

Elizabeth stood staring across at the blind shop window, her clear, green gaze taking in the smart paint, the roll of posh French chintz in the window, the bay tree in the doorway. The blind shop in Broad Street. Small 'b'. How stupid not to have thought of it before.

She looked at her watch. Two minutes past two. Why aren't they opening up? What the hell am I doing here, she wondered, wasting great lumps of time hanging around in shop doorways? When the wind has gone round to the north and there's a new chill in the air and I slept so heavily it took a brass band to wake me and I've been nursing a niggling headache ever since. I don't have to chase up villains and nutters for a living. I'm not rolling in it, but I've certainly got enough to suffer in comfort. Oh, get back in harness and like it, she told herself. Waiting is one of the great arts. Oh, yeah? What on earth would Jim say if he could see you? Well, old girl, everything changes, that's what he'd say. Was it possible he'd been gone ten years? Oh, yes, perfectly. These days time zipped by faster than the speed of light. But that's not the worst thing. The worst thing is the sense that so many things are decreasing. Life is getting thinner. My moods all over the place. I shouldn't be making Max suffer for trying to be a good friend, but fixing a blind date for me with a man young enough to be a toy boy? I ask you! Sometimes I wonder what he's got in his head instead of brains.

A movement across the way brought her back to the present. A girl in a blue jacket was unlocking the shop door. She looked frozen. Small, white face, thin legs in black tights. A waif in need of a good, nourishing cooked breakfast. Me, too, Elizabeth thought, crossing the street in pursuit of the girl.

Lizzie the lurcher loping into action.

'Excuse me. But do you have a Kirsty Andrews working here?'

'That's me. Sorry I'm late opening.' The girl smiled apologetically. 'A chunk of ceiling fell on us last night.'

'Oh, my.' Elizabeth listened as the girl filled her in on the rest of the story. Leaking roof to be mended; builders banging too hard; cracked ceiling; muffled thuds in the dead of night. What we seem to have here, she thought, is a perfectly normal, light-hearted girl making the best of a minor catastrophe. She asked her questions anyway.

'Was I in Buckland Slade the night of that murder? Well, yes, I was, actually. Averil asked me to deliver some blinds to a customer in the village. It's on my way home. Why do you want to know?'

Elizabeth told her. The girl looked puzzled. 'Someone thought I might have dumped that poor baby?'

'That's about it.'

She actually laughed. 'Well, I can assure you I wouldn't have had time to give birth that day! We were up to our ears here. Last hectic week of our sale. Everything reduced by fifty per cent. Ask Averil if you don't believe me.' She shook her head. 'Anyone who knows me will tell you I've been eight stone one since I left school. I'm afraid any new bumps and bulges would have been noticed.' She looked curious. 'So who told you they saw me near the vicarage?'

'A Mrs Pluess.'

Her brow cleared. 'Daisy! That explains everything. She's the village scandalmonger. What she doesn't know, she's perfectly willing to invent.'

Another blind alley, Elizabeth thought. Pardon the pun.

Five o'clock. Max parked his car in the garage behind the rugby ground and walked back down Edward Street towards his flat. The wind had dropped and the air was so still that the three-storey terraces looked like cut-outs against the night blue of the sky. A lone gull swooped, sailed then landed on one of the many chimney pots. That's odd, he thought. My dustbin's on the pavement. It's not bin day. Bloody kids again, messing around on the steps. He decided to leave it there for the moment. His back was aching from lugging furniture around and getting the thing back down the steps in the semi-darkness was an awkward business, involving edging sideways down with the bin held away from your body so that you could see what was happening to your feet.

He dawdled on the area steps as he often did, admiring the view. It was one that he was fond of. At the end of Edward Street was Great Pulteney Street, a thousand feet long and a hundred feet wide. Easily the finest street in Bath and probably the most stylish in England. Though – funny, this – there was nothing at all forbidding about it. He often rambled (the long way round), drunkenly and untidily back down Pulteney Street on his way back from the rugby club, right foot not quite knowing what the left foot was doing, gazing gormlessly up at these town houses of the old type. Civilised, he always thought, yet friendly.

But back to basics. What was he going to eat tonight? Was it to be a frying-pan job? He skirted the dustbin and picked his way down the steps. Or bread and cheese? Not sure I can be bothered to cook.

A shape moved at the bottom of the steps. There was someone standing outside his door.

'Christ! You made me jump,' he said.

'That so?' A big bloke. A Welshman wearing a rugger shirt – Cardiff – under his leather jacket. 'Max Shepard?'

'Who wants to know?' Max said, choosing to hedge his bets.

'I want to know.'

'OK.' He took a chance. 'I'm Max Shepard. What can I do for you?'

'You can answer a question or two. Are you the tosser who told my girlfriend she didn't want to know me?'

'I shouldn't think so.' He hadn't taken a girl out in ages, couldn't think of a single one that fitted the ticket.

'You're denying it, then?'

'I certainly am, Mr—'

'Evans.'

'Evans?' Max's voice had stopped working. The inside of his mouth was suddenly dry. The undischarged bankrupt.

'Right. Now you know who I am?'

'Now – listen – Mr Evans—'

'Mr Evans it is now?' A large hand had hold of Max's collar. 'You told her I didn't have any money. You told her I was a bankrupt. You told her all sorts of stories about me and now she's threatening to report me to the police.'

'You don't say?'

'I do say. And do you know what I'm going to do to you, boyo? I'm going to punch you through that wall.'

Chapter Thirty

'He got taken where?' Elizabeth asked.

'To the Royal United Outpatients.'

'Why didn't you call me last night?'

'Because it's not serious and he wouldn't let me.'

'What do you call "not serious"?'

'Cuts and bruises. It's lucky he did that judo course after the last time. He managed to flip the guy over, then scarpered and called Andy.'

'And?'

'Max gave them Evans's address. They're following it up.'

'Look – do you want me to come in?'

'No point, Elizabeth. It's Saturday. The office is closed. Max is OK and you've got your literary do.'

'Oh, that,!'

'Yes, that. You will go?'

A long pause. 'Not sure I can be bothered.'

'Elizabeth—'

'All right. All right. Fancy coming with me?'

'OK. If you like. Call me later, after I've called in on Max.'

That boy. Always in the wars. Of course, getting into the odd bit of trouble was par for the course in Max's line, even in a nice, well-behaved (well, on the whole) city like Bath. You lifted stones and all sorts of ugly things crawled out. Nasty creatures that didn't much care for the bright light of day. She just hoped Max wasn't too shaken up. Elizabeth stood with her back to the fire, thinking about the lectures on the poet who was born at Buckland Mill. Cory. Quinlan Cory. Oh, God, do I have to? Yes, you do. Can't sit around here all day with nothing interesting happening. Where's that leaflet that came with the tickets? She found her bag and dug it out.

Quinlan Cory Bicentenary Celebrations.
Buckland Slade Church Hall.

A cartouche with a square-jawed young clergyman in a Regency frock-coat standing by a mill wheel tastefully topped the flyer. Underneath it was the programme of events.

2 p.m. Church Hall. Quinlan Cory. Poet.
A talk by Dr Annabel Maskell, Senior Lecturer at the
University of Bristol.
3.00 Tea and biscuits.
3.30 Question Time.
4.00 Keats and his Circle. Carol-Ann Bowers.

Okay, so we'll put in an appearance. Show willing. You never know, some interesting little titbit might turn up along the way. And afterwards, Ginger and I will repair to the pub for a stiff drink . . .

But first I'm going down to Edward Street to make sure Max is OK . . .

Ginger, in a silver-grey top, was nibbling her way round the edges of a thin slice of pizza. Max, who hadn't eaten for over twelve hours, was attacking a bigger slab. He'd had a chunk of hair cut out over a particularly nasty-looking gash. The rest of it stood on end. He'd just come out of the shower and given it a good towelling.

Elizabeth told him he'd be better off in some different occupation. Like joining the army and getting himself sent to a war zone.

'Oh, ha ha, very funny.' But he seemed relieved to see her, delighted that she had deigned to come.

She looked at the strong, black coffee he was drinking. 'I could do with one of those.'

Ginger said sternly, 'I told you not to come.'

'I never do what I'm told.'

'So it seems. Sit down, if you can find a space. I'll wash another cup.'

Elizabeth moved a pile of discarded clothes and sat down next to the window. 'So he wasn't a happy chappy, our Mr Evans?'

'You could say that.'

'Think he'll come back and try again?'

'Always so cheerful.'

'I'm serious, Max. You should have the police keep an eye on this place.'

'I know. I know. I wasn't born yesterday.'

She sat there with her feet on the carpetless boards, while Ginger clattered away in the kitchen. 'Look, I'm not nagging. I'm just concerned about you. We've got enough problems on our hands with the Bartram case. You know what intrigues me?' she said suddenly. 'The business of the lights. Somebody put all the lights on in the house, that neighbour – Mrs Collinson – said, and Con always had a thing about saving electricity.'

'Perhaps just this once, he didn't bother.'

She shook her head. 'Once like that, you never change. They all went on one by one, she said. At nine thirty, it was lit up like a Christmas tree, which knocks on the head – sorry, kid – any theory that the killer was a random burglar.'

'He'd creep round with a torch, you mean?'

'Exactly.'

'Whereas a member of the family would have put the lights on without worrying.'

'Because it's perfectly natural for them to be there.' Elizabeth nodded. 'Except that none of them will own up to being anywhere near the house that night.'

'Except Rosie.'

'Except little Rosie. So if you were a betting man, Max, who would you go for?'

'I'd go for the obvious. I'd go for the man who owned the chisel. Nobody saw Kit Bartram get off the Paddington train at nine fifteen. He could have come back on an earlier one.'

'Uh-huh. But I don't have him down as a killer. Anyway, he wanted his mother to change the locks, have extra protection. That suggests he isn't our murderer.'

'Could be he's just playing clever. It's deliberate camouflage. He really hated his father.'

'I know. And he may be hiding evidence from us, but kill his father and his brother? I don't think so.'

'So who, then?'

'I've no idea, Max. That's the trouble.' She said, 'Did you find the little girl who cleans for Marian?'

'Oh, God. I clean forgot.'

She couldn't be too hard on him. 'Well, make it your first job on Monday.'

Ginger came in with the coffee and put it down in front of Elizabeth. 'So where do we go next?' Max asked.

'We just keep ploughing back over Con Bartram's life until we find something new.' Until something interesting started to push up through. At the moment it seemed to be barren ground. Nothing growing except the bruises on Max's head. She said, 'It's the early years of the Bartram marriage that interest me, I don't know why.' And yet she did know. 'If you want to know who a person really is, go back to the time when his character was being formed. In this case, when Con Bartram had a wife, a mistress and money worries.'

'You think?' Max said.

'I'm sure of it. Those expeditions of his must have cost a

small fortune to set up. I think we need to have another go at the Hughes woman.'

'I believed her story.'

'You took everything she said for gospel? Well, I don't. She was all over the place when we asked where she was the night Con was murdered.'

'Nothing strange about that. Can you remember what you were doing two weeks ago on Friday?'

She let the question go. 'She has no alibi, Max. She was at home all night on her own. Anyone can fake a migraine. And we should talk to that son of hers—' She had another thought. 'The Verey boys. Did anyone get *their* fingerprints?'

'They're not suspects.'

'Nevertheless.' She felt desperate enough at this stage to try anything.

Max heaved himself out of the sofa and limped over to a desk that stood against the wall. 'I just remembered – something I meant to give you, only somebody wasn't talking to me at the time.' He foraged through a pile of stuff in the pigeon-holes. Old bank statements (unopened), junk mail, racing papers. At last he came up with what he wanted. 'There you go.'

It was a slip of paper torn from a pad. On it was an address. 42 a, Preston Street, Battersea. 'It's where Juliet Lockie lived until her first marriage broke up.'

'Right,' Elizabeth said. 'So I'm to make a trip to London.'

'You said you were interested in that period of her life.'

'So I did.' Sometimes, Elizabeth thought, the worst thing about being me is having a big mouth. 'OK. I'll go next week sometime.'

But first she intended to have another chat with Mrs Hughes.

Chapter Thirty-one

Instead of having lunch (she wasn't hungry anyway) Elizabeth decided to drop in on the Hughes family. The little house with its Bath railings looked as plainly elegant as ever in the grey-green winter light. The terrace curved gently along on either side of it. Not a single mean modern window had been inserted to spoil the effect of the original design. Bijou but cultured. On the wobbly flagstones halfway along, a small black kitten was playing with a dead leaf flung along by the wind.

There was the sound of distant bells. Must be a wedding in the Abbey. She stood there listening and admiring it all for a moment. The doorways, the fanlights, the pale gold stonework, the sheer charm of the place. Juliet Hughes had done very well for herself. Juliet Hughes had a very pleasant life here; a lot to protect.

Mrs Hughes was alone in the house when Elizabeth pressed the doorbell, but she was still reluctant to let Elizabeth in. 'I told your young colleague all I know. I have nothing further to say to you.' She was holding a half-finished piece of needlepoint in her hand.

Elizabeth said, 'That's pretty. I can see you're an expert. Do you have any interest in patchwork – only my quilt shop may be of interest to you. It's in Pierrepont Mews. That sounds like advertising. I do apologise. Look – all I wanted was to check a couple of details.'

Lying through your teeth again, Betsey. But it worked. Mrs Hughes hesitated and stepped back. 'You can come in for five minutes. I have friends coming.'

'I won't keep you long, I promise. My, what a fine old clock. I almost complimented you on it the first time I called, but the English sometimes get, you know, funny if you get too fulsome. My old Pa used to make clocks back home in Turkey Creek. He used to say he'd sooner do that than rabbit hunt.' Elizabeth could assume a hill-billy style when it suited her, when she knew it would lighten the atmosphere, put clients at their ease.

Mrs Hughes led her into the tastefully laid out sitting-room. 'So what is it you want to know?'

'Well, firstly, I just wanted to check that it was you I saw at Mr Bartram's funeral.'

Juliet allowed herself a moment to think. 'Yes. I was at the funeral.'

'May one ask why?'

'Why?'

The question obviously bothered her. Her mouth took on a nervous look, as if she wanted to keep it closed, but didn't quite dare. 'I . . . went for old times' sake, I suppose.'

'But you hated the guy's guts. You told Max. Connor Bartram dumped you.'

'It was all a long time ago. I . . . felt I needed to go.'

'You were still holding a torch for him? Is that it?'

'No. I really don't know. Look – is this strictly relevant?'

'I think so. You see, I need to know more about your relationship with Mr Bartram. For example, I find it a little odd – a bit of a coincidence – perhaps that you should finish up living here in Bath, not ten miles away from your old lover's home in Buckland Slade?'

'It's not at all odd. My second husband happened to run a business in Bath.'

'He started the business in Teddington. You only moved down here after you were married.'

'Who told you that?'

'We check these things. It's what we're paid for.'

If looks could kill! 'We moved down here because Brian's family came from the West Country, but I don't see that it's any business of yours.' She was getting agitated. She had put the tapestry down on the sofa beside her but now she picked it up again and began to fiddle with a frayed end.

'I just wondered. I have to ask this: did you at any time after the bust-up resume your affair with Connor Bartram?'

'No. I didn't.'

'So you hadn't seem him at all recently?'

'I told you. I haven't seen him since I left his employment.' The blue eyes were now icy.

'I see. Tell me, did your son, Michael, ever know Mr Bartram, by any chance?'

'Michael? No. Why should he?'

'You tell me. How old is your son, Mrs Hughes?'

'He's twenty-five. Look – Michael has nothing whatsoever to do with any of this.'

'No?'

'No.' Her expression suddenly changed. She said, 'Has she been saying things about my son?'

'She?'

'Marian. What has she been telling you?'

'Well, now—'

'She's got a damned cheek. Slandering my son and coming round here to attack me—'

'She attacked you? When?'

There was a slight drawing back. 'A couple of days ago. She didn't attack me physically. It was just words.'

'And what did she say?'

A shrug. 'Use your imagination. She accused me of murdering her husband. There was a lot of vitriol. But what can you expect from such a family? I mean, from what I hear—'

'What do you hear, Mrs Hughes?'

'Nothing.' She had obviously gone too far. 'Only the gossip that's been in the newspapers.' She was trying to get herself back together again. 'There's no way you can connect me or any member of my family with these murders.'

'That wasn't my intention at all.' Elizabeth looked at her as if she meant it. 'I'm just trying to fill the gaps in our records.'

'Well, if my son's name is on your records, I'd be grateful if you'd remove it. I will not have you coming round here intimidating me. So just leave us alone, Mrs Blair, or I might be forced to call the police and file a complaint against you.'

Somehow I don't think so, Elizabeth thought as she walked away from the house. You're too tense. Frightened of something. Somebody. I wonder who. She walked to where she had left the car and stood by it thinking for a moment. Something was stirring in her brain, but no sooner did it surface than it was gone again. Something Juliet Hughes had said. She waited, but it didn't come back.

With luck, in time it would.

It was ten minutes past two by the time she eased her way into the lecture, sneaking apologetically into a gap in the back row. The hall was full and Dr Maskell (a young woman in a straight, dark trouser suit and a brown tee-shirt) was already in full, flow. According to Dr Maskell, Quinlan Cory, the eldest of six children born at Buckland Mill in the last years of the eighteenth century, had been a volatile character, his impulsive temperament always in extremes. (So who does that remind you of?) At the age of fourteen he had stopped getting himself into trouble in fist fights with the local toughs and had put all his considerable energies into writing poetry, beginning with a rollicking narrative poem about living a free and joyous life without money.

A ripple of muted laughter went round the room. A natural exuberance was apparently Cory's hallmark. His verses sometimes marched along in epigrammatic pairs, but there was a freedom of structure, a fresh, sensuous quality that boded well. From time to time Dr Maskell read selected passages from his poetry, which seemed to have in common a good many dusky vales, fading roses, lambs unshorn and millstreams flowing. . . It was all very soothing. Even soporific. Lamia and Appolonius; Truth and Beauty; Petrarchan sonnets and Chapman's Homer. The poet sang and after a while, Elizabeth slept. Until Ginger's voice whispering in her ear summoned her back to life. 'Tea and biscuits, Elizabeth. Wakey, wakey.'

'I wasn't asleep.'

'Of course you weren't,' was all Ginger said.

'I was deep in thought.'

'Very deep, by the look of it. Stay there and I'll fetch the tea. There's a scrum.'

The tea and biscuits were welcome. 'Village halls all smell alike,' Ginger said, snaffling the last biscuit from the plate. 'Dust and woollen curtains and floor polish.'

'Mmn.' Elizabeth spotted the vicar's wife, Mrs Fletcher, sitting two rows from the front. Her husband was on the stage talking to a blonde woman in a lilac jacket; in jovial mood, by the look of it. Enjoying himself greatly, which was more than you could say for Mrs Fletcher, who was sitting very straight in her chair, apparently not at all interested in refreshments.

The new session began. Dr Maskell invited questions. After an awkward silence, they eventually began to flow. Were any of Cory's poems still in print? Did he come back to the mill to live after he contracted consumption? His tragic death by drowning in a lake on the Mendips – wasn't it odd that a miller's son, living on top of the river, had never learned to swim? Dr Maskell debated the twin theories of suicide and accidental death by drowning.

And then, just as the question and answer session seemed to be over, there came a question from the platform. 'Vivienne McNeil,' said a well-modulated voice. The vicar's blonde friend.

'Do you think the romantic movement of the time was an attempt to reconcile the two opposites of poverty and hedonism?'

Hell's teeth, Elizabeth thought. Do we have to start on that when my rear end needs to prise itself free from this log of a chair? But Dr Maskell thought it an interesting question. 'The Romantics,' she said, 'tried to catch and hold together both the divine and the all too imaginable reality of this world. The taproot of romanticism is man's thirst for boundless expansion in a universe which has grave shortcomings. There devolved from this a kind of romantic restlessness—'

'You mean, the poet has a passion for transforming the world?' The Reverend Fletcher was leaning forward, a warm and boyish smile on his face. 'He's an idealist who—'

'An idealist – yes,' Dr Maskell half agreed with him. 'But his motives are quite complex.'

Two rows back, Mrs Fletcher moved in her seat. One hand went up to prop the side of her head.

'I like the phrase "romantic restlessness",' Philip Fletcher said. 'It smacks of sincere impulse.'

'Romantic restlessness?' There came an interruption from the second row. Catharine Fletcher was stiff-backed, her voice shaking with anger. 'Isn't that just a euphemism for the desire to commit adultery?'

A stirring in the serried ranks of the village literaries. Almost a collective intake of breath. But Catharine didn't notice. 'Isn't it? Mrs McNeil, I'd be interested in your opinion on this.'

'Catharine.' Her husband looked shocked, startled and rattled all at the same time.

But Catharine had only just got started. 'It seems to me that the so-called romantics have a lot to answer for. All that high-minded stuff about following your divine instincts. It's self-indulgence, isn't it, Philip? Isn't it? It's just an excuse for you to do exactly what you want and get away with it and damn your wife—'

A foolish laugh on stage. Her husband was searching desperately for some emollient reply with which to defuse the outburst. Catharine Fletcher stood up and glared at him. She said, 'You'd have made a better poet than a priest, Philip. Sex, wine and hot air without having to bother to offer succour to the sick and the weak.'

She pushed her way out along the row and turned to face the stage. 'I'm leaving now. Should have done it a long time ago,' she told him and was out of the hall before he could open his mouth to reply.

Chapter Thirty-two

And Elizabeth was out of there, too, faster than she would have ever thought it possible. She hadn't intended it. She didn't even ask herself exactly why she was chasing after Catharine Fletcher. Instinct took over. All she knew was that she needed to follow this up, that something useful might come out of it and that it would be uncommonly interesting to find out exactly what was going on at the vicarage.

Ginger must have been quick on the draw, too. The girl caught her up just as she reached the outer steps. 'What was that all about?' she asked breathlessly, 'and where are you off to so fast?'

'I'm going to talk to her.'

'Do you think she'll want to talk to you?'

'Probably not, but we'll cross that bridge when we come to it.'

'So what do you want me to do?'

'Push off back to Bath. Fill Max in. I'll call you later.'

Mrs Fletcher was way ahead of them and walking, head down, hands in her jacket pockets, in the opposite direction to the vicarage. Elizabeth gave Ginger a quick, dismissive pat on the arm and put on a spurt. She was out of condition after the flu bout, but in an emergency you could find hidden resources.

The fugitive was slowing down a little and the droop of her shoulders struck Elizabeth as tired and dejected. She called out, 'Mrs Fletcher. Are you OK? Is there anything I can do to help?'

'No,' she said. 'Go away.'

'My dear, you remember me?' Elizabeth said as gently as possible. 'Elizabeth Blair. I have a quilt shop down in town. Dottie Marchant introduced us at Mr Bartram's funeral.'

Mrs Fletcher stopped, turned, blank-faced. 'I don't remember.'

'No? Well, there *was* a crowd and Dottie does tend to rabbit on.' Elizabeth said, 'You look exhausted. Where are you heading? Can I give you a lift somewhere? I'm on my way back to Bath—'

'Bath?' she said.

'Of course you're probably heading back home eventually.'

'Home? No, I'm not going home.' Her eyes were very wide as if to prevent the tears from getting out.

'Then let me give you a lift. Is there anywhere in particular you'd like to go? I mean, it doesn't have to be Bath. We could go back to my place if you like. I'll fix some tea.'

'Tea?' She wasn't really functioning any more. She's in trauma, Elizabeth thought. Taking hold of Catharine's arm, she said, 'My car's just over here. Let's get out of here for a while. You look as if you need to.'

This time she didn't argue.

In the car, as they were driving away from the village, Mrs Fletcher said, 'The bulk of clergy marriage break-ups come after twenty to twenty-seven years of marriage. Did you know that?'

'No. No, I didn't.' Holy Moses, Elizabeth thought, what have we got into here?

'I read an article about it.'

'Uh-huh? Do you want to put your seat belt on?'

Catharine didn't seem to hear. Her fingers were hanging on to the car door like grim death. She said, 'We used to do marriage preparation classes together, you know. I should have lis-ened to my own advice. All I did was listen to him and look where it got me.'

Elizabeth stopped the car and fastened the seat belt around her passenger. She didn't object, so they drove on. Catharine was now so white that Elizabeth asked her again if she was OK. No reply. She didn't say any more until they reached the cottage. She seemed shell-shocked. It took fifteen minutes or so before she began to come out of it and by then Elizabeth had made tea and rooted out some cookies and settled her visitor into an easy chair by the fire.

She took the tea that was handed to her. Smiled wanly. 'I made a fool of myself back there.'

'You let some stuff out that had been bottled up. That's OK. Better out than in.'

'You reckon?'

'Definitely.'

She looked unconvinced.

'Drink your tea,' Elizabeth told her. 'Sugar it well. It'll make you feel better. So will talking about your problem if you need to.'

No reply.

'Look –I realise you don't really know me from Adam, but I promise that anything you say will be in strict confidence and will go no further than these four walls. Dottie will vouch for me.'

'Dottie?'

'Miss Marchant. She lives next door.' A look of alarm. 'It's OK. I was just using her as a character reference. There's no way I'm going to let on that you're here. All I'm saying is that if you want to pour out, you can. Sometimes a near stranger's more use than talking to friends and neighbours.'

Catharine said, 'A vicar's wife can't talk to anybody.'

'No? Your home life is supposed to be perfect, I suppose?'

'Exactly. But how can it be? We're fallible like anybody else.'
Mrs Fletcher put down the sugar spoon and sat staring into the

fire. 'Looking back over it,' she said, 'I've been a complete an-
utter idiot. I let him get away with it for years and years.'

'With what, my dear?'

'With adultery. There have always been other women in
Philip's life. He's always had affairs.'

Elizabeth must have looked shocked.

'You don't believe me?'

'Of course I believe you, but — no one found him out? How
did he get away with it?'

'It's easier than you think. Imagine how many lonely women
– parishioners there are in need of comfort and support. My
father used to say – he was a clergyman, too – he used to say that
it was dangerous to counsel attractive parishioners behind drawn
curtains. An ongoing hazard. The vicar is available at home and
on the telephone, you see. He costs nothing and physical contact
– sobbing on shoulders and so on – is hard to avoid with people
whose physical needs are extreme. My father used to say that a
pastoral visit should last precisely as long as it takes to make a
cup of tea and drink it. Philip never took that advice. Quite the
opposite.'

'But surely there must have been gossip? Some of his women
must have talked?'

'No. He's very charming. He somehow perfected the knack
of clean escape.'

There's always one bad egg, Elizabeth thought. She said, 'I'm
so sorry.'

'At the beginning, when things didn't go right, I thought it
was my fault. So every time it happened, we sat down and talked
and made extra time for each other. But—'

'But it wasn't your fault at all?'

Her eyes wore a frightened look. 'It'll be all over the village
by now. What I said. If it gets around – that he's involved with
Vivienne – he'll be forced to resign his living.'

Elizabeth put a hand out to touch Catharine's. 'Listen – you
did the right thing.'

'I wish I could be sure of that. I feel so . . . isolated.'

'Do you have family in the area? Anyone you can go to for a night or two?'

'No. My parents are dead.'

'No brothers or sisters?'

A shake of the head.

'Friends then?'

'Friends? Not in the village. Not real friends. There's only—' She stopped, flushed and looked down at her hands.

Elizabeth studied her, wondering what the heightened colour meant. A romantic involvement of her own? No, not the type. Too much integrity. What then? A man that she would like to be closer to in different circumstances? 'So where will you go?'

'I have no idea.'

'Look – Catharine – you need back-up. You can level with me. If there's someone you want to call, I can make myself scarce.'

'You're very kind,' she said. 'There is someone – just a friend, but he's got troubles of his own at the moment.' She shook her head. 'No, I can't involve him in this. It wouldn't be fair.'

'He lives locally?'

'No. His mother lives here, but Kit—'

'Kit Bartram?'

Catharine hadn't meant to let the name slip out. Suddenly she was begging Elizabeth to forget what she'd heard. 'We really are just friends. It's no more than that.'

A pause. A shuffling of options. Elizabeth thought, You have an interest in Kit Bartram. You've got to put her right about that or else she'll think you're deceiving her. Well, aren't you? You didn't chase after her for purely altruistic reasons. Face it, Elizabeth, you thought she might help you solve this case. She made up her mind to do the right thing. 'I have a confession of my own to make. I'm a private detective. If you remember, Miss Marchant told you about it when we met at the funeral.'

It was coming back to her now. Elizabeth's face. Her name. 'A detective?' A look of horror crossed her face. 'You're just fishing for dirt. And I've given you plenty.'

'No. Really.' Elizabeth tried to reassure her. 'It's not like that at all. What you've told me really will remain strictly confidential. Ellen Helmsley is paying us to help Kit. We're on his side. So if there's anything you know about Kit's movements on the night his father died, anything at all that will be of use to us—'

For a moment, Elizabeth thought she was going to refuse. Catharine picked up her bag and gripped it with both hands. But then she said, 'I suppose there's no reason now not to tell you. I did see Kit that night. He was with me during the later part of that evening. I wanted to tell the police, but he wouldn't let me. He said he didn't want me involved. Kit's a man of integrity. That's rare these days. Of course, I'd have had to own up if they'd kept him in custody.'

Elizabeth felt as if she'd struck gold at last, but her voice remained steady. 'Kit was with you. Where?'

'He'd been away in London. His train was due into Bath at ten to nine. It was twenty-five minutes late. I rang him on his mobile and arranged to pick him up at the station. I'd – I'd had a bad day. I needed to see him. We went for a drink in Bath. I can assure you there was nothing improper going on, Mrs Blair. Nothing physical.' A silence. Her face had flushed to a rose colour. 'I can't deny that we've become very close, but up till now, it's been purely platonic. I wouldn't . . . couldn't bring myself to let it go further.'

Elizabeth cut her short. 'My dear, I don't give a damn what you've been up to. As far as I'm concerned you're due a bit of happiness.'

'It isn't – really. Kit has been an emotional prop over the last few months. And maybe I've helped him, too. We've helped each other.'

'So how did this friendship begin?'

'He was working on the tower and one lunchtime when it was raining, he came into the church and found me crying. He asked me what was wrong. I didn't tell him at first, but eventually he got it out of me and we talked to each other a lot after that. He's very serious, very gentle. We have a lot in common. I know I'm ten years older, but we're on the same wavelength.'

'I wonder – do you have any idea – can you throw any light on this dreadful business about Piers?'

She said, 'He didn't tell me much. All I know is that he was worried because his brother owed a lot of money.'

'To whom?'

'Professional moneylenders.' She took a long, steadying breath. 'There's one more thing. I went over to The Old Vicarage that night.'

'The night Kit's father was murdered?'

'Yes.'

'For what reason?'

Lacing her fingers together, Catharine said, 'This sounds stupid – and it may be, I just don't know – but I'd convinced myself that Philip was the father of that poor baby. I was obsessed by the idea.'

'I'm sorry. I don't see—'

'The young girl who did the cleaning for Marian after Daisy Pluess left – Nina Harrison. She used to attend the church youth club. This is about eighteen months ago. And there was something, I'm sure, at one time, between her and my husband.'

'So why did you call at The Old Vicarage?'

'I decided I'd ask the Bartrams if Nina had been to work that day – the day the baby was left in our porch. If she'd been acting at all strangely. I couldn't stop thinking about her. I had to know.'

'So what time was this?'

'Ten past eight or thereabouts. I stood on the doorstep for ages, trying to pluck up courage. I felt desperate. I hurt inside. You don't know what kind of day I'd had. I was at the end of my tether. I thought Philip might have been sleeping with Vivienne

241

McNeil and this girl, Nina, as well. Anyway, I don't know how long I'd been there, but suddenly I heard voices.'

'Inside the house?'

'Yes.'

'What kind of voices? Can you describe them?'

'Two men. Shouting. At least, the younger one was.'

'You're sure of this?'

'Yes. I'm sure.'

'Con Bartram. was having a row with somebody. Another man?'

'I can't be sure – but it sounded as if he was telling someone to clear off.'

'One of the sons?'

'Not Kit. He was on the train from Paddington. I saw him get off. But Piers? I'm honestly not sure. I've thought about it a lot. It might have been. That's all I can say.'

'Did you tell the police this?'

'No. No, I didn't.'

'Why not?'

'I – didn't want them coming to the vicarage and asking awkward questions.'

'Awkward?'

'Questions about what we were doing that night. Questions about our arrangements at home. Stupid, I know. I mean, to all intents and purposes, Vivienne was just staying with us – a family friend. It's just – well, you get paranoid. You think everybody's looking at you, noticing things.'

Elizabeth sat there thinking. 'So did Mr Bartram answer your question? Did the girl – Nina – turn up for work that day?'

'In the end, I didn't ask. He looked in such a foul temper when he opened the door, that, like a fool, I took fright. I just mumbled something about coming back to see Marian in the morning and made my escape.'

'And did you continue your investigations about the girl at a later date?'

'Kit asked his mother later. She said Nina hadn't been at work for two weeks. I didn't dare ask the girl's family. They would have thought it peculiar.'

Chapter Thirty-three

The cottage was quiet. The fire snapping and crackling away, sleet on the wind outside – it hissed occasionally as a flake or two made its way down the chimney and came into contact with the hot logs. Elizabeth sat quietly thinking. She had driven Catharine Fletcher down into Bath in her Citroën and left her at the house of a friend, another clergy wife. There she had climbed out (without so much as a single bag) and taken her leave. 'Thanks for the lift,' she had said. 'And you won't—'

'Absolute discretion,' Elizabeth had promised. 'Keep in touch. And good luck.'

What is a member of the clergy? she asked herself now. A physician for the soul. Or should be. Someone who should light fires in a dark room and go on lighting them all his or her life. Richard Timms was a prime example. Goodness – a kind of light – shone out of him. But they weren't all like that. Oh, no. The odd misfit got up to antics the same as anyone else. Philip Fletcher was a bad apple if ever there was one. But retribution was no doubt belatedly on the way.

She picked up the Jacob's Ladder quilt and settled it on her lap. Kept on sitting there, looking at it as if it might offer her some key to the solution of this puzzle. Because no matter what she did, her mind would keep coming back to the story of Jacob and Esau. The loved son and the unloved one. But that's silly, she

told herself. Both Con Bartram's sons were unloved. So what is
it, then, about the old story – crazy story when you think of it
– that keeps ringing bells? Bits of it kept coming back to her in
no particular order. Isaac was forty when he married Rebekah,
Nothing odd about that. Happens all the time these days. He's
worried because she's barren. And then, twenty years on, she
conceives twin boys.

And the children struggled together within her. And the Lord said to her,
Two nations are in thy womb.

And the first child – Esau – came out all red and hairy. And
after that, his brother, Jacob, came out, grabbing on to his
brother's heel. Sibling rivalry, if ever there was. Climbing that
particular ladder almost before he'd taken his first breath.

Esau, his father's favourite, was, if she remembered rightly,
the outdoor type, always out hunting, always as hungry as a
hunter. Jacob the introvert, hanging around indoors, a Mummy's
boy, but ruthless. Jacob tricked Esau out of his birthright for a
bowl of lentil soup. Then, fearing his father's curse, he tricked
the old man into blessing him. Covered his lily-white hand with
a piece of goatskin that smelled of the fields. Pretended to be
Esau.

Fairy-tale stuff.

Only one blessing. They can't both have it.

Daft plot, Max would say. And he'd be right. But it's the
characters that you believe in. They're spot on. The emotional
intensity of Esau's bitter cry. 'I want your blessing too.' So true
to life. And what was Isaac's reply? Sorry, son. You'll have to put
up with it for now, but you'll win in the end.

After that, Esau hated his brother.

So is there any application of all this to Kit Bartram and
young Piers? The valuables missing from the house, perhaps.
Daisy Pluess swore she hadn't had them and Piers was short of
money. But surely he wouldn't steal from his own parents?
You'll steal from anybody if you're desperate enough. And Kit,
if he found out that his brother had been misappropriating the

family silver— Would he be mad enough to attack Piers?

You tell me.

So Esau went crazy because he lost his birthright and Rebekah told Jacob to take himself off until his brother's fury had died down. Protective. How far would Marian go to protect one brother from the other? She certainly hadn't been able to protect poor Piers from his tragic fate. Anyway, Jacob took himself off until he got to the place where he was forced to lay his head upon a stone. He did OK in the end. God promised him that his seed should be spread abroad to the west, and to the east, and to the north, and to the south. Funny old God, Elizabeth thought. No just retribution for stealing from his brother. No matter what their actions, some people go up the ladder of life and some come down. And some go sideways.

It was no good. She'd still caught no more than a glimpse of what the quilt had started in her mind. All she knew was that it fascinated her, the relationship between Kit and Piers. Brother and brother. Her finger smoothed out a bump in the feather quilting. That young man shouting at Con— Let's make a list of the likely candidates. Kit. Piers. Michael Hughes. All of an age. All born within five or six years. The Verey boys? No, that was fanciful. Con didn't even know them.

Back in Edward Street, Max was talking to Fran on the phone. 'So who told you?' he asked.

'Ginger, of course.'

'She had no business.'

'She thought I ought to know.'

Max said, 'Are you eating?'

'Mm. Chicken sandwich. I'm starving.'

'I thought Ginger said you'd decided to go veggy.'

'That was last week. I've given in to temptation. It was all right, though, that stuff she made for supper. Cracked something-or-other with Chinese eggs. She's all right, is Ginger. I'm surprised you haven't got in there.'

'Got in there?'

'Don't play innocent with me, lad. I've known you too long. I'm surprised you haven't taken advantage.'

'How do you know I haven't?'

'Because I asked.'

'You didn't?'

'Where I come from, you want to know something, you ask.'

'So what did she say?' Max asked, not knowing if he wanted to hear the answer.

'She said office relationships were murder. Anyway, you didn't fancy her. That right?'

'Call you back later,' Max said. 'Got to go. Somebody at the door.'

When he put the phone down, he thought, *Don't fancy her? Bloody hell!* But maybe there's a reason she thinks that. Maybe you should make some kind of move instead of just sitting on your arse thinking about it.

The phone rang again. This time it was Elizabeth. 'Hi. How are you feeling?'

'OK.'

'Good.' That was that. She got right on down to business. 'Nina Harrison. Did you find her yet?'

'Er – no.'

'Well, get on to it. It's urgent. Guess what happened at your literary do today. . .'

Kit Bartram had heard. When Elizabeth called on him the following morning (hang church for once, this was more important) he looked as if the vicarage rumpus had done him some good. He still looked drawn around the face, but his eyes registered a quiet satisfaction on hearing at first hand how Catharine Fletcher had at last committed her act of rebellion.

'You took her down into Bath, you say?'

'To stay with a friend. I'll give you the address.'

'Thanks.' The cottage was quiet this morning. Rent-a-Mouth had taken the kids off to a birthday party, so that was lucky. A CD was playing – something soothingly pastoral. 'Grab a seat,' Kit said. 'So that's what you came to tell me? About Catharine walking out on him?'

She said, 'Not exactly. I assumed you'd know already. I assumed she would call you.'

'Yes. She called me at the workshop yesterday evening.'

'You work late.'

'Yes, well.' He reached down and flicked a speck of white stone dust from his shoe.

'Then you'll know as well that Catharine and I had a good long talk?'

'Jumped in there like a flash, didn't you?'

'I don't hang about. But I try not to take advantage of people either. I liked her. I liked her a lot.'

'You still pumped her for all she was worth.'

'Not pumped. No. She was rather in the mood for pouring out. She told me about your friendship. How you tried to help her.'

'And now you've come to see what you can get out of me?'

'No. But I'd like to hear the truth about your movements on the day your father died.'

'Catharine told you. I was with her that evening.'

'You were with her for part of the time. She saw you get off the train at nine fifteen. I'll accept that. What puzzles me is that she heard a young man shouting at your father when she went round there earlier that evening.'

'Wasn't me. I was on the train.' He saw her face. 'You don't believe me? You think I was in Buckland at eight fifteen and doubled back to Chippenham to hop on the train that Catharine met?'

'No. Not really.' It was plainly ridiculous. There wouldn't have been time.

JACOB'S LADDER

'Look — if I level with you, will you shove off and leave me alone?'

'Sounds like a deal.'

'OK.' He seemed to have come to some sort of decision. 'I did see my father that day, but much earlier. I went round to the house in the morning. I didn't want anyone to see me, so I cut across the field and went in the back way.'

'I thought you weren't speaking to your father.'

'I wasn't, but I had to go there to try and help Piers.'

'Piers was in some sort of trouble?'

'He had financial problems. He owed an enormous sum of money to a loan shark and he couldn't keep up the payments. He came to me for help. I gave him what I had — a pittance — but it was a drop in the ocean. So — this is not for anyone else's ears — he started helping himself to valuables from our parents' house and selling them to raise money. In the end, I decided I had to talk to my father whether I wanted to or not. I had to tell him what a fix Piers was in. I went round there that morning to ask him to help.'

'And what did your father say?'

'What do you think? He said if Piers had got himself into a hole, he would have to dig himself out. I said that wasn't possible, so he said he'd damned well have to take the consequences. At which point I lost my temper and said wouldn't it be better to give Piers the money rather than have him turn himself into a common thief? I told him Piers had been pinching stuff from the house. He said Piers didn't come to the house. I said he doesn't while you're around, but there are other people here he might want to see, people who really care about what happens to him. I told him I thought Piers was in danger and that he had a duty to help him. He really hit the roof. If Piers wanted money, he said, he'd have to ask for himself. Then he told me to clear off and he told my mother to clear off when she tried to intervene.' Kit sat staring at a point of space. 'She was so terribly afraid that one of us had killed him. You know? But she was wrong.'

'Are you quite sure?' Elizabeth said, 'I don't like to say this, but your brother could have driven back from the Cotswolds that night. It's possible that he got into the house, as you did, without being seen.'

He shook his head. 'No. I know – I knew Piers. He wouldn't – couldn't have killed his own father.'

'Not even if he was desperate?'

'Not even then.'

'They had quarrelled,' she reminded him.

'I know. But that didn't matter. Not in the long run. Piers still idolised him, more's the pity. He was devastated by our father's death. Anyway, you're forgetting something.'

'What's that?'

'The murderer was left-handed. Piers was right-handed and so am I.'

Elizabeth leaned back in the chair. 'So you have no idea who the young man was that Catharine heard shouting at your father that evening?'

'None at all.'

'Have you met Michael Hughes?'

'Michael Hughes?'

She explained who Hughes was. He sat there a minute absorbing the information, pale, more tired than ever, gazing at her as if there were a glass partition between them.

'You didn't know about your father's involvement with this woman?'

He shook his head. He seemed to have turned to stone, become petrified.

'I'm sorry if it upsets you.'

'It doesn't.'

She didn't quite believe him, but she had no idea what he was thinking at that moment. Was he wondering about Michael Hughes? His mind seemed to be far away. He was staring blankly out of the window and drifting. That was the only word for it.

Chapter Thirty-four

⚫══◆◆◆══⚫

Max had imagined that Nina Harrison would live in Buckland
Slade, but when he asked at the pub, it turned out that though
she had attended the village school, and had sometimes turned
up at the church youth club, she now lived a couple of miles
away over at Compton with her Aunt Stella, a hard bitch, according to the landlord of The Gardener's Arms, with a hard hand
and an unpredictable temper. Aunt Stella had taken Nina in
when her mother had gone off with a double glazing salesman —
or did he have his own window cleaning business? Either way, it
was always the children that suffered and what with Nina's dad
going totally to pieces and her mother not leaving a forwarding
address, things were never the same for poor little Nina. Nice
girl. Pretty girl. Amazing red hair. Tawny skin. A bit — well,
simple was too strong for it, but a bit vague, a bit stargazy. You
know what I mean.

Max next phoned Andy to find out if Nina had been
checked out by the police. After that, it all seemed to move into
another gear. 'You're too late, mate,' Andy said. 'We've found her.
A Mrs Fletcher called last night with the same information.'

Andy brought him up to date. Seventeen-year-old Nina had
broken down and confessed to leaving the newborn in the vicarage porch. Contrary to what the village gossips were now
putting around (among a thousand other rumours), the father of

the child was not Philip Fletcher, but the result of a one-night stand with a boy she had met at a club. The Reverend Fletcher had, nevertheless, been interviewed about an illicit relationship with the under-age girl, his wife having let out certain information when being questioned about Miss Harrison.

The girl had hidden her pregnancy from her Aunt Stella, who would – Nina's wording – have larruped the living daylights out of her. The child had been born in the bathroom at home while Aunt Stella was out at work. Nina had bundled her inside her coat and had walked across the fields to Buckland Slade, taking a little frequented footpath and cutting up through Buckland Wood. She had chosen the vicarage not because she wanted to incriminate Philip Fletcher (indeed she still remained disconcertingly fond of him), but because Catharine had always chatted to her at the Youth Club and had been kind to her. She had known the child would be in safe hands and had thanked her lucky stars, that fateful afternoon, on finding, just inside the vicarage porch, a ready-made nest in which to lay the child – a sound, dry box stuffed with second-hand jerseys left by one of the parishioners for the January rummage sale.

Finally and most importantly, the girl had given them one very interesting bit of information. She had returned to the vicarage at approximately eight fifteen that evening to make sure the baby had been found. She had seen Mrs Fletcher re-entering the vicarage after having left the Bartrams' house across the way. And immediately afterwards, she had seen the figure of a young man in a dark jacket at one of the Bartrams' upstairs windows.

'Can she identify him?' Max asked.

'Too far away. But she definitely saw him.'

'So what'll happen to the girl?' Max asked.

'Not sure yet. We're conferring with social services, but for the present she's in a safe house being kept well away from the press pack. They think it's Christmas all over again. They don't know whether to doorstep the vicarage, Aunt Stella's or the Bartrams.'

Monday afternoon. By the time Max got to All Saints, it was drizzling. He parked the car next to the church wall and went in through the lychgate with his jacket coat collar turned up. Elizabeth was waiting at the top of the path by the storm porch. It was three fifteen p.m. Anybody with any sense was within doors – except a couple of reporters hanging around by the Bartrams' gate and a photographer who was taking a shot of the Fletchers' place across the way.

Elizabeth said, 'Fancy a trip up the tower?'

'Do I have to?' Max asked. He had no head for heights.

'Might be interesting. I want your opinion on something.'

'Won't it be locked?'

'I got a key from Kit Bartram.'

She thought of everything. Max didn't know what pressed her buttons and said so. She pretended not to hear him. Led the way round to the vestry door, and thence into the church. 'Over here,' Elizabeth said, her footsteps clacking on medieval tiles. Max followed her through a door at the base of the tower. Then they were climbing the circular stone stairway. It was freezing cold. You could hardly see a hand in front of you and Max could think of things he'd sooner be doing on a Sunday afternoon, like watching the footy on the sofa at home with a lager can in his hand.

Elizabeth said, 'Almost there.' Reaching the top step, she pushed open yet another ancient wooden door.

Max said, 'I'll look from here.'

'You won't. You'll come on out.'

'Bossy bugger.'

'You're in church. Quit swearing.'

And then they were out in the rain again and Max felt . . . afterwards he could never work out why . . . the world was sud-

denly lopsided. There was this enormous, swinging silence. And
wet green fields and sky and clouds and the river wandering aim-
lessly around in the valley.

Elizabeth said, 'Don't ask me why I had to come up here. I
guess I wanted to let my mind stretch out. Take in the whole
picture. The answer to all this is down there somewhere, Max, if
we can only get our heads around it.'

'Yeah. Right.'

She fixed her eyes on the bend of the river. On the mill.
'There's one thing I want to put to you,' she said.

'What's that?'

'Hard hats.'

'Didn't bring one.'

'No. Kit's hard hat. What colour, do you think?'

'Yellow,' he said.

'Correct. How did you know that?'

'Easy. It's down there on the scaffolding.'

'Well spotted. He leaves it there.'

'So?'

'So anyone could climb the scaffolding and put it on.'

'Right.' Max knew he was supposed to make something of
that.

'Now if I happened to be down there by the pub and you
were up here working with that hat on, would I necessarily be
able to say who you were?'

He thought about it. 'Not necessarily. You'd probably assume
it was Kit.'

'Good boy! The point I'm making is that anybody – any
peeping Tom – could have come up here night after night to
keep watch without too much notice being taken.'

'Such as?'

'You tell me. Find out who and maybe – just maybe, we have
our killer.' She said, 'I've a mind to visit the Vereys again.'

Max thought it a waste of time and said so.

'Maybe,' Elizabeth said. 'Maybe not. We shall see.'

* * *

Juliet Hughes checked her watch. It was six p.m. She had cleared away the tea things. Her husband lowered the paper and peered at her over the top of it. 'You're restless,' he said.

'I can't help it, you know I can't help it. I don't think I'll go to Eve's tonight.'

'Big mistake.'

'Why?'

'You'll only sit here waiting for the phone to ring.'

'So what else is there to do?' she snapped.

He was wearing a crisp white shirt and a navy tie. He looked like he'd got prospects, had always had prospects. Why did he always have to look so damned pompous?

'Look — you've done everything you can.'

'But is it enough?' Had she done enough to put them off the trail?

'How can one tell?'

'You want to save his soul, I suppose?'

Hughes said, 'His soul is his own affair. I used to think I could make a difference, but now I know I can't.'

'So you're wiping your hands of him, is that it? Leaving it all to me? You don't even care, do you? You don't give a damn.'

'I should have contacted the police. I didn't. Do you know how much that lies on my conscience?'

'Conscience!' she said. That was a luxury she could no longer afford. There were times, now, when the word made no sense at all.

'Mrs Blair?'

'Speaking.'

'It's Richard Timms.'

Elizabeth sat up, raked a hand through her hair and then felt foolish for having done so. 'Oh, hi.'

'You weren't asleep?'

'No.'

'Only it's rather late.'

She looked at her watch. Ten past ten. 'No, I was watching some god-awf— a very boring programme on the box.'

'The one about criminality?'

'Should have switched it off, but I couldn't be bothered to pick up the zapper.'

'Monday night. Low spot of the week.'

'But—'

'But what?'

'You can't feel like that. You're a parson.'

'Parsons are people, too.' There was a wry smile in his voice. Hadn't Max said the same thing? Put it up on a hoarding.

He said, 'I told myself I wouldn't ask, but this business up at Buckland Slade. Did you know all the facts when you asked me about Philip Fletcher?'

'No. It was just a feeling I had. If I'd known it all, I would have told you.'

'Yes. Of course you would.'

'It's a bad business.'

'Sad.'

'Sad for poor Catharine. The world isn't made of apple pie. The more you see of it, the more you realise that.'

'Yes. Well, she'll get all the support we can give her.' He said, 'So how are you feeling? Better, I hope?'

She couldn't tell him the truth. I feel like an old hag. Haggled. 'Oh, fine,' she said. 'I'll survive.'

As no doubt she would. After she'd put the phone down, she switched off the television, raked the fire, stood in front of it for a moment enjoying the flames kicked up from a log she had turned over. She wondered if the Bartram murders would ever be solved. If that poor little newborn would be allowed to grow up with her mother or be given to a foster family permanently. Better to be with her mother, if at all possible. In an ideal world, that's how it would be. But it's not an ideal world. Far from it—

As the log flickered, a light suddenly went on in her head. Babies . . . There was always a risk. Now why didn't I go down that particular path before? I'm not usually so thick. She said, 'I wonder—'

Never taking her eyes from the fire, thinking hard, she started to put it all inside her head. Con Bartram, the wife, the mistress, the children, the ex-nanny. Jealousy, resentment, the need for revenge. What if— A wild, new idea was about to crack open in her mind. The expression on her face didn't alter, but something had jerked her on to a new course.

Chapter Thirty-five

——◦∘◦——

'You'd better sit down,' Marian Bartram said.

'I'd just as soon stand,' Max said. Elizabeth had told him not to be soft on them.

'As you wish.'

'I hope you've got a good reason for disrupting our day?' Serena Bartram, tall and angular, glared at him from across the drawing-room carpet. She wore a shirt of crushed velvet the same colour as the bowl of red tulips on the sofa table, and long pewter ear-rings. It was a quarter past eleven. Max had arranged to be there at eleven, but had deliberately kept them waiting. Rosie Angel, perched on a stool beside an armchair on the opposite side of the room to the other two, was very pale and, in so large a room, she looked small and fragile.

'I think so.'

There was no sign of Elizabeth, though she had arranged to meet him there at five minutes to eleven.

'So what is it that you want?' Mrs Bartram asked.

'Let's start with Juliet Lockie. Now Hughes.'

'Who's Juliet Lockie?' Serena asked.

'She's the woman your father-in-law had an affair with twenty-five years ago.'

Marian Bartram said nothing at all. She sat silently staring down at her hands, which were clasped tightly in her lap.

Serena said, 'Look – don't you think she's been through enough.

'She's been through a lot, yes.'

'So why don't you bloody leave her alone?'

'I will when you've all stopped giving me a load of bull,' Max said. 'Your husband did have an affair with her, Mrs Bartram, didn't he?'

No reply. She just sat there in her grey sweater, her hair very sleek.

'You went to see Mrs Hughes recently, I believe?'

Marian's face hardened. A heavy, awkward silence fell over the room.

'You hated her, didn't you, because she used to be your friend and she betrayed that friendship?'

No reply.

'You hated her and in the end, you hated your husband too.'

'I didn't hate him.' Marian's voice was harsh now.

'No? You had grounds.'

'I had grounds, but hate would be too strong a word. Yes, he had an affair with her years ago, but he finished it because I was the one who held the purse strings. He needed my money to help keep his office running. I said he had to choose between us. Between her and his career.'

'Juliet Hughes says you accused her of killing your husband.'

'That's a lie.'

'One of you is lying, that's for sure.'

'Well, it isn't me.' Marian was very white and she spoke with a trembling voice.

'So why did you go to see her?'

'I was at my wits' end. We were friends once. And . . .' She hesitated.

'And?' Max prompted.

'And I found her name and telephone number on a pad in my husband's desk.'

'I see.' He didn't, but maybe in time . . . 'Do you have any idea why it was there?'

'None at all.'

'So you went over there to ask?'

'Yes. And that's the truth.'

Maybe.

The older woman got up and began to walk around the room. 'I had to lower my pride considerably to go over there. But I'd just lost my son and I was desperate. I thought she might know something. Anything that would put Piers's killer behind bars.'

Piers. Not her husband. The loss of a husband was bearable, but losing the boy had cut her to the quick.

'And did she have an explanation for the phone number being on his desk?'

'No. None.'

'She had no idea?'

'That's what she said. She told me she hadn't seen him in years.'

Max's brain was chasing itself in circles. 'Did Piers know the Hughes family, by any chance?'

'Not to my knowledge.' A long, shuddering sigh. But with it a certain relief that came from talking.

'Mrs Hughes's ex-husband is a wealthy businessman, I understand?'

'I believe so. Yes.'

'Would Piers have tried to borrow money from Lockie?'

'I don't know. You'll have to ask Oliver that.'

'I already did. And he didn't. But Piers was in trouble financially. Kit told Mrs Blair.' Max glanced across at Serena, who was looking distinctly agitated. 'Where is Kit, by the way? I tried to call him at the workshop this morning.'

'I haven't the faintest idea. He didn't come home last night.'

Max hadn't expected that one. 'Did you contact the police?'

'No. Not yet.'

'You mean it's normal for him to stay out all night?' Max glanced across at Marian Bartram. She was as white as a sheet.

'He does it occasionally. Usually when he's had a skinful.'

'Did you try his mates?'

'Kit doesn't have mates, as you call them. He just has his blasted stones.'

'So you have no idea where he is?'

'No. And if I did, I wouldn't tell you.'

'No, I don't suppose you would. But Miss Angel might.'

Rosie seemed on the point of panic. 'I don't know where he is. Why should you think that?'

'Well, I might be wrong, but it seems to me you were a bit of a favourite. Con treated you like the daughter he'd lost, the daughter who might just have saved his marriage. Kit had a soft spot for you.' He was watching Serena's response out of the corner of his eye. 'You know, I still have the feeling there are things you're keeping hidden. Things Con might have told you over a glass of whisky when he was feeling low.'

'He didn't tell me anything.'

'He didn't ask you why Piers had been stealing from his own father?'

'What are you talking about?' Marian asked.

'You didn't know?'

'Know what?'

'Your son took valuables from this house and sold them.'

'It was Piers?' Marian wasn't a very good actress. 'But why would he steal from us?'

'Ask Rosie. She'll tell you.'

'Shut up, both of you,' Serena said. 'Don't you see what he's doing? Playing us off against each other—'

It was as if Rosie hadn't heard her. She said, 'He didn't want to, but he was desperate. Con didn't believe me—'

Now we're getting somewhere. 'You discussed Piers's money problems when you went to the house that night?'

'Yes. Yes, I told you. Con called me the afternoon of the day he died.' Rosie was growing increasingly agitated. 'He wanted to talk to me, he said. Could I come round? I told the police it was just a casual visit. If I'd told the truth they might have found out how much trouble Piers was in. Kit was worried about that, too. He told me not to say anything.'

Max looked at Serena. He had by now sized her up. You had to catch her sideways on, come in from an angle; otherwise she would knock you for six. 'Of course, Kit may be in danger, too. Did you think of that?'

Serena didn't think so. Or else she was brazening it out. 'Don't be ridiculous. He's probably gone off on one of his ecclesiastical rambles.'

'Where, for instance?'

'God knows. He takes off and tramps for miles taking in churches.'

'He's done it before?'

'When the mood takes him.' Quickly she said to Marian, 'There's nothing to worry about.'

'Can you be sure of that? He told me to change the locks, remember, after the second break-in.'

Max walked over to the window and stood looking out. 'Did Juliet Hughes get a mention in your husband's diaries, Mrs Bartram?'

'I told you. I've never set eyes on the diaries. I didn't even know they were there.' She added, 'I should have made him talk to me.'

'Piers?'

'Con. That's where it all started. If we'd been able to talk to each other more. You get out of the habit. If only we'd been more open.' The thin mouth twisted into a grimace. 'There was the phone call,' she said suddenly.

'What phone call?'

'The day before Con — before he died. A voice said, "Is he there?" '

'Meaning your husband?'

'I took it to mean that. Yes.'

'Anyone you recognised?'

'No.'

'Describe the voice.'

'It's difficult. A male voice. Young, I think.'

'You didn't mention this before?'

'I'm sure I did.'

Max looked at her for a moment in silence. Marian broke it and got to her feet. 'I can't talk any more,' she said.

Chapter Thirty-six

———— ≫∘∘ ————

Anne Verey was about to get into her car when Elizabeth walked up the drive. She was reaching into her briefcase for her glasses case – maroon suede. Elizabeth waved a hand and said, 'Hi. Just caught you.'

Mrs Verey didn't look too thrilled about that. 'Have we met?'

'I'm sorry. Should have introduced myself. Elizabeth Blair of the Shepard Detective Agency. My colleague, Max, came to see you a while back.'

Mrs Verey remembered, but she still wasn't keen to talk. She was late for work, she explained and had a thousand things to do when she got there. 'I was off sick last week with flu. Didn't get any essays marked. And I was hoping to pile into a few before the afternoon session.'

'You work part-time?'

'Since September, yes. My husband retired and he wants—' She stopped. 'Look, what can I do for you? Only I really have to get on.'

'I won't keep you more than a minute or two. Honestly.'

'But I already told you—'

'I know that. And we're very grateful. I just wondered if you would possibly show me a photograph of your elder son – the one I met at Buckland Mill two or three weeks ago.'

'A photograph?' Mrs Verey snapped the briefcase shut. Swung

herself into the car. 'Look, I can assure you that Stephen has nothing whatever to do with your case. So is this necessary?'

'I think so. Yes. Absolutely vital. And I don't believe he's involved for one minute.' You mean you hope he isn't. She smiled sweetly. 'It's purely for the purposes of elimination.'

A long sigh. 'All right. I have some photos in my bag here. Just had them developed.'

'Thank you. I'd be most grateful.'

There followed some ferreting around in the briefcase, which looked rather like one of Elizabeth's – a complete hell-hole. Best not to look. She stood there with a politely averted gaze while Mrs Verey searched. At last, 'Here we are. No – that's the other pack. My study week. But they're here somewhere. I know they are.'

At last she opened a pack of photos in a mustard-yellow slip-case. 'Yes. Here we are. These were taken at Christmas. Stephen is the one fooling around on the left and that's James centre front.'

Elizabeth asked her again in case there had been some mistake.

'No. There and there.' Mrs Verey's finger pointed them out again.

The final piece in the puzzle. Elizabeth's eyes glowed with satisfaction. She said, 'Thank you, Mrs Verey. You've been a great help.'

'I can't see how.'

You don't, but I do, Elizabeth thought as she strode back to where her car was parked out on the road.

'Fancy a drink?' Max said at one thirty.

Ginger wasn't sure. 'Hadn't we better wait for Elizabeth?'

He looked at his watch. 'She won't be in now.'

'She might.'

'Oh, come on.'

'But she might fancy coming with us.'

'No. No, she won't.'

'You said she needed company.'

'Not a chance,' Max said. 'She went up to London yesterday, so she'll be resting after her exertions.'

'What did she go to London for?'

'To take a look at the flat where Juliet Lockie used to live.'

'But that was twenty odd years ago.'

'I know. But if Elizabeth gets a bee in her bonnet— So are you coming or what?'

Ginger tapped a few keys and closed a file. She appeared to make up her mind. 'OK. Only I'll have to go back to my place first to check on Henrik.'

'Henrik?'

'The dog I'm minding.'

'Bloody silly name.'

'Named after the playwright.'

Max looked blank.

'Ibsen.'

'Oh – that Henrik!' Max said. 'Isn't it time you got shut of him?'

She sighed. 'Only another week, thank goodness.' She leaned over the desk to reach the tin of paper clips and her hair was almost under the lamp. It glowed russet. But that didn't get anywhere near the real colour. There was red and gold, burnt umber and copper. Max was fascinated. She didn't notice, but grabbed a couple of clips and snapped the tin shut. She stepped back not realising where he was. There was only about a foot between them. He said, 'I'll run you up to your flat and then we'll have a drink.'

'OK. Ready then?'

For what?

'Something wrong?' she asked.

'No. Nothing at all.'

'Good. Then let's go.'

He'd been to her flat before, but only to pick her up. He'd liked the look of it then – the bare boards, the kelim rugs, the flowers, the throws, the warmth of it. The blasted dog he could live without. It leapt at them – went berserk – as soon as Ginger opened the door. 'It's all right. It's all right,' Ginger said. 'You're OK. Yes, you're fine. Really you are. Come on now – settle down.'

Just shove him in a cupboard, Max thought. He stood gazing at her like someone in a trance, until she said, 'Are you hungry?'

'Me or the dog?'

'You, stupid.'

'Now I think of it—'

'Because I'm starving. Right. What's quickest? Mint and watercress soup.'

'Watercress? In soup?'

'Mm. What's wrong with that?'

'Oh, nothing,' Max said.

'You'll like it. And it only takes ten minutes. Want to take Henrik for a walk?'

Was that a rhetorical question? Probably not. 'There's a bottle on the table,' she said. 'You can open it as soon as you get back.'

'That was great,' Max said, after his second bowl of soup.

'You didn't expect it to be?'

'Well, no. But if something tastes good, it tastes good. Doesn't matter what's in it.'

She sliced into a chunk of bread and said, 'More wine?'

'There isn't any more.'

'Did we drink the whole bottle?'

'Better open another one then.'

'Right.' He really had intended to take her out for a drink, but events seemed to have led them in another direction. He grabbed a bottle of something red and tasty-looking (a bit like Ginger – he stifled the thought) from the top of the cupboard and peeled off the seal, 'So who does the dog belong to?'

'A dotty uncle.'

'Dotty how?'

'Hippy romantic. He's gone off to India to find himself.'

'In three weeks?'

'Sometimes it's possible,' she said.

He supposed. 'Uncle on your father's side or your mother's?'

'Father's.'

'So what does your father do?'

'He's a counsellor.' She fetched some cheese from the fridge.

'Planning committees and stuff.'

'No. Sorting out people's heads and stuff.'

'Oh – that sort.' He watched her stroking the dog's soft, brown head. Wish she'd do that to me. He was trying to wrestle the cork out of the bottle, but it was being predictably tough.

'Want me to have a go?' Ginger asked.

'No,' he said, although the bloody thing wasn't moving an inch.

'Oh, give it here.' She came round the table to take the bottle off him. The way she knew she could tackle the thing when he'd failed amused Max. He was at that stage when the wine was unsettling his brain, but hadn't quite upended it. Watching her struggling with the corkscrew delighted him. She looked funny and gorgeous at the same time. Forget the bloody wine, he wanted to say. Just come to bed with me. What he actually said was, 'Give up?'

'No way.' She was very determined.

'For god's sake—' He reached over and took it from her.

'Max!' She got mad and reached out to try and grab it back. Max, grinning, went to hold it above her head, but he must have misjudged the angle. His hand happened to brush the bare skin of her neck. And that was it. He was gone. She was standing there almost in the crook of his arm, her face turned up, her mouth in a little O of annoyance. The next thing he knew, he was kissing her.

And everything in his life was turning inside out.

Chapter Thirty-seven

Her mind elsewhere, her legs taking her down across the field almost automatically, Elizabeth made her way down to Buckland Mill. The woods hung close and deep on the far side of the river. Heedless of her surroundings, on she walked, still working it all out inside her head. Now for the first time she thought she knew who had killed Con Bartram and his son, Piers. It had been like taking a leap into the dark, but for the first time in weeks she had felt absolutely sure of herself. She had had to have it confirmed and she had been right. Speculation had turned to mild anticipation; excitement to certainty. How strange, she thought, to have had to go all the way to London to solve the thing.

Inexplicable crimes don't exist. You don't kill someone without a very important reason.

And she had found that reason in a quiet back street in Battersea, in an old lady's well-worn ground-floor flat. Bed at one end of the room, table in the window at the other. Morning sunshine, a jug of plastic daffodils, a little terrier giving off doggy smells, May Lynch with her crocheted blanket over her knees. 'And who did you say you were?' May had asked. 'A friend of Mrs Lockie's? My stars, that was a long time ago. Poor thing. She used to come in here for a bit of company. After he left, you see. Oh, I know she'd done wrong, but isn't it human nature? I was tempted myself once, when Harry was away with the war.

Blackouts, bombs dropping, everything gone to pot. In the end, I drew back, but I might have given in to him. Who was to know – except if you got caught. Which she did, poor soul. Such a pretty girl. Said she didn't know how she was going to manage. You'll manage, I told her. I had four and a husband lying in a cemetery somewhere in France. You'll manage. And I'm glad to hear she did.'

Elizabeth stopped on the wooden bridge and gazed down into the water. Adrenaline was coursing through her. She felt alive again, lively, energised. All that remained was for her to try out her theory. The quiet around the mill seemed to hover in the air. She remembered the young man she had met in the field that day. Saw his hard, blue-eyed stare, thought of the words they had exchanged. She hadn't rumbled him. Hadn't realised just how brilliantly he was improvising.

Clever. All that chat about the builders and the bank loan. He talked so easily that I didn't have an inkling.

The morning was quiet except for the babbling water. She dropped a twig in and watched it reappear on the other side. She watched it float downstream and saw it disappear into the millpond. The water down there was deeper and clogged with weed. She walked on until she reached the far bank, turned right and went through the wicket gate into the overgrown mass of weeds that used to be a garden.

In front of her an old well, a shaggy lilac tree, the millhouse. She walked slowly and deliberately (madness, she thought afterwards) to the front door. Lifted the knocker and let it bang down a couple of times.

It was as she lifted it to knock once more that she saw the face at the window . . . A face she recognised.

The path round to the back of the mill sloped down to a clump of willows. Elizabeth pushed her way past them, slithered on a patch of mud and, turning right, crossed a patch of sodden grass until she came to a small cobbled yard. There had to be another door. Yes, there was, over there by the steps leading up to what looked like a raised barn.

'I'll show you round, if you like.' A voice behind her, steady, cold, firm.

She turned sharply. He was standing perfectly still, one hand behind his back. The young man she had met on her first visit. Reddish hair, light blue eyes, strong hands. 'You were here before.'

'Yes. Yes, I was.'

'Snooping. Trespassing.'

'I guess,' she said quietly. 'But then, if I'm right, so are you.'

'You've got a cheek. I live here.'

'No. I think you're squatting. There's a difference.' With infinite caution, she eased herself sideways.

'Don't move. I could crack your skull open.' His left hand came into view. It held a length of iron piping.

'I'm sure you could. You've killed before.'

He didn't react immediately, but she saw the slight tremor in his hand as his eyes met hers. 'Me? You don't even know me.'

'I know you. At least, I can make an intelligent guess.' She said, 'You're his son. Con Bartram's eldest son. And Juliet Hughes is your mother.'

His face tightened. It looked wasted. The blue eyes remained blank. Was he on drugs? Possibly. Take it gently, Elizabeth told herself. She said, 'You took your father's early diaries. It had to be you. Who else would have been interested in that period of his life?'

No reaction.

'What's your name?' she asked suddenly. 'What did Juliet call you?'

'Mark.'

'Mark Hughes?'

'Lockie,' he said forcefully.

'Ah, yes.' Wouldn't be seen dead wearing the name of Hughes. 'You've got the missing diary, Mark, haven't you?'

He raised his head and stared at her. 'So who the fuck are you? Turning up here with your stupid questions.'

Take care, Elizabeth. 'I'm – I'm a friend of your aunt.'

'My aunt? I haven't got any aunts.'

'Oh, but you have. Your father's sister. She very much wants to know who killed him. And why. You've got the diary, Mark, haven't you?'

'I wanted to know.'

'About Con and your mother. Of course you did. So how did you find out where he hid them?'

'He never drew the curtains at night.'

'I'm sorry. I don't see—'

'I kept a watch on the house with binoculars.'

'From where?'

He was proud of this. An involuntary smirk crossed his face. 'Where do you think? From the scaffolding on the church tower.'

'Just across the way.' Obvious really.

'I could see everything. He used to get the diary out at the same time every night. Creature of habit, my father.' There was irony in his voice, and dislike. 'But they were a big disappointment.'

'The diary?'

'It didn't tell me anything. What he wrote was crap.'

'It didn't help?'

'He turned out to be a tin god. Somebody who should love you but didn't.'

Elizabeth watched him as if from a long distance. 'I expect this place was quite handy for you as well?' Her eyes moved up across the slope of the field, on the far side of the river. 'You could watch the back of the Bartram house from here?'

'Know it all, don't you? You'd be surprised how much I saw.'

'Lucky for you that the Vereys practically abandoned the

place. I'm surprised the police didn't search it.'

'They did, but I saw them coming. I got my stuff out and watched from the woods. As soon as they left, I was back again.'

'And no one else noticed?'

'Nobody much comes down here. Except poetry nuts.' His eyes were odd, but not without cunning. 'You know too much. Get inside. Up the steps. Don't try and run for it. You wouldn't make it.'

He was right. What an absurd idea it had been to come on her own. She saw that now. Reckless. Got to do everything yourself. Got to show them you're not past it. Them? Who? Max and Ginger? They're your friends, for God's sake. She went ahead of him up the six deep steps and into the oldest part of the mill. Inside, there was ancient machinery, a dusty smell, with traces of old flour clinging to everything. The sound of water was more noticeable, the light more dim.

'Stand over there, where I can see you.'

Keep him talking, Elizabeth thought, while you get your brain going. 'So did you always know Con Bartram was your father?'

'No. She didn't tell me.'

'When did you find out?'

There was a sleeping bag over in the corner under the window and next to it a rucksack and some blankets. He propped the piping against the wall, reached over and picked up the rucksack. He extracted a packet of cigarettes, eased one out and lit it. He took a deep whiff then relaxed a little. 'I found a pile of press cuttings. And a letter from him. I was ten. Michael – my half brother – would have been about five.' He drew slowly on his cigarette.

'How did you get on with Brian?'

'Hated him. I did my best to break them up.'

'I expect you did.'

'He used to tell the teachers I was a difficult child. They agreed with him. My reports said: "Always in trouble. Attention-seeking. Delusions. Good at English, but some of his essays are disturbing." ' He flicked imaginary ash from the cigarette.

You're almost enjoying yourself, Elizabeth thought. You've got an interested audience. You're making the most of it. 'I wasn't a very lovable kid. But then, Brian wasn't a very lovable man. Religious. They're the worst kind.'

'In what way?'

'If you had a devil, he liked to beat it out. I got out of there fast, as soon as I was old enough. He suffered. Michael. Poor little sod. I told him he should get out as well, but he didn't listen. Religion!' He spat hard on the ground.

'So why do you think she married him? Brian?'

'God knows. She was desperate for money, I suppose, and he had it.'

'You said you found some press cuttings. And a letter from your father?' Elizabeth had been standing in one position, hardly daring to move. Her leg had gone to sleep. She tried to move it, but that made him nervous.

He said, 'Stand still. One bad move and you'll know it. I'm not kidding.'

She attempted to shift her weight to the other leg, but without moving, or at least without appearing to move.

'The fucking letter.' He almost laughed. 'God knows why she kept it. It was rubbish. He didn't even dare put "love" on the bottom. But it was about me – the baby – so I knew he had to be my father.'

'What did the letter say?'

'It said he was too poor to send money but that he would see us right one day. That's a laugh, but I believed it at the time.'

'Did you tell your mother what you found?'

'Yes. She said I was to forget about it. I wasn't ever to talk about him again. But then I saw him on television. It must have been a couple of years later. I thought he was great. A hero. That's when I started to buy the videotapes about his expeditions. I used to save up and buy them. Kept them hidden under my bed and watched them over and over again while Mum was out. It was like – like pressing a pleasure button. Like giving yourself a dose of something.'

'But the actual man didn't measure up to the imagined one?'

Silence.

'So when did you first meet your father, Mark? You did meet him?'

'About a year ago. I read his autobiography.' A wry laugh. 'Nothing about us in it, but there you go. It said he lived near Bath and then one night he was on the local news, making an appeal for the church. So I looked him up in the directory and rang him up.'

'That was brave.'

'I didn't feel brave. I was terrified, but I was determined to do it.'

'So what did you say to him?'

'Just who I was. Who my mother was. I said I wanted us to meet.'

'And?'

'And he said it was out of the question.' He dropped the cigarette on the floor and stubbed it out with the toe of his shoe. 'I rang him again a couple of weeks later. And again and again until he agreed to see me. Half an hour, he said, no more. I was to come to the house at a set time and leave when he said.'

Elizabeth waited.

'That first visit I don't think anything I said to him really went in. He sat there with a polite smile on his face. I didn't ask for money or anything. All I wanted was for him to acknowledge me as his son. All open and above board. I came away thinking he would consider the matter. He seemed mildly interested, but I realised afterwards that it wasn't even that. He was just somewhere else. He didn't give the idea any thought at all.'

Elizabeth said, 'He didn't think about his other children much either.'

The words didn't get through to him. He went on reliving it

all in his head. 'I expected to hear from him, but I didn't, so called him again. He put the phone down on me. He was rattled though. I could tell that from his voice.'

'And after that?'

'After that? I went back to the house and I made him see me.'

'Was his wife there?'

'No. She was out. I didn't ask him for money, though it would have been useful. I wasn't demanding that he put me in his will or anything. I just told him again that I wanted him in my life. But he refused.'

'Did he give a reason?'

'He said he didn't even like me. He made me feel I was nothing. Worse than nothing. I wasn't even worth spending two minutes' thought on.'

He wouldn't even let you on the first rung.

'That made me wild with anger. I said I thought my brothers might want to meet me. And he laughed. He said, "You don't seriously think I'd tell my wife and other sons about you?" But I'm your son too, I said. My mother can prove it. He said he very much doubted it. So cold. And he suggested that I should leave. And don't try and blackmail me, he said. Don't go to the newspapers. You'll regret it.'

'That must have been hard.'

He lit another cigarette. 'It was like a douche of icy water. I didn't believe it at first. I thought I must have got him on a bad day. That he'd come round when he'd had time to get used to the idea. I used to watch him on TV, you know, and think, That's my father. I was so proud of him. I savoured the idea. But—'

'He rejected you?'

'He called me a bloody little liar. And yet, it was him that was lying. He found out where we lived and he came to see my mother. He'd had an affair with her that lasted almost a year. He knew she wouldn't lie to him, but he still denied I was his son. Who else were you sleeping with? he asked. I was upstairs, listening. I didn't believe the things he was yelling at her. I saw red. I think I decided there and then that I was going to kill him. I wanted to. I dreamt about it that night. At first I kidded myself that it was for Mum. But it was really for myself. For rejecting me, when he looked after the other two.'

The bottom line, Elizabeth thought, always turns out to be yearning. It doesn't take long for love (even imagined love) to turn to hate. 'So you broke in here and you watched and waited and bided your time? You stole a chisel from your brother's bag?'

'That wasn't difficult. He used to leave them up there. I took it home and hid it in the shed. Michael saw me. He asked me what I was up to, but I wouldn't tell him.'

'I thought you said you weren't living with your mother.'

'I got chucked out of my flat and had nowhere to go. I stayed there a few weeks, that's all.'

'So tell me how you did it. How you killed your father. You went to his house that night?'

'I thought I'd have one last go.'

'You went to see him – your father – that night.'

'Right.'

'So what time was this?'

'Just after eight.'

'And he didn't appreciate the visit?'

'He was in a foul mood for some reason. Vicious.'

Wrong time. Wrong moment, Elizabeth thought. One son up to his ears in debt and demanding money, the second having a go at you for not coughing up and the third saying, 'Daddy, love me or else.' Not good timing.

'He said—' Mark Lockie stopped suddenly. The hand holding the cigarette paused in mid-air.

'What's the matter?'

'Shut it!'

'I didn't hear—'

'I said shut it!' And to make sure that she did so, he hit her with such force that she went down like a ton of bricks. 'That's better,' he said. 'You'll do what you're told next time.'

Chapter Thirty-eight

Three in the afternoon. It still felt strange to be on the bed with her. It wasn't just that it was in the middle of the day or the newness of it all. Nor was it the other bottle of wine. They hadn't even managed to open it. It was more than that. Something deeper, but he couldn't quite define what.

'Max. This has got to stop.'

'Why?' A faint, snowy drizzle was falling outside the window. She pushed him away, leaning up on one elbow. 'Because somebody has to open the office.'

'Damn the office,' he said.

'And Henrik's whining.'

'Damn Henrik.' He had shut the thing in the kitchen. He reached out a finger and happily traced the shape of her eyelid. 'Not pebble-shaped,' he said. 'Almond-shaped. I can't think why this never happened before.'

'Because you didn't even know I was there.'

'You are joking?'

'All right, so I gave you some hassle.'

'You can say that again.'

'I gave you some hassle, but you never wanted to—'

'Wanted to what?' His hand was now pushing itself into her hair and lifting it, strand by strand.

'Well—' A slow flush was spreading up from her neck. It

hadn't occurred to him that she would be so vulnerable. He felt oddly touched. And excited and tender and bloody responsible all at the same time. His voice seemed to be playing up, like there was a frog in it. 'Well, what?'

'You know.'

'Do I?' He was playing with her now. His mind as well as his body seemed buoyant. He lifted her arm and dropped a kiss on her slim wrist. Covered with freckles, it was. Hundreds and hundreds of freckles. He wanted to kiss them all.

'Max—' She was trying to stop him.

'Don't say we've got to go back to work.'

'We should.'

'You don't really want to?'

'No. But—'

'Then forget it.' He reached for her again to stop her talking. Because he was simmering nicely. The earth wasn't just moving. Live volcanoes sprang to mind. 'Ginger,' he whispered into her shoulder. 'Ginger, Ginger . . . Listen, are you – er – on the pill or anything? I mean, is it all right?'

And she said, 'Yes, I'm all right,' and off he went again, his body totally out of control. She, too, it seemed. Breathing his name, sliding under him, winding herself all over the place.

But then she seemed to stop.

Sighed, twisted away from him, sat up and said, 'It's no good. I've got to tell you. I don't feel right about it.'

'About what?' Bloody hell! 'So what's the problem?'

'I told you my father was a counsellor.'

'So?' He just wanted to get on with it.

'So I lied.'

'Lied?'

'Yes.'

He didn't understand. 'What for?'

'Because people get funny about it. Because you'd have run a mile. Men always do.'

'Ginger – what's this all about?'

'My father isn't a counsellor.'

'So what is he?'

'You won't like it.'

'Do I have to like it?'

She didn't answer.

'Ginger – what's this all about?'

It was then that she uttered the killer words. 'He's a vicar.'

That was when he lost all his oomph. 'Bloody hell!' he said.

Chapter Thirty-nine

Elizabeth sat watching Mark Lockie tearing the pages of his father's diaries, one by one. She was cold. Cold all over and the world had turned darker and her hands were tied behind her back and then fastened to a metal ring in the wall.

She thought, I hope I get old before I die. Really old. Get me out of this, Lord, and I'll never moan about anything ever again.

Now calm down. You've got yourself in deep, but there'll be a way to get out again. You think so? Well, I've got news for you. This young man's a real weirdo. Look at him. Enough suppressed anger to fuel a rocket to the moon. You don't stand a cat in hell's chance. Her face hurt where she had hit it against the corn trough as she went down. She wanted to touch it, wipe the blood off, stop it aching, but it was impossible with her hands tied. She'd have to grin and bear it. Talk to him, she told herself, even though it feels as if he's knocked half your teeth out. Talking's the only chance you've got.

So what do I say? Where to start?

She said, 'You only told me half the story. I'd like to hear the rest.'

'Nosy bitch.'

'Always was. I have to admit it.'

Elizabeth wedged her back less uncomfortably against the wall.

Lockie said, 'He liked danger, so I gave it to him.' That note in his voice was almost exhilaration. He's dangerous, she thought. He's got nothing now to lose except his freedom.

'You went to your father's house that night and you had a bitter row?'

'I went there just after eight. He told me to get out. I called him a few choice names. We had a right old ding-dong.'

'And the doorbell rang in the middle of it? The vicar's wife decided to call.'

He couldn't understand how she knew so much. It seemed he was about to ask, but then he said, 'She didn't stay long.'

'Your father got rid of her. And then—?'

'And then he got rid of me. Or so he thought.'

'He asked you to leave?'

'Not so polite as that. He slung me out.'

'Physically?'

'Yeah. He took me by surprise. I didn't expect him to be that strong.' There was a scowl on his face.

'But you hung around and somehow you got back in later?'

'It was easy. I went round the side of the house and forced the kitchen window.'

'And you were hanging around in the back of the house when Ellen Helmsley – your Aunt Ellen – called?'

Light blue eyes gazed at Elizabeth: cold, dismissive. 'I listened to them talking. I waited until she had gone and then I followed him upstairs to his den.'

'You took him by surprise?'

'He went mad. Started bollocking on about what a pest I was. Calling me names. Making me feel I was nothing. Worse than nothing. Not even worth him spending two minutes' thought on. I didn't say a word. I went right up close to him as if to tell him what I thought of him, but I gave him the chisel instead of words. It went in quite easily. I was surprised. Somehow I thought it would be more difficult. He was surprised, too. You should have seen his face—'

As he spoke, he was tracing the shape of a C in the dust on the floorboard. He said, 'Shall I tell you something? He activated a part of my brain I'd never used before. I found that interesting.'

'You don't say.' She tried not to sound revolted. Or frightened. And yet at the same time, she wanted him to say more, as if only talk could now get her out of this hole she had dug herself into. There was a smell of violence around the place. He kept glancing at the lead piping. Brooding about it, as if deciding when to use it and where. The Lord looks after His own, she told herself.

That's what I'm worried about. I haven't been to church in weeks.

'I put all the lights on afterwards.'

'Really?' said Elizabeth with caution. 'You weren't worried about being seen?'

'I thought, I'm a member of this family and I can do anything I like. I can put lights on, walk round the place. Pick things up, put them down. Help myself to whatever I fancy. He's not in a position to stop me any more.'

A seriously disturbed young man, Elizabeth thought, I must be careful how I respond. From where she sat, she could see the door behind him and the iron latch, black-painted, so heavy it stuck out inches from the oak boards. As she went on looking at it, there was a faint noise, no more than a clinking sound, behind her at the window, followed by a small click.

He said, 'What's that?'

Elizabeth didn't have any idea. 'The wind? A loose tile?' She was about to try something. Only got yourself to blame if it all goes wrong, she thought. But if it works, it might make him have second thoughts about doing away with me. She cleared her throat, said, 'I told you a little fib earlier.'

'What's that?' He was still nervously watching the window. On the deep sill lay his camera and a set of binoculars.

'I told you I was a friend of your Aunt Ellen. That was true, but it wasn't the whole truth.'

He was looking at her now, giving her his full attention.

'I'm also a private detective. And I've got a file on you back at the office that my colleague will send to the police if anything happens to me.' It wasn't true. She hadn't a thing in writing. It would serve her right if it all went wrong. Bad practice, keeping stuff to yourself.

'You're a detective?' He didn't believe it. 'You're spinning me a line.'

'Well, now I may not look like one. But I tracked you down, didn't I?' She sat there trying to get her pulse rate down to normal. She thought, It's now or never. She said, 'Well, do you believe me or not?'

Another clink, this time at the other window, the one nearest the door. This time Lockie moved. He picked up the length of piping and went over to look out.

'Probably birds,' Elizabeth said.

'Shut up. Just shut up.' His voice was sharper now — sharp enough to show that he was fussed, although he didn't want her to know that.

'Your brother, Piers. Did you intend to kill him?'

'I expected the other one to cop it — the one that was working on the tower, but I didn't really care. I hated them both.'

'Which is a shame really, because they disliked their father almost as much as you do. Well, Kit does. Con gave them both a really hard time.' You might have been better off without him, she wanted to say. But discretion is the better part of valour, especially when your face is aching fit to bust.

'Yeah, well, I used to see him up there on the tower.'

'Kit?'

'The one who's supposed to be so good with his hands. Bloody fool. All that money — public school education — and he sits tapping away at old stones. But the scaffolding was useful. I used to go up there at night and watch them all.'

'And that's when you thought about tampering with the ladder? You thought you'd take revenge on your brother, too?'

'Why not?'

'But you got Piers instead.'

'Piers! Bloody stupid name.'

She said, 'I suppose if you got rid of them both, you'd maybe inherit? Is that what you're thinking?'

'Who knows?'

'It was you who made the calls to the solicitor?'

Silence.

'Then they'd know you existed? No one could ignore you any more?'

'You watch your mouth. It's too big.'

'I know. That's what my husband used to say. But I guess I'm too old to learn. You haven't got Kit stowed away here, by any chance?'

'No.'

'Is that the truth?' She added, 'Actually, you're very like your father.'

'Bullshit.'

'No. It's true.' There was something very vital. A force inside him. He was like Con physically, strong and wiry. 'Really.' They both liked danger. It was a turn-on. Unfortunately.

'Don't bother with the smarm. Won't do you any good.'

'No. It's true. I saw the videos, too.'

He half wanted to believe her. She almost felt sorry for him. For one moment, there was such a look of need – or something very like it – in his eyes. He was a child again, desperate to connect with the father who had rejected him. The cynicism on his face mixed with expectation. A lost child. The reverberations of that phrase seemed to give her surroundings a piercing clarity: the twisted beams, the uneven floor, the cold light coming in through the deep-framed window.

'You know something?' he said.

'What's that?' They faced each other across the room, Elizabeth huddled into the corner behind the beam, Lockie standing with his back to the door. Neither of them was at ease.

'I can't let you walk out of here. You know too much.'

'That's what my Grandma used to tell me. You know far more than is good for you, my girl. Believe you me, it will get you into trouble. And she was right.'

'I'm not joking.'

'I realise that.'

Lockie, now, was gazing at her almost furtively. Now, she could see him thinking how to dispose of her. Her stomach churned and her heart thumped. I must not panic, she thought, that won't help. So what will? Not a lot that I can think of, except prayer. A gust of wind rattled the window. Lockie picked up a length of timber that had been standing against the wall. Felt its weight. Looked at her with a slight frown. At which point, Elizabeth noticed a movement behind him. She sat bolt upright, staring over his shoulder.

The door was opening . . .

A gust of wind almost took it, but a hand was holding it firmly in place. Someone was letting himself silently in. Kit Bartram . . . Don't look round, she thought. If you look round now, you'll see him. Kit put a finger to his lips, but it was too late. Lockie must have sensed the movement, because he spun round.

Kit said, 'Well, now . . . Who do we have here?'

'Boy, am I glad to see you,' Elizabeth said.

'You told him.' Lockie was white with fury.

'No.' Kit pushed the door shut behind him. 'I work on the tower, remember. I saw her going down across the field and wondered why she didn't come back.'

'Kit — take care. He killed your father and Piers.'

'I know.' Kit was still coming forward. 'Michael Hughes came to see me last night.'

'Michael?' A confused, startled look crossed Lockie's face.

'Yes. Your mother wouldn't go to the police, so he came to warn me. He brought me a recent photograph.'

'You're lying.'

'Don't call me a liar, you murdering bastard.' Kit drew something out of his pocket. A sharp blade. 'I'd have got on to you anyway, sooner or later. I saw your mother at the funeral and I remembered her coming to the house. She was pregnant. I was only six. But I knew that much.'

Elizabeth said, 'Kit — look out!'

There was a crash as the length of timber swung in a great arc, hitting the wall instead of Kit. Then a tinkling of glass as it swung back again and shattered the window.

Kit said, 'Not so clever with that. Dab hand with a saw, though, aren't we?'

Mark Lockie lashed out again with the wood caught his half brother a glancing blow on the back. Kit went reeling backwards, but more out of self-defence than anything else. He came back almost at once. 'I'm going to get you for Piers's sake. If it's the last thing I do.'

Elizabeth twisted her wrists in a futile effort to get herself free.

Lockie caught Kit another blow on the side of the neck and Kit slashed the blade across the other man's wrist. Lockie swore and came rushing at him, had Kit trapped against the wall. But he'd forgotten the power in Kit's wrists. Lockie went backwards and at last Elizabeth found some way of contributing. She stuck out her feet and tripped him. As he crashed down, he struck his head on the grinding stone.

After that, he didn't get up.

Epilogue

Max said, 'Friend of yours called to ask how you are. Your tame vicar.'

'Richard? That's nice.' Elizabeth held the Jacob's Ladder at arm's length to study it. Not bad, she thought, though I say it myself.

'He said to be careful in future. I said, it's because she's a Yank. She thinks she's got to be the cavalry.'

'Did he say if Catharine Fletcher's OK?'

'She's fine. He's given her the address of an organisation called Broken Rites. It was formed by a group of ex-clergy wives. They'll help her deal with financial problems and such.'

'I suppose her most pressing need is somewhere to live.'

'Yeah. Did you know that the breakdown of clergy marriages is on the increase?' There was a pause. Max glanced in Ginger's direction. There was something odd going on between them. Ginger hadn't said a word and Max was being — well, overly formal. 'Apparently the McNeil woman has left the village. She's now residing in a hotel in Bath.'

'Shouldn't think she'll have the nerve to go back to her cottage, even when her renovations are finished. And Philip Fletcher?'

'He's well and truly in the—' He stopped when he saw her face. 'In the mire.'

'Serves him right,' Ginger said. 'Men like him give the church a bad name.'

'Quite right,' Max said. He looked at Ginger, and then out of the window; seemed vaguely embarrassed, though Elizabeth couldn't imagine why. What *was* wrong with him?

'What put you on to the rogue son?' Ginger asked Elizabeth. 'I mean, as far as we knew, he didn't even exist.'

'I'm not sure,' Elizabeth mused. 'I've been trying to pin it down. Jacob and Esau perhaps.'

'The son who desperately wanted his birthright. His father's blessing?'

'You got it.' Elizabeth was impressed. 'Not many kids these days know their Bible stories.'

Ginger fiddled with the handle of her coffee mug. 'I'm the exception.'

'And then there was something Juliet Hughes said when I went to her house. "There's no way you can connect me or any member of my family with these murders." *Any member of my family* . . . That phrase kept coming back to me. And then the vicarage baby – poor mite – was never far from my mind. I guess she took my thoughts back to the nanny's story about Juliet coming to the house and screaming at Con. And I thought, quite suddenly, out of the blue – what if Con's mistress just happened to be pregnant? What if we made a few enquiries in that direction?'

'Women's logic,' Max said. 'It never fails to amaze me.' He saw Elizabeth's expression and sensed danger. 'So – how are the bruises?' he asked, deftly changing the subject.

'On the mend.'

'Good.'

'I feel fine. I feel myself again.' What she'd had was a monumental fit of the winter blues. But it was over now. Coming face to face with death and surviving was a pretty good antidote. Yes, I'm glad to be here, Elizabeth thought. She felt her spirits lift. Her smile wrinkles came out for the first time in ages. 'You're good kids,' she said. 'I haven't deserved you lately.'

'Thanks, Grandma,' Max said. His eyes met Ginger's. And held.

There *was* something going on between the two of them. This place, she thought. It never stays the same two days running. Still, the only consistent people are the dead. While you're alive, you can change your mind, blow with the wind, chop and change as much as you damned well like. She smiled at them again, feeling light with happiness.

LIZBIE BROWN

DOUBLE WEDDING RING

Elizabeth Blair, American widow and quilt-shop owner, is discovering that behind Bath's tranquil façade lies a morass of betrayal, blackmail and revenge.

When Johnny Mulligan's wedding is cut short by his furious – and pregnant – lover, Kat Gregg, it causes a local sensation; a sensation that becomes more serious when Kat is killed on the night of the ruined ceremony. When the jilted groom is charged with her murder, his mother turns for help to Max Shepard, private detective, and his partner Elizabeth Blair, to prove her son innocent.

The Double Wedding Ring quilt is a symbol of love and loyalty. But there wasn't much fidelty in Johnny Mulligan's life and it seems that he isn't the only one with secrets to hide. More than one person had reason to want Kat Gregg out of the way. And as Elizabeth knows, lift the lid on one lie, and suddenly you discover another. It is up to the enterprising sleuths to expose the truth . . .

HODDER AND STOUGHTON PAPERBACKS